Letters of FATE

The premise of this historical western romance series, Letters of Fate, started out with the idea of writing a Mail Order Groom series.

As I pondered the idea, I decided rather than an agency or newspaper announcement bringing a woman and a man together, I'd have a man receive a letter that changes his life and brings him to the woman he can't live without.

This element also made the books in the series standalone. One book doesn't have to be read before the other as they are only connected by the hero receiving a letter.

Brody
Letters of Fate

Paty Jager

Windtree Press
Hillsboro, OR

This is a work of fiction, Names, characters, places, and incidents either are the product of the author's imagination or are used fictitiously, and any resemblance to actual persons living or dead, business establishments, events, or locales, is entirely coincidental.

BRODY: LETTERS OF FATE
Copyright © 2016 Patricia Jager

Contact Information: info@windtreepress.com

Windtree Press
Hillsboro, Oregon
http://windtreepress.com

Cover Art by Christina Keerins
Photo by Paty Jager
©Can Stock Photo Inc. /refairusta

Published in the United States of America
ISBN 9781944973094

Acknowledgements

Each book is a special journey for me in the writing and researching. This one is special because it is set in an area not far from where I live. Digging into the local history has been fun and has introduced me to other people who are interested in our history.

Special Thanks to:

Harney County Historical Museum
Karen Nitz- Harney County Library

New York City
1891

Chapter One

Brody Yates stood in the sweltering August heat of a New York City courtroom. He swiped a sleeve across his forehead, mopping the sweat that ran down into his eyes. He'd hoped the courthouse would be cooler than the jail where he'd sat for the last week. Those hopes were dashed as soon as they'd trudged up the stairs to the second floor.

A week ago he'd been found guilty of stealing, and for some reason, his sentencing had been stalled. And he'd sat wondering and waiting among the thieves and murderers in the lower east side jail.

The tall, thin judge with a full head of gray hair who'd presided over his case last week entered the courtroom and everyone sat.

Just as Brody relaxed into the chair, Mr. Peck, his attorney, grabbed his sleeve, tugging him to his feet once more.

"Brody Yates, you have been a thorn in the side of

many police officers the past ten years. Today, we are happy to say we will be rid of you." The judge had a smirk on his narrow face.

He glanced at his attorney, wondering how bad of a sentence he would be given. He'd stolen food for the mother and small child who lived in the room next to his in a tenement. Granted, the police hadn't caught him the day before slipping money from a well-dressed man on one of the busy streets. But that had also been to help a friend. It wasn't his fault the ways he'd learned to stay fed and alive on the street also provided him with ways to help other people in his building. The judge's glee as he spoke worried Brody. He had a feeling they were going to put him in prison, or worse. He stared at the judge and stood with his shoulders back, ready to take whatever the judge gave him.

"I have a letter from a Judge Abner Radley of the Double R Ranch in Oregon." The judge leaned forward. His dark eyes stared hard and cold at Brody. "I have considered the judge's request and think it is the best way for you to become a responsible citizen."

He shook his head. He didn't know any Judge Radley or anyone who lived in Oregon. "I don't understand. Why would this judge send a request?"

Mr. Peck grabbed his arm, again, and shook his head. "I'll read the letter to you after the hearing," he said in a low voice.

Brody stared at his attorney. He knew about the letter and hadn't told him? Now, he was just plain mad. He crossed his arms and glared at the judge. Then a thought struck him. This was his chance to get clear of New York and head out west. He for sure wouldn't go to Oregon, but there were lots of other places he could live.

"Bailiff, hand this letter to the defendant's attorney and let's get on with the next case." The judge held out a crisp, official looking document and the bailiff took it, walking to Mr. Peck and holding it out.

He wanted to snatch the paper and find out more about this judge in Oregon. His attorney tucked the document into his leather case and nodded for him to follow.

Out of the courtroom and on the street the heat was only slightly less offensive. Smoke from factories and dung from the horses added a foul odor that hovered in the streets with no current of air to lessen them. Summers in New York. He had often wondered why he'd stayed.

"How did you know about the letter?" he asked, as they dodged people hastily moving along the street.

"I've had it in my possession for some time." Mr. Peck didn't even look at him. He just kept walking. The attorney's average build made it easy for his long legs to keep up with the man.

He stopped. "You've had the letter? How? Why?"

Mr. Peck spun around, grabbed his sleeve, and pulled him along the walkway toward his office down the block. "It's a story best told in the confines of my office and not here on the street." He nodded behind them.

Brody glanced over his shoulder and noted a patrolman following a short distance behind them. "Judge Adams wants to make sure I leave his city, doesn't he?"

"Yes. Precisely why you need to follow me to my office and hear the letter." Mr. Peck picked up his pace, pushing his wire-rimmed glasses up his perspiring nose.

Curiosity kept him from ducking down an alley. Finally, they turned into the brownstone that housed the offices of Lester Peck, Attorney at Law. Inside the main office a large man sat in one of the waiting chairs. Mr. Peck nodded to him and continued into his office.

"Have a seat." Mr. Peck placed his hat on the wooden stand by the door and his leather case on his desk. He opened the case, pulled out the letter the judge had waved around, and sat behind his desk.

Curiosity won out. He sat and noted the office was cooler than the courtroom and the street. "Why have you had this letter for a while?"

"Let me read the letter, then you may ask questions." Mr. Peck cleared his throat and began, "To the Courts of New York City, I, Judge Abner Radley, take full responsibility for Brody Yates. He is my estranged grandson. I will put him to work on my cattle ranch, the Double R, in Harney County, Oregon and make sure he learns a good work ethic and stays out of trouble. I have a man who is willing to escort him to my ranch saving the courts the cost of time and money. The honorable Judge Abner Radley."

A grandfather? Why hadn't I heard from this man before when I really needed help? He didn't believe it. "How do you know this man is my grandfather? He could be some person who sells young men to ships or other countries as slaves." He'd heard stories of men shanghaied in the west coast cities and working on ships for years.

"He is your grandfather. He was your mother's father." Mr. Peck slid a small stack of papers across his desk. "These are the official papers linking your mother to Judge Radley."

He shook his head. His mother never spoke of her father, only that her mother had died when she was fourteen and she'd met Brody's father when she was sixteen. She'd never mentioned where she grew up. He'd assumed it was New York City, the only place they'd ever lived.

His hands shook as he reached out to read the papers. One was an affidavit from a preacher and a doctor saying Mary Elizabeth Radley was born May 2, 1852, in Oregon City. He couldn't believe what he read. Mary Elizabeth was his ma's name. But it was Yates, not Radley. He mentally thunked himself. Yates was his father's last name. The next paper was a report stating Mary Elizabeth Radley had been kidnapped in August of 1868 from Canyon City, Oregon. Below that paper were letters addressed to Judge Radley from lawmen across the country saying they could not find his daughter. The next to last letter was from the Pinkerton Agency. He'd known who it would be from before he read the words. It had the one eye symbol for the agency on the top of the page. They had discovered Mary Elizabeth Radley Yates had passed away January of 1881 and her son was now seventeen and working, it seemed, at the docks.

Five years ago his grandfather had found him, and yet, he did nothing. "Why didn't he contact me then? When I was seventeen?" Brody glanced up from the papers and found Mr. Peck watching him with sympathy glimmering in his eyes.

"He thought you'd made your life as you wanted. But he also had received information about your habit of irritating the law. That was what prompted him to write this letter five years ago and send it to me to keep in case you were to be sent to prison or worse."

"So even though he thought I was doing all right, he didn't think I would stay that way." That rankled more than knowing he'd had a grandfather out there watching over him and not showing his face. The fact the man believed he would falter or fail. He wasn't his father who couldn't keep a job to save his family. His father died a drunk in a gutter, killing himself on the money they needed for rent.

Brody stood, tossing the papers onto the desk. He'd been just fine all these years on his own. He didn't need a stranger to help him out now. "What if I don't want to meet this grandfather or work on a cattle ranch?"

"You'll go to prison for stealing." Mr. Peck leaned back in his chair. "Wouldn't meeting your grandfather and trying a hand at cattle ranching be better than being stuck in prison?"

The fleeting thought he'd had about heading toward Oregon and stopping somewhere along the way seemed like his best option. He wouldn't have to be beholden to anyone. "I've heard enough stories about prison that an Oregon cattle ranch sounds better." He started for the door and stopped. "How am I to get there? Did my grandfather send you money for my travels?"

Mr. Peck stood, walked to the door, and opened it. "Marshal Evert, would you come in please?"

Brody backed up as the large man who'd been sitting in the waiting room stood and walked into the office.

Mr. Peck shut the door behind the man and faced them. "This is your escort to your grandfather. U.S. Marshal Jake Evert. Marshal Evert, this is Brody Yates, Judge Radley's grandson you are to see gets to the Double R Ranch in Oregon."

"Yates." The marshal stuck out his hand.

Brody didn't like the idea of someone taking him to his grandfather like he was a criminal or a small child that needed an escort, but he knew better than to let the man know. "Marshal." He shook hands and stepped back. "When do we leave?"

"The train pulls out headed west in two hours. We'll gather your things and head to the station." The marshal shook hands with Mr. Peck, who slid him an envelope.

Keeping his eye on the envelope, he noted the marshal placed it in his left inside jacket pocket. Good to know, considering he'd need funds to get him anywhere but Oregon.

Chapter Two

Brody's body ached from the hours sitting on the hard benches in the train. He knew there were softer seats. He'd managed to get away from the marshal early in the trip and had darted into the car behind theirs. It had soft seats that changed into beds. Why couldn't his grandfather have paid for better accommodations? After all, they'd been traveling on the train for seven days.

Marshal Evert appeared to be sleeping, but he'd learned it was the man's ruse to see if he'd try to get away. The marshal had smiled, a knowing smile, the first time he'd managed to get as far as the next car. He'd also tried to get away on a long stopover in Denver. But the marshal had been right on his heels and his smile wasn't as friendly when he'd grabbed Brody by the back of his jacket and hauled him back to the train.

So he sat, grumbling and cursing the man sitting across from him as the train slowed and the conductor called out, "Baker City!"

"This is our stop." The marshal knocked Brody's crossed leg off his other leg and stood. "Grab your gear."

He reached under the seat and pulled out his small canvas knapsack with one extra set of clothes and a photo of his mother and him taken before she'd grown sick. He didn't have any photos of his father and didn't want any. Even thinking about the man made him angry. If it had been his father's father who arranged his not going to prison, he would have chosen prison. That was how bitter he felt toward the man who'd fathered him and left him and Ma fighting to survive every day until she lost the battle.

The train chugged and puffed, sifting more black soot into the open windows. He coughed and followed the other passengers off the train and onto the station's platform. Hard heeled, pointed-toed boots, the men with wide-brimmed hats wore, thunked with an interesting cadence as they crossed the raised wooden walkway. The knee-high footwear was fascinating. He'd never seen anything like it. A crowd of people stood back watching the train. He wouldn't have known if his grandfather stood with them or not. He couldn't picture a male version of his mother.

The marshal pushed on his back. "Move along. We'll go by stage from here."

Brody walked to the edge of the people and faced Marshal Evert. "Are we going straight from the train to a stage? I don't think my legs can take being folded up any longer." He shook first one leg and then the other to emphasize how cramped they'd become from days and nights sitting in the confined space of their seats on the train.

"We'll spend the night in a hotel and get on the stage tomorrow." The marshal waved his empty hand toward the street. "Keep walking down this street. We'll bunk at the stage hotel, it's a few streets down."

Stage hotel. He had a pretty good idea it would be like the hotel they'd stayed in one night on the train trip. One big room with bunks. There had been a dozen men sharing the space. He might have grown up in the slums of New York, but he liked to be clean and right now he wanted a bath and to change into clean clothes.

"Any chance we can stop at a bath house before the hotel?" He plucked at his sweat-stained shirt. "I've been living in these clothes for two weeks."

The marshal narrowed his eyes. "You'll have to promise not to try and run if we go to a bath house."

"I don't know where I'd go if I did run." He smiled sincerely and shrugged. This move had worked when he was younger and had plucked an apple from a store. From the narrowed stare the marshal aimed at him, he had a feeling it didn't work on hardened lawmen.

Marshal Evert started walking. "Come on. If you so much as try to get away, I'll have this whole town looking for you in five minutes. This is my territory."

The way people on the street nodded, smiled, and greeted the marshal, Brody believed the man.

They crossed over five streets before Marshal Evert entered a building with the sign, Boarding. It was next to the Baker City Livery. Across the street, he noticed a Chinese laundry. Inside, Marshal Evert paid for two beds and then headed back out to the board walkway.

"There's a bathhouse at the back of the laundry across the street." He pointed beyond the dung littered, dusty width of dirt between the two buildings.

Brody followed the marshal, dodging horses pulling wagons and men on horseback, to the small wooden structure with a laundry sign.

They stepped inside and were greeted by a Chinese man who stood only as tall as their chests.

"Chang has the cleanest baths in town," the marshal said.

"Yes. Yes," the man said, drawing the curtain aside and revealing two metal bathing tubs half full of water.

"Step on in. You get the tub in the back." Marshal Evert grabbed his knapsack as he walked by. "I'll keep these until I'm done and dressed."

He relinquished his bag and stepped to the back of the narrow area. He shed his clothes and slipped into the tub.

"I get hot water then wash clothes." Chang picked up the dirty clothes and hustled out of the room, drawing the curtain closed behind him.

Brody leaned back in the tub, enjoying the luke warm water. He closed his eyes, savoring the idea of getting clean.

"Don't fall asleep." The marshal's voice reminded him he wasn't alone.

Chang returned with two steaming buckets of water. He poured one in Marshal Evert's tub and the second one in Brody's tub.

"Stir." Chang moved his hand back and forth.

He swirled the water and sighed as the hot water hit his sore back. Bouncing and sleeping sitting up in the train had his body aching in places he didn't know he had.

He slid down, dunking his head under the water and came up sluicing the water from his face.

"Soap." Chang held out an earthy smelling bar.

"Thanks." He slid down in the water again and scrubbed the soap across his short cropped hair. Until he'd been sent to jail, his hair had brushed against his collar. The first thing they did before putting him in with the other prisoners was shave his head. All the men he'd been jailed with had their heads shaved. The rumor was it prevented an outbreak of head lice. For that reason, he didn't mind losing his hair. He'd had head lice as a child. Ma had shaved his hair off and then coated his scalp with petroleum jelly and made him sleep sitting up.

The soap smelled unlike anything he'd used before, but it cleaned the sweat and grime from his skin and made him feel like a man and not a street urchin. He rubbed a hand across his face, the whiskers rasped across his skin and felt longer than his hair.

"I shave," Chang said, standing to the side of the tub.

"I'd appreciate that." He leaned his head back against the tub edge and closed his eyes.

A hot towel covered his face for several moments before a stiff brush scrubbed lather on his face. Swift strokes of a blade cut the whiskers. The hot towel returned.

"I could use a good shave, too," Marshal Evert said.

Brody finished scrubbing and stood, pulling a

towel from a peg on the wall. His clothes were in the knapsack hanging on a peg by Marshal Evert's head. Chang had placed the hot towel on the marshal's face at the end of the shaving ritual.

Glancing at the man relaxing in the tub, he stepped along his tub and the marshal's tub. His fingers touched the strap on his knapsack. A hand grasped his leg, clamping tight enough to make his leg buckle. He grasped the sides of the tub to keep from falling into the water with the marshal.

"I said you'd get your clothes after I'm dressed. Sit on that chair." Marshal Evert pointed to a chair near the curtain.

He'd known better than to get his clothes, considering the warning he'd been given, but damn, he was a man and he didn't need to be treated like a child. "Can I grab my clothes and dress in the back of the room?" Sitting on a chair without a stitch of clothing on, waiting for permission to dress, angered him far more than any other wrong he'd ever encountered.

Marshal Evert stood, wrapped a towel around his lower body and placed the knapsack in his hands. He pointed to the tub where Brody had bathed. "There."

Clutching his knapsack to keep from saying anything, he walked to the back of the small room and dressed with his back to the marshal. If he didn't have the man keeping an eye on him, he'd have strolled through town, looking for fun and money to get away from the marshal. If the marshal's vest had been hanging near the knapsack, he'd have gone for that. He'd learned long ago, the only way a person could survive was to get their hands on money.

Dressed, he waited for Marshal Evert to pay the Chinaman, noting the marshal took money from the envelope in his vest pocket. The big man had worn the garment to bed the one night they'd slept off the train. Until this bath, he'd never had the garment off.

A plan formed in his head. He smiled and followed the marshal back out onto the street. "My stomach's grumblin' any chance we could eat a real meal?"

Marshal Evert stopped at the edge of the walkway and peered both directions. "There's a restaurant couple streets over." He pivoted to his right and strode down the walkway.

The thunk of his boots drew Brody's attention. The marshal wore boots similar to the ones the men in the wide-brimmed hats wore. He took a good gander at the marshal's hat. His hat was shaped near the same as the other fellas but the brim wasn't as wide.

At the restaurant, waiting for their food, he took in how the people were dressed. Half the men had the pointy-toed boots and wide-brimmed hats. If they had a woman with them, she didn't wear a fancy dress and her hat was small or functional. The clothing was pretty and clean and didn't show any skin but her hands and face. The men in suits reminded him of New York— dressed fancy, with gold watch fobs and chains. The women with these men wore fine dresses with lace showing off their necks and giving a peek at the creamy skin on their chests. They had on big fancy hats that were more for show than keeping the sun off their skin.

The young women where he lived in New York only wore a hat if they were going to church or a special event. He'd noticed while walking the streets, every female over school age, wore a hat or bonnet.

Staring out the window, he wondered over the small buildings, the tallest two stories. He'd only seen houses that were this small, not businesses.

"What can I get you tonight, Marshal?" the woman, he'd figured out was the owner, asked.

He could tell by the way she and the marshal eyed each other that if the marshal weren't escorting him, he'd be keeping the woman's bed warm tonight. That gave him an idea.

"I'll have my usual, May," Marshal Evert said. His eyes twinkled.

"And you, young man?" May asked, not even looking at Brody.

"I'll have a steak, roll, and pie." He figured if his grandfather was paying for the trip he could pay for a steak.

"No potatoes with your meal?" May finally looked at him.

She had a round cheerful face and a mouth that was constantly turned up at the corners.

"No taters for me," he said, shaking his head.

"Tater?" May and the Marshal said at the same time.

"Tater, potato." Everyone knew a tater was a potato.

"Why do you call a potato a tater?" the marshal asked.

"That's what we called it when I was growing up." He shrugged.

"No taters for you," May said playfully, and put her hand on the marshal's shoulder before walking away.

He nodded toward May's retreating body. "If you want to visit her later, I can go to bed early."

Marshal Evert narrowed his eyes. "You won't be going anywhere that I don't go. May understands I'm doing a job."

Brody smiled but on the inside he was seething. He had to find a way to get loose from the marshal or he'd be facing his grandfather soon.

Chapter Three

Lilah Wells couldn't concentrate on the conversation with her friend, Sarah. She and Judge Radley had driven the wagon to Venator to meet the stage and the grandson the judge had never seen.

Five years ago when the judge had received the letter stating they'd found his deceased daughter and her son, he'd cried. At first tears of grief for a daughter he hadn't seen in years and then at the joy of having a part of her still living—her son. From what the judge told her, she hoped Brody liked the ranching life. Judge Radley wanted to leave his ranch in good hands and he preferred those hands to be his grandson and legacy.

Shouts and the sound of jingling, creaking harnesses drew her attention.

"The stage" she said, feeling the excitement of a child awaiting a gift. "I have to go."

Without a glance at her friend, Lilah hurried down the dusty street to the post office where the stage would stop. Judge Radley had waited in the wagon, parked in the shade of the post office. She watched him climb down. She'd wanted him to bring the buggy, it provided a smoother trip and was easier for him to enter and exit. He had said he didn't want the boy to think he was putting on airs. He'd feel more comfortable being picked up in a wagon.

She wasn't so sure, noting the way the younger man on the top of the stage coach winced as a wheel dropped into a hole before the conveyance came to a stop. Taking in his appearance, she was pretty sure the man was the grandson. His angular features and touches of red in his whiskers reminded her of Judge Radley when she'd first met him. She'd been about six when he'd visited her father and mother. He'd been considerably older than Brody and his hair was graying, but there was a definite resemblance between the two.

Once the stage stopped swaying, the passengers inside the coach stepped out.

Lilah drew her gaze from the man and noticed Marshal Evert on the seat next to Willy, the stage coach driver. That settled it. The man on the top of the coach had to be Brody Yates.

A shiver skittered up her backbone when he looked her way. His light blue gaze held hers for a moment before scanning the street. She didn't have time to decide if the shiver was good or bad before noticing him grimace and appear disgusted with what he saw. That he found their little settlement distasteful annoyed her.

Venator wasn't Baker City or even Burns, but it was her home and she was proud of the small settlement. They had the necessary businesses to survive. A post office, small mercantile, livery-blacksmith, and a boarding house.

Marshal Evert climbed down off the stage and glanced back up. "Yates! Toss down the bags and get down here!"

The man she had already dubbed Brody, glared at the marshal and tossed the bags down to the lawman with a bit more force than she deemed appropriate.

Judge Radley stepped up beside her. "As I figured, he's going to be a handful. Growing up the way he did, I pegged him as independent. Probably rubbed him wrong having a lawman escort him here."

Lilah wrapped her arm around the judge's and squeezed. "You'll bring him around. You have a way with unruly orphans."

The judge patted her hand. "You were easy, my dear, you had two loving parents before I took you in. My grandson has had a tough lot so far. I'm sure he isn't thrilled with me having him escorted here after hearing I've known of his existence for five years."

The last bag hit the marshal in the chest, and the younger man swung down from the top of the stage. He scanned the area again. His gaze stopped on his grandfather. He had to know he was looking at a reflection of himself in forty years.

Marshal Evert tossed a small knapsack at Brody, pulling his attention from the judge. The marshal nodded their way and he and the younger man walked over.

"Judge Radley, this is Brody Yates." Marshal Evert put a hand behind the man, urging him forward.

The judge held his hand out to the marshal. "Thank you, Marshal Evert. Is there enough money left to pay you for your services?" he asked, not glancing at his grandson.

Lilah watched the gap between the younger man's brows narrow as his frown grew deeper.

"Yes." Marshal Evert shook hands with the judge. "Good luck."

Judge Radley chuckled and turned his attention to the angry man standing in front of him. "Brody, grandson, it is a pleasure to finally meet you." The judge held out his hand.

She held her breath, hoping the man wouldn't be so rude as to ignore his grandfather's offered hand. She could tell by his hesitation, it had crossed his mind.

Finally, he reached out and shook hands. "Judge."

The older man smiled and clutched their clasped hands with his other hand. "We have much to talk about, but let's get back to the ranch."

Clearing her throat, she interrupted the grandfather's study of his grandson.

"This is my ward, Lilah Wells. She's staying at the ranch until she heads off to the university." Judge Radley patted her arm. "Come along," he added, walking toward the wagon.

At the wagon, Brody grimaced.

The judge held out his hand, helping her onto the wagon seat. "Hop in back, son. I'm sure you're sore from all the travel, but we'll be at the ranch in an hour."

***

Brody tossed his knapsack into the wagon and crawled up, sitting at the back as far from the man claiming to be his grandfather and his ward.

The old man glanced over his shoulder. "No need to sit clear back there. You can come stand behind the seat if you're tired of sitting."

He didn't want to accept the man's offer but his sore backside said different. The judge waited for him to walk to the front of the vehicle and grasp the wagon seat before he clucked at the horses and slapped their rumps with the reins.

The wagon lurched forward and he bumped the old man's shoulder and the middle of Lilah's back.

"Sorry," he mumbled to no one in particular. Inhaling the air near the young woman brought about memories. The soft floral scent swirled memories of his mother, holding him, reading to him, and hugging him tight as they waited for his father to come home. Those first years, she'd been happy, kept herself presentable, and always smelled like a fragrant flower.

He shook his head and realized the judge was talking to him. "Pardon?"

"I was saying, I'm sure this country is nothing like what you're used to," the judge said, raising his voice.

"All I've ever known were cobbled streets and tall buildings that block the wind and the sun." He had to admit the fresh air and unfiltered sunshine was something he could get used to. "The air here is fresh."

"What is the air like in New York City?" Lilah asked, tipping her face up, her dark green eyes peering into his.

"Thick. Soot from the factories fills the air and makes it hard for many to breathe." His gaze slid from her eyes to the sprinkling of faint freckles scattered over her nose and across her cheeks. Her rosy lips were full and tipped up at the corners. Her dark brown hair was pinned up under the hat that matched the color of her skirt and jacket. Where the sunlight touched her hair the strands had a copper color.

"Yet, I read New York City has a population of over a million people." Lilah stared straight ahead. "I can't even imagine that many people."

Brody smiled. "There were days it felt like every one of those million people watched every move I made."

"Why is that?" the judge asked.

He didn't think the man wanted to know how he supplemented his meager wages and helped others out. Being as how he was on the side of the law, Brody doubted he'd look kindly on his kin stealing. "Walking the street to and from work, you were bumped and jostled. Women up in the tenements hung out the windows calling to their men and children or one another."

"Where did you work?" Lilah asked.

"At the docks. I unloaded wagons." It was hard back-breaking work, but it paid more than anything else he could find. But barely enough to pay for the room he rented and food.

"From the work you've been doing, you shouldn't have any problems working in the hay fields." The judge nodded to a field with several men pitching hay onto a wagon.

"That your field?" he asked, watching the men and thinking the work looked as hard as the work on the docks.

"No. That belongs to Alphena Venator. He owns most of the land around the community. It was named for his family. The Double R is five miles from the community." The older man clucked to the horses and they picked up a bit faster walk.

Five miles from even the small community of Venator. Brody was getting itchy to see more people and some action. Any kind of action. The marshal had kept him close at hand the whole trip. He wanted to jump out of the wagon and head back to Venator, find a card game, and catch the next stage out of here.

"The ranch has a year-round supply of water running through the meadows creating good hay for the cattle and horses in the winter. The last few years I've cut back on market cattle and have been striving to breed hardy stock that carries good beef traits." The judge continued talking about the ranch, mentioning words he didn't understand.

Brody tuned him out and studied the countryside. Rugged flat-topped hills surrounded wide areas of tall grass and lines of short, willowy trees or vast flat areas scattered with rocks and a bush the marshal called sagebrush. This country didn't look like anything he'd seen in photographs, magazines or advertisements. The dust curled up behind the wagon, settling on his shoulders and the shoulders of the judge and Lilah.

He coughed and spit the grit out of his mouth.

"Get used to the dust. It's even worse when the wind kicks up." A heavily veined hand handed him a cotton cloth. "It's a bandana. Tie it around your neck loosely and pull the larger part up over your nose."

Staring at the square of cloth he couldn't

understand what the man meant.

Lilah turned in the seat. "Here, like a bandit." She folded the square into a three-sided shape and held it up to his neck. He bent down and she tied it loosely around his neck. Before he straightened, she pulled the folded part of the cloth over his nose.

"You'll wear something like this a lot when you're working the cattle." She faced forward.

Not if I'm not here. Brody was beginning to think the crushing bodies and sooty air of New York City was favorable to this country.

Chapter Four

Brody's legs finally gave in to the bouncing and he sat behind the wagon seat, staring into the cloud of dust following the wagon. After twenty minutes or so, the wheels crunched on gravel and the wagon bounced more, but the dust didn't curl up as much behind them. Glancing to his right, he spotted a stream.

"You're on Double R land. We own close to four thousand acres, a thousand head of cattle breeding stock, and a hundred head of ranch stock horses. We hay two hundred acres of meadow ground to feed the livestock through the winter. Some winters we barely make it and others we have hay left over. The winter of eighty-one we lost a couple hundred head due to the deep snow and long cold spell." The judge waved his arm. "I homesteaded on this creek after my wife passed. Two years later your mother ran off with your father." The older man sighed. "At the time, I thought he'd kidnapped her. He'd shown interest in her, but she'd not let on to care a lick for him."

"It wasn't your fault, Judge," Lilah said.

Brody glanced over his shoulder. The woman had a hand on the old man's arm. He narrowed his eyes and studied the two of them. Was there more between them than her being his ward?

"If Mary Elizabeth's ma had been alive, she'd have noticed what was going on. Perhaps could have prevented it."

The judge, his grandfather, wished he hadn't been born. His chest ached. He'd hoped he'd finally found family, have someone who cared again. Now he wondered why the judge even sent the letter to the courts. It was obvious he wished the union between Brody's mother and father hadn't happened.

Two riders charged through the dust behind the wagon. They had bandanas pulled up over their noses and their horses charged toward the wagon.

"Judge! Judge!" one hollered over the crunch of the rocks under the wheels, the jangle of the harness, and the thumping of the wagon box.

"Whoa!" The judge pulled the horses to a stop and turned to watch the men stop next to the wagon.

"What's wrong?" Judge Radley asked.

"Found one of your best cows dead and skinned up over the ridge along that crick that don't stay full." The man talking sat taller and was slender while the other man was as wide as he was short. The shorter man stared at Brody as the other man talked.

"Thieves!" The judge shouted. "Get Clem and Roy to help you round up all the cattle in that area and bring them to a valley closer in. Then Sandy, you and Angel, see if you can't find some tracks and figure out who killed my cattle and took the hide."

"Yes, sir." Sandy settled his hat on tighter and his horse shot forward. "Come on, Stubbs!"

The shorter man clasped his hat to his head with one hand and took off in a cloud of dust after the one the judge called Sandy.

Brody pulled his body up to stand behind the wagon seat as the judge whipped the horses into a trot. The wagon bounced twice as much as before. Lilah clutched the seat. She bounced toward the edge and he grabbed her arm, keeping her from falling over the edge of the wagon.

"What's the hurry? You told that man, Sandy, what to do." He kept hold of the young woman as the wagon rocked back and forth.

"I want to send out more men to check for any other skinned cattle. I won't tolerate thievery." The judge bounced forward, but caught himself from going over the front of the wagon.

"Judge. Slow down, if you're killed in a wagon accident, you can't do anything about the cattle." Lilah nearly shouted to be heard above the sound of the wagon banging, bouncing, and rattling.

The horses slowed to a walk, and she breathed a sigh of relief. She also noticed Brody didn't release the arm he'd been holding since she nearly went head first over the side of the wagon. His fingers held her tight but didn't dig in. With the heat of the afternoon, she wouldn't have thought she could feel heat from his hand, but she did. It was a warmth that trailed up her arm and settled in her chest.

She glanced up at him and tugged on her arm. He

looked down and gazed into her eyes a moment, then at the hand still clutching her arm. His fingers opened, and he rubbed his palm on his pants.

Why had he wiped his hand? Was she perspiring that much? She glanced at her arm. The jacket she wore to keep the dust off her shirtwaist wasn't thick, but it did make her perspire more than without wearing it. She noticed a slight dampness where he'd held her. But it appeared to be from his hand and not her arm.

They now drove through the meadows allowed to grow to make hay. The grass was nearly up to her waist. The judge had set the cutting to start next week. She studied Brody. He looked healthy enough to do the work. But would he balk when he saw what all it entailed? She even helped with the haying. The last three years, she'd driven teams of horses that ran the cutting machine and that bucked the hay. At first Judge Radley had been against it, but she'd asked Buster Malone, the foreman, to show her what to do and then she'd shown the judge she had the skills.

"This is the hay ground. We'll start harvesting next week." The judge glanced up at Brody. "You'll be part of the haying crew until you've had time to learn about the cattle and horses." He turned his attention back to the team pulling the wagon. "I don't suppose you had much experience with animals living in the city."

"Stray cats and dogs. Not getting run over by a horse or team." His tone reflected boredom.

But his gaze scanned everything, eyes wide with surprise as he studied the area.

"I figured as much. That's why you'll start out helping with the hogs and chickens while haying. After that I'll have someone teach you to ride and you can follow Buster, my foreman, around to learn about the cattle." The judge clucked to the horses.

Lilah thought she might as well offer her help. "I can teach Brody to ride. That way it won't take one of the hands away from their duties."

The judge looked at her. "You'll be headed to the university after the haying is done."

"I've been thinking about that. With Agnes in the family way it might be best if I stay until after the holidays. The baby will come in November and I can start the university at the beginning of the year." This was one thing she planned to dig her heels into. She would not leave poor Agnes stranded. She had two little ones already and had admitted this time she wasn't feeling well. Not like she'd felt with the other two.

"Mrs. Fellowes can help Agnes," the judge said, his face hardening into the stern, stony expression he'd perfected as a judge.

She had learned long ago his "judge" face was scarier than his bite. "She doesn't have the time to help Agnes. You have to remember she's slowing down and won't admit it."

"If Lilah doesn't want to go to university, I'd think it's her decision," Brody piped up.

"I didn't say I didn't want to go. I don't want to leave when Agnes needs my help." She loved studying and the community of learned women as much as she loved the ranch and Venator.

A growl erupted from the older man sitting beside her.

"You've only been at the ranch fifteen minutes and

you think you know what is best for my ward?" The judge hauled back on the reins stopping the horses. He stood and turned to face his grandson. "When I accepted to care for Lilah at her parents' request, I also promised them she would get all the schooling their funds allowed."

The younger man didn't back away or say I'm sorry. "You might have taken over the responsibilities of a parent, but that doesn't make you her Lord and master." Brody glanced down at her and then back up to his grandfather. "Not everyone has the opportunity to go to a university, but not everyone wants to go."

The judge threw his hands in the air and sat. "You wouldn't understand." He gathered up the reins and slapped them on the horses' rumps with a curt smack.

Lilah studied the judge as he set the horses in motion. Something Brody said had upset him. Was it that not everyone wanted to go to university? Had he had hopes of sending his grandson? She understood the judge's need to fulfill her parents' wishes. He always followed through on his promises. But just because her parents had taught at a university, didn't mean she wanted to follow in their footsteps. She loved the ranching life and had voiced that opinion several times, but the judge always pretended he didn't hear her. She had a few more studies she wanted to attend but then, she wanted to come back and live here, on the Double R Ranch.

She glanced up at Brody. His jaw clenched tight and a muscle along his jawline twitched. She had a feeling this wouldn't be the last time the two men, who were so alike, would clash. The judge had hoped for this day to come since receiving the file five years ago from the Pinkertons. She had asked him once why he didn't go to New York City and visit his grandson. He'd said after all these years, the boy may not see him and he couldn't bear the thought of being shunned by his own flesh and blood.

A quick glance at the man stole her breath. He stood tall, his face forward, but she witnessed vulnerability in his eyes when he glanced down and back up. He needed his grandfather and family as badly as his grandfather needed him.

It's up to me to keep the two stubborn men together. I owe it to the judge for taking me in and to Brody for having spent so many years of his life alone.

Chapter Five

What the judge called the ranch buildings looked like a small town to Brody. He stood in the wagon counting the buildings. A two-story ranch house, a long low building Lilah pointed out as the bunkhouse, a cabin she said Buster Malone, the foreman, lived in with his wife and their two children, and two large barns. That didn't even count the smaller buildings scattered around between the other larger buildings. This looked like a town compared to the sparse little buildings that had dotted the one street in Venator.

The wagon stopped in front of the large barn. A tall man with broad shoulders, large arms, and a leather apron walked out of a small addition to the barn.

"Didn't expect you back until dark, Judge." The man took hold of the horse on the left side.

"I didn't expect to come back to thievery." The judge climbed off the wagon. "Brody, help Lilah down," he barked.

He leaped out of the back of the wagon and held his arms up to the young woman. He didn't usually jump when given an order, but when the order allowed him to put his hands on a pretty girl, he didn't balk.

She blinked a few times, then slowly leaned down into his upraised hands. He caught her at the waist and lifted her down. She wasn't a wispy girl. He could feel her body was hard from working. He'd held several girls who worked hard every day of their life. They had muscles as hard and strong as men.

He set her feet on the ground and continued to study her. He liked the smattering of freckles, it gave her a youthful appearance. She licked and opened her full rosy lips.

"You can let go of me. My feet are on the ground."

He released her and stepped back. Glancing around, expecting a lecture from the judge for holding onto Lilah too long, he found the old man in a deep discussion with the man who still held the horse.

"Who's he?" Brody nodded toward the big man.

"That's Smithy, he's the blacksmith. He can shoe a horse and fix anything made of metal."

Screeches and barking dogs came from the smaller barn across the road moments before two dogs and two small children burst out the open door of the building.

"Those two are Buddy and Betsy. Buster and Agnes' children. The dogs are Red and Hound." Lilah laughed and hurried toward the two children, her arms spread wide.

The dogs jumped around her, yapping and showing their delight in seeing her. The children's faces lit up, and they both launched at her. She held one on each hip and walked back toward him.

The discussion between the three of them was animated. It reminded him of the Irish family next door when he was a child. There had been four children and the mother and father always played and made time for them, even though they were struggling to keep food on the table as much as he and his mother.

The girl held out a tiny finger. There was a thin path of blood the length of the finger.

"Did you hurt yourself?" he asked, kissing the tip of the finger.

"Ma cat. She swatted at Bets," said the boy.

"Kitties," Betsy said, pouting.

"It seems Betsy wanted to hold a kitty and Ma cat didn't like the idea," Lilah said.

"You know, mommies are protective of their babies. You'll have to wait until the kittens come out to play with you." His heart warmed at the way the two children hung on his every word. "If they come to you, then their ma knows you aren't a threat."

Buddy nodded. "That's what Papa says. Ain't it—"

"Isn't it," Lilah corrected him.

"Isn't it, Bets?" he finished.

Betsy nodded her head, making the straight brown hair flop into her face.

"Woo hoo! I have cookies made!"

A short, plump, white-haired woman with a brown dress and ruffled apron called from the side porch of the main house.

"We're coming!" Lilah replied, sliding Buddy to the ground. He took off at a run for the house. Betsy still clung to her. She took two steps and turned. "Come on, she made the cookies for you."

He glanced to where he'd last seen the judge. Smithy was unharnessing the horses and the older man was gone.

"Where'd Judge Radley go?" he asked.

Smithy looked up. "He went to saddle up a horse. Wants to see the skinned cow himself."

His first thought was he should be riding along, but he'd never ridden a horse. The thought of cookies and hopefully a soft seat, sent his feet heading to the door of the house that Lilah disappeared through.

He stepped into the house and was surrounded by the scents and chatter he'd yearned for since his father's death. His mother was never the same after his father died. He'd put more meals on the table than she had. And he'd brought in the money or stolen the food that fed them.

"Welcome to the Double R," the plump woman said, stepping forward and extending a hand. "I'm Mrs. Fellowes."

Brody clasped her warm, soft hand and smiled. The woman's genuine smile and twinkling eyes were the first real welcome he'd experienced since getting off the stage.

"Brody Yates," he said, squeezing her hand and releasing.

Lilah cleared her throat and pointed to the cap on his head.

"Hats aren't worn in the house," Mrs. Fellowes said.

"Sorry." He pulled the cap from his head and held it in front of him.

"There's pegs by the door for hats and coats." The round woman waddled over to the stove. "Would you prefer coffee or milk with your cookies?"

He hung the cap on a peg. Milk. He couldn't remember the last time he'd tasted it. "Milk, please."

Brody sat in a chair at the table where Lilah and the children sat already dunking cookies in milk.

Mrs. Fellowes placed a tall glass of milk in front of him and pulled the plate piled with golden cookies toward him.

He grasped the glass and found it pleasantly cool to the touch. Cold milk. He'd never had it cold. The few times his ma had purchased milk the liquid was warm by the time he'd taken a drink.

Lifting the glass to his lips, he tried to remember the taste. The memory was nothing compared to the real thing sliding across his tongue and down his throat. He drank half the glass before picking up a cookie. The sweet treat melted in his mouth and sparked recollections of a time long ago. Tears burned the back of his eyes at the memory of his mother baking cookies and handing him one still warm from the oven. He had so few of those remembrances that he clung to them tightly.

A hand patted his back. He started and opened his eyes, realizing he'd had his eyes closed reliving memories he'd tucked to the back of his mind.

"It's good to have you here," Mrs. Fellowes said and added more cookies to the plate.

He glanced around the table. The children studied him with wide, innocent eyes. Lilah stared at the sweet in her hand.

"This is one of the best cookies I've ever eaten," he said and plucked another one from the plate. He savored another drink of milk and bit the treat.

Lilah had noticed Brody's reaction to both the milk and the cookie. What kind of a life had he led all those years? She wanted to ask, but knew it was too soon. Even though he'd held her much longer than was appropriate when helping her off the wagon, she didn't think he thought of her as an ally. After his comments to the judge about university, she'd almost sworn, he'd wanted to go to a university, but then he'd contradicted that claim. She bit the cookie in her hand and raised her gaze. He was an interesting man.

He watched her as he emptied his glass of milk.

"Would you like more?" Mrs. Fellowes asked, hovering around the man as if he were her long lost son and not the judge's long lost grandson.

"I don't want to take more than my share," he said.

The housekeeper laughed. "There's plenty for everyone. The milk cow gives more than we can drink, but the hogs love it." She poured more milk in his glass.

The way his brow furrowed, Lilah could tell he found it hard to understand there was plenty of food.

"I'll show you around when you've had your fill of cookies and milk," she offered.

Chapter Six

Brody shoved another cookie into his mouth, chewed, and swallowed the rest of the milk. His mouth and stomach were happier than they'd been in years. This trip he'd eaten more food than he'd had all of last year.

He grabbed his hat from the peg by the door as Lilah stepped out the door ahead of him.

She led him to three small buildings behind the main house. "That's the privy for the house." She pointed to the smallest building that was closest to the house and farthest from the stream running down the crevice behind the house. "That's the ice house where the milk and other foods are kept cold by large blocks of ice we haul from Malheur Lake in the winter." She waved a hand toward a sod building with two doors. "The other side is the cellar where we keep the canned goods."

"You have a whole building just to keep canned

goods?" he asked, wandering toward the side she'd said was the cellar.

"We live a long way from the nearest store and have to feed those of us in the house and the ranch hands." She stepped beside him and tugged on the door. "This place is large enough and cool enough to keep food supplies good until we need them."

He grasped the handle and helped. "Why is this door so tight? Doesn't that make it hard for Mrs. Fellowes to get things?"

"It's a tight fit to keep the rain and snow out." Lilah motioned for him to enter.

Stepping into the sod building the scent of earth overwhelmed him. The low ceiling and shelves along the walls closed in around him. His breathing quickened and his heart raced. He pushed by Lilah, who stood in the doorway.

Out in the sunshine, he bent at the waist, inhaling the warm, fresh air.

"Are you all right?" she asked, placing a hand on his back.

Brody shook his head and caught himself. The earthy scent was new, but the dark and damp confined space reminded him of what he'd escaped. Prison.

He stood, took one more deep breath and exhaled. "I'm good now." Drawing in more breaths and easing the tension in his neck and shoulders by rolling his head around on his neck, he said, "You didn't say how Mrs. Fellowes gets that door open."

"She puts her weight behind her tugging."

Peering at Lilah, he saw mirth in her eyes and her lips quivered. He laughed and she joined him.

Her sparkling laughter lessened the tension. As she slowly brought her laughing under control, he wished he could think of something that would keep her laughing. He was surprised by the humor and warmth of her laugh. Being a woman who wanted to be smarter than most men, he'd expected her to be more uppity.

"Please don't tell her I said that. But it's the truth. She latches onto the handle with both hands and practically sits down when she throws her body backward."

"I would like to see that, but I don't think I could keep from laughing." He shoved the cellar door closed and waved his hand to the front of the house. "What else do you have to show me?"

They walked through a small grove of trees with white bark that shaded the side of the house.

"What kind of trees are these? I've never seen ones with white bark." He stopped and ran his hand up and down the slick trunk of the tree. A breeze fluttered the leaves, and they rustled pleasantly.

"They're aspen trees. The judge went up to the Steens Mountains and dug them up to transplant here. He believes houses should have shade. In this country with the hot summers it's nice to find a spot of shade." Lilah reached up and rustled the leaves on a lower branch. "I love the sound of the leaves. It's a joyous sound, like bells."

The staccato thud of racing hooves, drew them out of the trees and to the front of the house. Three men on horseback raced up to the large barn and jumped off their horses before the animals came to a complete stop.

"Something's wrong." Lilah picked up her skirt

and ran toward the barn.

Brody followed, keeping in step with her and watching the men talking to Smithy. The barn was the farthest building from the house.

They arrived as the largest of the three men demanded, "What do you mean he went looking for the dead cow?"

Smithy backed up. "Buster, you know how he is when he's upset. I tried to talk him into waiting for you, but he wouldn't listen."

"Damn!" Buster handed the reins of his horse to Smithy. "Get my other horse saddled. I'm going after him."

"Buster, what's wrong?" Lilah grabbed the man by the shirt sleeve.

The man's gaze drifted over her and landed on Brody. "You must be the grandson. Why didn't you go with him?"

Brody stared at the man. "With who?"

"Your grandfather, the judge. He's rode off on his own." Buster fidgeted with his gloves. "He's getting too old to do such a fool thing."

"I didn't know about it until he'd left, and I don't know one hill around here from another." He ignored the comment the judge was getting too old. What he'd seen, the man had seemed in good health and faculties. Better than most of the men he knew in New York that were the judge's age.

"He knows this land better than all of you," Lilah said.

"I know that. But if he runs into the person responsible for the cow killing, what do you think is going to happen?" Buster turned to the other two men with him. "Go take care of the evening chores."

They nodded, but their gaze was on Brody. He didn't smile, just stared back until they both led their horses around the side of the barn.

Smithy returned with a large horse.

Buster swung up on the animal. "Any idea where he's gone?" His gaze landed on Lilah.

"When Sandy stopped us, he said they found a dead, skinned cow up dry creek."

The foreman nodded. "I'll find him."

"He told Sandy to get Clem and Roy to help Stubbs round up the cattle in the area and push them closer to home and Sandy was to get Angel to help him track whoever did this."

"The judge did the right thing, except for riding out there. I'll bring him back, but it's going to be late." He kicked the horse into a run and headed down the road from the ranch.

Lilah sighed. "The judge thinks he's still the young man who homesteaded here."

"He looked healthy to me," Brody said.

"He is for a man his age. There's days, I find him sleeping in the chair behind his desk. He doesn't even realize he sleeps."

The question that had been nagging at him popped out. "Do you know why the judge didn't contact me five years ago?"

She opened the barn door and motioned for him to follow.

The main part of the building had a loft. He stared up at the floor and waited for her to answer.

"That's where we store the hay for the horses after it's cut and dried." She walked between the wagon and buggy standing in the open area.

"You're avoiding my question." He followed her deeper into the barn.

She stopped at a horse stall and whistled. A pretty grayish horse stuck its head over the gate. "This is my mare, Dusty." Lilah continued to pet the horse's head.

"Are you avoiding my question?" he asked, leaning against the stall gate on the other side of the horse's head. Was she stalling to avoid hurting his feelings or because the judge wasn't planning on treating him like family?

"That's a question you'll have to ask the judge. All I know is when he received the information from the Pinkertons that your mother was dead and you were working the docks, he cried. First from grief, then from joy. Why he didn't contact you, only he knows." Her hand stopped and she studied him. "I don't know why he changed his mind about you coming here or why he had Marshal Evert escort you, but I do know if you don't stay it will break his heart."

Brody pushed away from the gate. "What else do you need to show me?" He wasn't going to let her pretty eyes and pouty lips change his mind about cutting his ties with the judge. He didn't need family. Even as the thought rolled through his head, his heart wasn't as set on getting away.

"Come on then." Lilah led him back to the main door of the barn and turned left. "This is the corral for the working horses. The horses the men ride and the horses used to pull the wagon and buggy. They're brought in at night so the ones needed for the day can be caught each morning and the rest graze up on the hill."

Past the corral sat a small addition connected to the long, low building she'd already told him was the bunkhouse.

"This lean-to off the bunkhouse is the kitchen for the men. Sourdough makes the meals and sends those out riding with some grub to hold them over until dinner." She waved a hand. "That's the bunkhouse where all the hired hands live, except Buster. He's the foreman. He and Agnes, his wife, and the children live in that cabin in front of the garden." She stopped and stared at the garden. "I've been trying to keep the garden up but it's hard without Agnes's help. She's having a hard time just getting through a day of her regular work."

Brody remembered her arguing with the judge about needing to stay to help Agnes. "I've never heard of a woman being poorly when they were in the family way." His thoughts went to all the women living in the tenements who carried on with their daily chores and lives as if they didn't have a swollen belly and a child on the way.

"I've tried to get her to ride into Burns and see the doctor, but she refuses. She wasn't this poorly with Buddy and Betsy." Lilah chewed on her bottom lip and her brow furrowed under her hat brim. "I'm worried something bad is going to happen."

He saw her worry but didn't know how to ease it. "I'm sure with your help she'll be fine."

She shook her head and started across the road. "I

don't think my being at the birth will be enough."

Brody followed her to the smaller barn. Hogs squealed, chickens squawked, and a cow bawled.

"This is the barn that houses the animals who feed us. You'll get to know these animals well since the judge said you'd be caring for them until after haying." She started on the side farthest from the house. A tan cow with big brown eyes, horns, and a bell on her neck stood in a small enclosed area with grass. "This is Daisy, the milk cow. You'll be milking her twice a day. The morning milk goes to the hogs and the evening milk is put in a crock in the ice house. Gus, the hired hand who usually deals with these chores, will show you what to do tomorrow."

"I've never milked a cow." He stared at the four teats about four inches long sticking out from a large bulge between the animal's back legs.

"You'll learn tomorrow morning." The smile in her voice made him wonder how hard it was to milk a cow.

She walked into the barn and he followed. "These animals are kept inside during the winter to ensure they are healthy. That's the area Daisy will stay. The hogs can go in and out all year round." She walked to the back of the barn.

Brody covered his nose with his arm. "What's that smell?"

"The hogs."

"We eat something that smells that bad?" He'd seen drawings of pigs and heard them squeal behind the butcher house but he'd never smelled one.

"They are actually a clean animal. It's the manure you smell. They tend to pile it in one spot. Outside it's

not so bad, but the boar likes to pile his in the barn."
She turned to him and smiled. "That's one of your jobs,
removing the manure pile from the barn."

He didn't like the chores he'd be taking on. If I'm
the grandson of the ranch owner, I should be following
him around. With this thought foremost in his mind, he
followed Lilah out a side door that led directly into a
room full of chickens. They squawked, flapped their
wings, and ran out of the room through a small hole in
the outside wall.

"You'll feed and water the chickens and clean out
the coop. You won't have to gather the eggs, Buddy
likes to do that." Lilah walked back out the door they'd
come through and closed it when he stood inside the
barn. "That's everything you'll be taking care of in the
morning and evening before you help with the haying."

"How long should these chores take?" He was
thinking at least half a day, noting the water for all the
animals would need to be hauled from the creek
running behind the other barn.

"Gus gets them done in an hour in the morning and
evening." Lilah walked to the main door of the barn.

He scanned the barn, moving from the cow's pen
to the hogs, and the chicken coop. All this was done in
an hour? If he stuck around long enough, he could
probably get it done in two hours. But he wouldn't be
here long enough to get fast at the chores.

Chapter Seven

Darkness had settled around the ranch an hour earlier. Brody paced the sitting room while Mrs. Fellowes and Lilah did needlework. The last fifteen minutes he'd told himself he wasn't worried about the judge, he wanted to go to bed and neither of the women seemed obliged to tell him where to find his room.

He started to ask when they heard hoof beats in front of the house. Not wanting to appear anxious, he hung back as the young woman and the housekeeper hurried to the front door. The judge stepped through the door, his face haggard, his shoulders drooping.

"Judge!" Lilah surged forward, putting his arm over her shoulders and leading him into the sitting room. His outing had taken more out of him than anyone had suspected. "Mrs. Fellowes bring him a cup of tea with honey and the dinner you had warming."

"Yes, Miss." The housekeeper hustled toward the

kitchen.

Brody stepped to the old man's other side and helped ease him into a chair. He stepped back, leaving room for Lilah to fuss over him.

A knock on the door drew his gaze from the old man in the chair.

"Don't stand there, go see who it is," she admonished.

He didn't like being ordered around by the woman but it beat standing there staring at the old man. Crossing the sitting room, he pulled the door open.

Buster, the foreman, stood at the door, his hat in his hands. "I need to talk to you," he said.

"Why me?" Brody followed the man as he backed out onto the porch, closing the door.

"You're the judge's only kin. He can't take off like he did today. I found him nearly falling off his horse. He forgot to take water and he's..." Buster shoved his hat on his head and rubbed a hand over his face. "I wasn't supposed to tell anyone, but seein' as how you're kin and here now, when he and I went to Canyon City for supplies this spring, he saw a doctor."

His gut squeezed. Here it came. The one thing that would keep him here.

"The doc told him to slow down and his heart might make it another ten years. But if he kept up working alongside the men and taking fool rides like today, he may only last five or less." Buster shoved a finger at his chest. "Now you're here, you need to help take on the responsibilities."

He slapped the foreman's hand away. "I don't know the judge, I don't know ranching, and I sure as hell don't care about this place." Even as he said the words his heart lurched. He wanted to belong, he wanted to be needed. But so far every person he cared for had left him. He wasn't going to care for the judge, from the sound of things, he'd leave too.

Buster took hold of Brody's shirt and lifted him onto his toes. "You damn well better get to know your grandfather and learn about ranching. He's set on giving this ranch to you, but only if you can run it. It would break his heart and his spirit if you rejected what he's offering."

The door creaked and opened slightly.

Buster leaned closer. "And I know how you came to be here. No one else does, but the judge wanted me to know, since I'll be the one showing you around. Believe me, I would like nothing better than to send you back to where you came from, but Judge Radley and I go way back, and I owe him his family."

"Is everything all right out there?" Lilah asked from the doorway.

"Yes." Buster released him and stomped down the steps.

He took a moment to let the man's words sink in. The judge planned to leave him the ranch. He'd never owned more than the clothes on his back and a dollar or two his whole life. He could have a home. That was if he didn't mess up—like his father.

***

The following morning, the judge roused Brody out of bed just as the sun peeked through the window.

"Come on, boy. Gus is waiting in the barn to show you how to do the chores." The old man tugged the covers back.

He opened one eye. Judge Radley was dressed and looked rested. Which was more than he could say for himself. After the women had taken care of the old man, they'd finally sent him to a room upstairs. The bed was comfortable, but he'd heard snoring all night long. He was used to people talking, screaming, crying, even footsteps at night, but he had never heard someone snore to the likes of the judge.

"What time is it?" he asked, rolling away from the old man.

"Five. When the chores are done, we'll have breakfast. After that we'll do an inventory of the hay equipment." The judge shook his shoulder. "I'm not leaving until you are dressed and headed down the stairs."

He groaned, rolled over, and sat up.

The old man held his pants out to him. "We'll go to Burns the end of the week and get you some working clothes."

"What's wrong with these?" he asked, putting on the pants and grabbing his shirt off the end of the bed.

"I don't know what you did on the docks, but these clothes aren't going to hold up to ranch work." He held the door to the bedroom open and waited.

Brody stuffed his feet into his boots and laced them up. They were the footwear of dock workers. The soles were made to grip wet wood and give leverage when pulling on hoists. They weren't anything like the boots he saw on the hired men.

He stood and walked out the door, yawning. Walking by Lilah's bedroom, he noticed her door stood ajar. Was the educated woman allowed to sleep in while he had to work before he could even have breakfast?

He entered the kitchen and found the housekeeper and young woman busy working dough.

"Good morning," Lilah said, smiling. "I told you the chores started early."

"I didn't think you meant this early." He grabbed his hat from the peg by the door and headed outside. The coolness was welcome even if it sent a chill up his arms. The room he'd slept in had been stuffy. He'd opened the window when he went to bed but didn't get any real relief until a few hours ago. But he hadn't had to share the room or bed with anyone. He'd been lucky when his ma passed that he could make enough money to live in a room by himself. Granted it was only a room with a cot, but he was better off than others in his building who shared not only a room but where they slept with family.

As he walked toward the barn, squealing hogs reminded him of the children in the tenement who screeched and screamed when getting their paddlings. The deep bawl of the cow echoed the low, deep moan of the ship's wind stacks. The noises might have reminded him of New York, but the cool, clean air was a welcome reminder he was out of the city. He went to the enclosure where they'd looked at the cow the day before. Daisy wasn't there. Retracing his steps, he entered the barn.

A man, older than the other hired hands he'd met, stood by the cow. She was raising a ruckus, bawling and moving her back feet as if agitated.

"You need to get out here on time. See the size of

her udder, she's in pain and needs the relief of being milked." Gus held out a small stool and a bucket.

"You could have started." Brody grabbed the two items from the man and walked over to the cow. He didn't have any idea where to start or what to do with the stool or bucket.

"Plunk that stool down next to her by the udder," Gus said, motioning for him to move closer to the moving back feet.

"What's the udder?"

Gus's jaw dropped, and he stared at him like he was dimwitted. "The udder is that big hard bag of milk with four teats." He stepped up beside Brody and placed the stool just in front of the moving back legs. "Sit down on that stool, poke your head into her flank, and start milking the teats. She'll stand still."

He had a pretty good idea where to place the bucket but wanted to fluster the man. "What do I do with the bucket?"

"For Pete's sake." Gus placed the bucket directly under the cow's udder. Now take hold of those two back teats, one in each hand, and pull down."

Brody wiped his hands on his pant legs and took hold of the teats. They were soft, supple, and engorged. He wrapped his hand around one and pulled down. Nothing happened other than the cow letting out an outraged sounding bawl.

"Start at the top, squeezing with your thumb and first finger, and slowly squeeze each finger down the teat." Gus made the motion with his hand. "Use both hands. Pull on one, and then pull on the other, and don't stop in between. Daisy will let her milk down. She wants the relief and knows it's her job."

He studied the pot-bellied man. How did he know the cow knew her job? She was just a stupid animal. He pulled on the teats like Gus told him.

A stream of milk shot into the bucket. He pulled on the teat in his right hand and another stream zinged into the pail. The cow dropped her head and started crunching on grain.

He started at the top of the teat, squeezing his fingers.

"Keep going, over and over again."

His fingers made the motion in a continuous flow and milk squirted into the pail. Soon the milk came so fast foam formed on top of the milk in the bucket.

"See how the back, where you're milking has gone down and the milk isn't squirting as hard, she's gettin' empty back there. Switch to the two front teats," Gus said. He stood a moment watching, then wandered over to the hog pens.

Squealing and woofing filled the barn.

Brody kept his head tucked against the cow and kept the milk flowing. He had to admit without Gus watching him, it was a peaceful chore. Him, the cow, and the sound of the milk filling the pail. The front teats became thin and barely any milk squirted. He pulled the bucket out from under the cow and picked up the stool.

Gus stepped out of the chicken coop. "That stool hangs up on that hook." He pointed to a metal hook made from a used horseshoe on the pole by the cow's pen.

Once the stool was hung up, Gus walked over to where Daisy stood. "This is a stanchion. It holds the cow in place to milk. In the morning when you come to milk, pour oats in this trough. She'll stick her head through, and you move this board over." He pulled a wooden peg from the stanchion and a board slid to the side. Daisy lifted her head and backed out.

He nodded. That was a clever way to hold the animal and not harm it.

"Bring the bucket of milk. Mornings you give it to the hogs. It keeps them busy while you clean out the pen." Gus pointed to a long trough on the other side of the wooden fence.

Brody poured the milk and the two large hogs and two medium sized hogs pushed at each other trying to get more of the liquid.

"Put the bucket down, grab that shovel, and hop in the pen." Gus pointed to a shovel leaning against the wall by the pig pen.

He grabbed the shovel but was hesitant to hop in the pen with the large, noisy animals.

Gus waved for him to get over the fence. "They won't hurt you. They know the routine."

Brody crawled over the fence. The largest hog raised his head and smacked, staring at him.

"The boar won't hurt you. You're cleaning up his mess."

Sliding the shovel under the foul pile of manure, he picked it up and asked, "What do I do with it?"

"Best to shovel it in a pile then slide it out the door. Them walking through it will move it around out there."

He did as he was told and hurried back over the fence as the hogs finished the milk and started milling around inside the pen woofing at him.

"I fed the chickens, but I'll show you where the feed is and where to put it." Gus showed him that chore and handed him two buckets. "Walk to the creek and bring back water for the animals. Fill the trough out in Daisy's pen, fill the trough you poured milk in for the hogs, and then the pan in the chicken pen."

His stomach growled.

"When that's done you can have breakfast." Gus slapped him on the back and headed out of the barn.

Carrying the two buckets, Brody followed and crossed the road to the opening between the cabin and bunkhouse. He found the spot it looked like was used to scoop water. He filled the buckets and hauled them back. The cow's trough was half full. He filled it with the two buckets and returned to the stream. The next two buckets took care of the hogs. Thinking ahead, he filled both buckets again, but it only took half of one to water the chickens. He left the bucket sitting by the hog's pen. It would save time this evening when he did the chores again.

The scent of the hog pen followed him to the house. He looked down and noted the soles of his boots that were so good for traction on the dock, held the pig manure in their crevices. He sat on the porch and unlaced his shoes. Mrs. Fellowes and Lilah wouldn't appreciate him bringing that into the house.

When he stood, the judge opened the door. "I was just coming to see how those chores were going."

"My boots brought back the pig pen. Thought it best to take them off." He stood and reached out to open the screen door.

"Wash up in that basin." The older man pointed to a tin basin with water, soap, and a towel on a bench.

He washed up and walked by the man. Fresh sweet rolls and bacon aromas filled the kitchen. "Smells good in here," he said, taking a place at the kitchen table.

"Don't get used to it," Judge Radley said.

His head whipped around so fast his neck popped. The judge had on the stern expression he'd witnessed yesterday when Sandy rode up and told them about the cow.

Chapter Eight

Lilah couldn't believe the judge had said something so mean. All he'd talked about since learning his grandson was coming to the ranch was getting to know the boy. And here he was making insinuations Brody wasn't welcome.

"Judge, what are you talking about?" she asked, taking a seat across from Brody at the table. She didn't think the judge would send his grandson away so soon after finding him. It didn't make sense. She looked across the table at the younger man. His face had turned to stone, making him look even more like his grandfather. Had they had words that she didn't know about? Had the younger man said or done something to upset the judge?

The older man stared at her. "I've decided that until you go to university, it would be best for your reputation to not have Brody in the house." He turned his attention to his grandson. "You'll stay in the bunkhouse and take meals there except for dinner. I'd like you to spend dinner and the evenings with me so I can get to know you."

"That's not fair," Lilah argued. She was the outsider, he was family.

"It's fine," Brody said. His head was tipped down and he stared into his plate.

"No, it's not." She wasn't giving up on this. "You belong in this house more than I do." She put a hand on the judge's arm. "You can't put him out in the bunkhouse, he's family."

His rough hand patted her hand. "Yes, he is. But he has to learn how this ranch works from the hired men to the daily chores. The best way to learn is for him to hang out with the men who do the work."

She glanced at the younger man. He nodded slightly. Did he agree to this because he didn't want to be around his grandfather? He hadn't shown much concern last night when the older man could barely walk through his own door.

"Besides, he'll only have to stay in the bunkhouse until the end of September when you go off to the university." The old man's eyes glinted as if he'd put one over on her.

She stood and glanced back and forth between the two men. "I told you, Agnes needs me. I'll not be going to university until January. This trying to make me feel bad about Brody staying in the bunkhouse isn't going to make me change my mind. He can stand the bunkhouse as long as I need to take care of Agnes." She picked up her dishes, placed them in the sink, and headed out the back door.

Her body shook with anger as she walked through the trees and headed toward the foreman's house. That was the first time the judge had tried to manipulate her. She didn't like it. In the past they talked things over, but lately, he seemed to think he could tell her what to do rather than ask her opinion. Like go to the university in September. She'd only been home a month from the finishing school and he was ready to send her off to Denver. And she did plan to go, just not before she saw Agnes and Buster's next child.

She stepped up to the cabin door, knocked, and walked in. The smell of a morning meal didn't linger in the air. Since the beginning of this child growing in Agnes' belly, she couldn't tolerate any food smells. Buster and the kids took their meals in the bunkhouse.

"Agnes? Are you up?" She walked through the cabin to the bedroom in the back. The children slept in the loft up above their parents' bedroom.

Agnes lay curled in a ball, still in her nightgown, in the middle of the bed.

Lilah hurried across the room and sat on the bed. "Agnes?" she said softly.

The woman's eyelids fluttered up. Her once vivid blue eyes were sleepy. Gray skin rimmed her eyes. She'd lost weight, but that was due to the first three months she'd had trouble keeping food down. Now she did small tasks and went back to bed, exhausted.

"Come on. You have to get up and eat. Think of the baby." She gently uncurled the woman and sat her up, leaning her against the pillows placed behind her. "I know for a fact Judge Radley is going to Burns this

Friday. I think you should come with us and see the doctor."

Agnes turned her head one direction and whispered, "No. No doctor. I didn't need one for the other two."

"You weren't this tired with the other two. He may have something that will make you feel better." She stood. "I'm going to make you some tea and we'll get you dressed."

Agnes just stared at the wall in front of her.

In the kitchen, Lilah put the kettle on to heat and spooned tea into the teapot. If Agnes refused to go to the doctor, perhaps she needed to persuade the doctor to make a house call.

***

"Come into my office," the judge said to Brody, standing and walking out of the kitchen.

He glanced at the housekeeper. "That was a good breakfast. Sorry I won't be having more of them." He walked through the kitchen door and found the old man in a room between the kitchen and the sitting room.

"Come in." The judge sat in a chair behind a large wooden desk littered with papers. A ledger sat in the upper right corner of the desk. "Have a seat."

He sat in the chair in front of the desk. There was a seat long enough for two under a painting of two people on horseback in what appeared to be this country.

"I meant what I said. You'll stay out in the bunkhouse to get to know the hired hands and to learn from them. They know everything that goes on here. It's the fastest way for you to learn how this ranch operates." He leaned back in his chair. His eyes narrowed as he studied Brody. "It seems you aren't too keen on the idea."

"Sir, I haven't a choice whether I like it or not. It's live where you tell me or go to prison." He studied the old man as intensely as he was watched. This first meeting alone with his grandfather would determine if he stuck it out or took out on his own. The idea of heading out didn't settle well, knowing this man, his grandfather, was ill. He also wanted to know what Lilah's intentions were toward his grandfather. Being as she was educated it made him wonder why she wasn't off looking for a well-to-do husband.

Judge Radley leaned forward, placing his arms on his desk. "You had a choice when you stole that food."

He shook his head. "No, I didn't. If I hadn't stolen food for Maria and little Emma, they would have starved to death."

"Did you leave behind a wife and child?" Distaste twisted the judge's mouth and darkened his eyes.

"No. They lived in the next room in the tenement. Maria's husband was killed in a factory accident. She couldn't find work that would allow her to bring her daughter along. She took in washing to pay for the room where they lived, but they didn't have any for food. I could barely pay for my room, my meals, and the clothing necessary for working on the docks." He didn't understand his need to make his grandfather see his thieving was to help others, not himself.

"This woman. She didn't have any family?"

"No. Her husband brought her over from Spain. She had no one other than her husband and her little girl." He leaned back in his chair. "I would steal again if it helped feed someone who could not afford it."

"What will happen to this woman and her child with you gone?" Again the man studied him closely.

That was his biggest worry as he'd traveled farther and farther from New York City. "If Maria gives in to the need to feed her child, she could become a prostitute."

The judge shook his head. "I can see why you were compelled to help. But stealing is never the way. Which brings me to the rules you will abide by. No drinking, whoring, stealing, or killing. And most importantly, no getting familiar with Lilah. She doesn't need any more reasons to keep her from continuing her education."

Brody had nodded to all the rules. He wasn't much of a drinker, didn't like to pay for a good time, and had never shot a gun. The stealing for him wasn't a compulsion. He'd learned the art as a child when his mother needed food or medicine. He didn't see a need to use that skill while at the ranch. Lilah. That was another thing. She was the only person on the ranch close to his age and he enjoyed ruffling her feathers.

Judge Radley rose and held his hand over the desk. "Do I have your word you will follow my rules?"

He stood, grasped the man's hand, and looked him in the eye. "I'll do my best."

A tear glint in the old man's eye. "That's all I can ask for, son."

They released hands.

Brody's chest tightened. He wanted to make this man proud. Wanted to prove he wasn't anything like his father.

"Head on out to the bunkhouse and find Buster,

he'll show you around this morning. We'll deal with the inventory this afternoon." Judge Radley sat down ay his desk and pulled papers toward him.

Without a word, he pivoted and headed for the room he'd occupied during the night. He might only have one set of clothing besides the ones he had on, but they were his belongings and they went where he'd be sleeping. The bunkhouse.

***

Brody couldn't believe he'd just spent three hours riding a horse. He still had a lot to learn, but he and Buster had covered a lot of ground as the foreman showed him the boundaries from the top of the highest point on the ranch and down to the herd kept closest to ranch headquarters. These breeding cattle were the papered stock worth more money than the cattle sold to the beef market.

The foreman had pointed out the hay fields and the sequence in which they would be harvested. Now they walked the horses up the road toward the barn.

Buster glanced up at the sun. "Sourdough'll be puttin' the noon meal on the table. Best get back and put your horse up if you want any."

"Aren't you going to eat?" Brody asked, stopping his horse in front of the barn.

"Going to check on Agnes and the kids."

All morning Buster had appeared distracted. He'd been worrying about his family.

"Lilah said your wife wasn't well. Sorry to hear that." He dismounted and found his legs wobbly.

Buster smiled. "Takes some getting used to being in a saddle for hours." He spun his horse and trotted over to his cabin and dismounted.

Brody wondered what besides the child in her was causing the woman problems. He wasn't a doctor but living in a tenement with people who couldn't afford a doctor, he'd picked up information on a lot of home remedies.

He led the horse into the barn and stared at the straps holding the saddle on the animal's back.

"Need help greenhorn?"

He spun around. Lilah walked in from the door leading to the corrals.

"I can't remember which strap needs to be unhooked." He hated to admit that to a woman, but he had a feeling she wouldn't have walked on by and let him figure it out eventually. He backed away, holding the reins in one hand.

She smiled and started messing with the widest strap. "This is the cinch strap. You have to loosen and unhook it. Then the belly strap. Now lift it off and set it on that pole." She pointed to a long pole that had a couple of saddles sitting on it.

He pulled the saddle from the horse and did as he was told.

"Did you have a good ride?" Lilah asked, picking up a brush and brushing the horse's sweaty back.

Brody leaned against a stall and watched her, keeping his distance. "It was interesting. That's the first time I've ridden a horse. It's a much faster way of getting around than walking."

She laughed. "It is. What did you think of the ranch?"

"It's big. Lots of hills and valleys."

"Buster must have taken you to the tall hill." She moved to the other side of the horse.

To keep her in view, he ducked under the neck of the horse and resumed his position against the stall. "It was quite a climb. Thought I was going to go off the back of the saddle and horse a couple of times."

"There's a knack to staying in the saddle when going up and down hills. I'll show you after the hay harvest." She put the brush back in the wooden box that held half a dozen brushes. "Put your horse in the corral and go get your noon meal. Sourdough won't serve you if he's already cleared the table."

His gaze followed her out of the barn. It was as if the judge making her off limits made him more interested in her.

Chapter Nine

Brody and the judge stood in front of a large metal contraption with many pointed pieces and a wide metal seat.

"This is a mower," the judge said. "It's pulled by two horses."

The mower had a long bar with jagged teeth. "How does it work?"

"A driver sits on that seat and drives the horses along the edge of the field cutting a swath of grass. The wheels move the cutting teeth back and forth. The horses are driven around the outside of the field so they don't knock the grass down before it gets cut."

He counted three mowers. "Who drives the mowers?" He wasn't volunteering. He'd never driven a wagon and had no desire to run a piece of machinery that looked this dangerous.

"Gus, Stubbs, and Lilah."

He stared at the older man, touching the pointed

pieces on the mowers. "Lilah? Isn't that dangerous to have a woman using one of these machines?"

"Buster taught her how to drive the mower and the sweep rake three years ago. She does a better job than the men." Judge Radley moved along through the side of the barn that stored the equipment. "These are the sweep rakes. They gather the windrowed hay and haul it to the barn or stack yard, depending on which field is being harvested." He walked farther along. "These are rakes that put the hay in windrows, so the sweep can pick it up faster. That large thing at the end is the stacker."

Brody stared at the equipment. The stacker was the only thing that he could figure out. It had mechanics like the hoists they used on the docks. He hoped that was where the judge put him to work during the harvesting.

"I have my list of repairs for Smithy to work on." The judge shoved a small book into his pocket along with the pencil he'd used to make his list. He headed for the outside door.

"Did you figure out who killed the cow?" Brody asked. The men had talked about the killing during the noon meal, but the ones who knew anything weren't there, Buster, Sandy, and Angel, the hand he'd yet to meet.

"Won't know anything until Sandy and Angel get back. They've been gone long enough they must have picked up a trail." Judge Radley stepped out into the summer sun. He held a hand to his eyes even though he had a wide-brimmed hat like all the other men in this area.

Brody wondered if he should say something to Lilah or Buster. The foreman already knew the judge was sick. What he didn't know was if the light bothering the judge was part of that illness or something different.

The older man pulled his hand away and continued walking toward the corrals. Unsure if he was to follow or not, he walked a few steps behind the man.

"Get up here, son. It's hard to talk to a man when he's trailing behind you."

He picked up his pace and walked alongside the older gentleman.

"You need three saddle horses. You can pick them out of the ones we plan to sell." Judge Radley stopped at the corral and put a foot on the bottom rail. "These are all five-year-olds that Angel and Sy have trained to work cattle."

He looked into the corral. Thirty horses of every color milled around in the corral. "You said I wouldn't be riding until after harvest, why do I need to pick out the horses now?"

The older man peered at him and smiled. "You don't have to pick them today. Hang out here by the corral when you have spare time. Watch them. Get to know them. See if you like how they move, if they come over. Curious horses make good horses. Don't pick them for their color, pick them for their brains." He laughed. "That's sound advice for picking a woman too. Your grandmother and your mother were smart women. And they both knew how to pick horses." Sadness filled his eyes and drooped his shoulders. "My Madeline would have loved seeing the horses I raise now." He put a hand on Brody's arm. "There's not a day goes by I don't miss both my girls."

The judge confiding in him, tugged at his heart. He missed his ma. There wasn't a day went by he didn't talk to her. He knew the loss the man standing next to him felt. He didn't want to cause his grandfather or anyone that misery.

***

Lilah spotted the judge and Brody standing by the corral that held the horses to be sold in the spring. They both stared at the horses, but she could tell by their dropped shoulders and arms resting on the top pole they weren't discussing horses. Her heart ached for both of them. The grandfather who so desperately wanted family again and the man who kept his distance. It was apparent he didn't want to get close because he called his grandfather Judge instead of the endearment the old man wanted to hear.

She settled her riding hat firmer on her head and entered the horse barn. After helping Agnes with her household chores all morning it was too hot to work in the garden. She'd tend to that after dinner when it wasn't so hot. Right now a ride would make her own breeze and ease some of the heat.

In the barn, Dusty nickered. She was ready for a ride as well. Lilah led the mare out of the stall, brushed and saddled the horse, and led her out of the barn.

Brody was alone by the horse corral. He turned and watched her.

She waved and mounted.

Buster said the younger man had rode better than he'd expected when they set out that morning. She was looking forward to giving him lessons. Clicking her tongue, she set the horse into a trot and then a lope down the road and around the edge of the hill. She knew better than to ride near where the cow was killed. Her path today would be the small patch of willows where the runoff from the snow settled, making a natural watering hole for the cattle.

Days like today would be only a memory once they started harvesting the hay. Right after that would be rounding up the cattle and getting ones they missed in the spring branded and settling them in the hay fields for the winter. And the baby would be coming.

Dread squeezed her chest. Without a doctor she didn't think Agnes and the baby would live. Why was the woman being so stubborn about a doctor? She'd tried to talk to Buster but he said if his wife didn't want a doctor, then don't make her see one. They were both being pig-headed.

Dusty nickered as they neared the watering hole.

Lilah peered ahead, studying the willow bushes. The only thing that would make Dusty nicker would be another horse. No one should be out here.

"Who's there?" she called, watching the willows for movement.

A horse snorted. Her gaze hovered the direction of the sound. Reaching down to grab the rifle in her scabbard, she realized she hadn't brought it with her. Not having her rifle on a ride, proved her mind had been occupied with Agnes and her troubles. That was the first thing the judge taught her. Never go out riding without a rifle. There could be four-legged and two-legged critters a rifle would scare off.

"What are you doing on Double R land?" She called out again.

"Didn't know I was trespassing." A scraggly-looking man stepped out from the willows. He'd not shaved in some time, his clothes were filthy from dust and sweat stains. "Saw the willows and figured there'd be water for my horse."

"Water your horse and move on. You are trespassing." As she talked, the man took small steps, closing the distance between them.

"What's a fine filly like you doing out here all alone?" He took several more steps.

She pulled on the reins, backing Dusty away from the man. "I belong on this ranch. I'd advise you to get on your horse and head back the way you came."

He grinned, showing dirty teeth. "Can't. There's men on my tail."

Scrutinizing him with a more critical eye, she noticed stains on his pants and shirt that looked like dried blood.

She spun Dusty around and dug her heels in. The man would be foolish to follow, but if she could get to the ranch, the judge would send men out to see about the man.

The wind whipped at her hair. Her hat slid, bouncing against her back, the rawhide she'd tied under her chin kept it from falling. She didn't hear hooves following her, but she looked over her shoulder anyway. Only the patch of willows getting smaller could be seen.

Dusty didn't slow until they neared the barn. The dogs ran out barking at her. Buddy and Betsy burst out of the small barn. And Brody and Smithy walked out of the horse barn.

Brody hurried toward her, his hands raised. He pulled her off the horse and stared into her face. "What's wrong?"

She shoved out of his hold. "I have to tell Buster and the judge."

"What?"

"A man was by the watering hole. He…he…"

"Did he hurt you?" Anger blazed in his eyes.

"No. But I think he's running from the law." She put a hand on his arm. "Please, find Buster and bring him to the judge." She spun and headed to the main house. Judge Radley would be reading stock reports about this time.

Brody headed for the cabin. He didn't like how disheveled Lilah looked when she'd raced back to the barn. There hadn't been any noticeable signs she'd been hurt, but he was damn sure going to go look for the man who scared her. He'd scratched his knuckles on the faces of several scumbags when a woman he knew had altercations with a man who was out of hand.

He knocked on the cabin door.

"Come in," Buster called.

Stepping into the quiet home, he was surprised to see it resembled a room housing with a lazy woman running it. With Lilah helping Mrs. Malone, he had expected the cabin to be as tidy as the main house.

"What do you want?" Buster asked, turning from the stove with a steaming kettle.

"Lilah just rode in like a wind storm and said there was a man at the watering hole. She wants you to go to the house so she can tell you and Judge Radley about him at the same time." Brody nodded to the other room. "Want me to stay here?"

"No, Agnes is resting." Buster grabbed his hat from the peg by the door and waited for him to exit before he did.

They strode to the house without talking and entered the front door.

"They're in the office," Mrs. Fellowes said, without missing a stroke of the cloth she used to polish the table in the sitting room.

At the office, neither knocked. The judge sat behind his desk studying Lilah who paced back and forth.

"Good you're both here." She motioned for them to sit. Buster took the chair in front of the desk. He took the one by a small table.

She stopped pacing and glanced at each one of them as she talked. "I rode down to the watering hole to the south. Dusty nickered and I figured someone had to be there. I called out twice before this man stepped out of the willows. He was dirty and said he was watering his horse. I told him that was fine, but to go back the way he came when he finished. He said he couldn't. Someone was following him. Looking him over again, I noticed he had dried blood on his clothing."

Brody's heart sped up. "What were you doing riding around by yourself?"

She spun toward him. "I've been riding on this ranch by myself for ten years."

"Well, you shouldn't." He held her gaze, waiting for her to back down, but she didn't. Her eyes only narrowed more.

"Enough. Buster, round-up whoever is here and go see if you can find this man. Even if he didn't kill my cow, he sounds like he's untrustworthy and I don't want him on Double R land." Judge Radley stood. "As for Lilah riding alone, I agree." He stared at her. "It's not a good idea as long as there is someone out there killing cattle."

She sputtered and Brody grinned.

"Come on," Buster said to him.

"He can't go. He doesn't know how to ride a horse," she said, pinning him with a glare.

"I think I mastered it fine this morning." Brody put his fingers to his cap brim and followed Buster. He heard Lilah pleading her case for riding alone as he closed the door.

"Glad you're willing to take me along," he said, falling into step alongside Buster.

"Got no choice. Everyone else is either out riding fence or chasing the person who killed the cow." Buster walked into the barn, picked up two bridles, and handed him one. "Catch the same horse you rode this morning."

Chapter Ten

Brody kept up with Buster even though the foreman's long-legged horse took one stride to every two strides of the horse he rode.

At the watering hole, they found evidence of the man and the horse. Buster dismounted and studied the tracks. "He must have headed out as soon as Lilah headed home." He walked around the edge of the watering hole and stared up the ridge. "He's headed deeper into the ranch instead of heading off."

The idea the man was using the Double R to hide had his hands gripping the reins tight and his teeth clenching. "Let's go find him." He dug his heels into the horse's side. It lunged forward.

"Wait!" Buster hollered. "You don't know where you're going. The boys are out checking fences. They'll come across him. When they come in tonight, I'll tell them to be on the lookout and to catch him when they see him. He's got some talkin' to do."

"But that ridge goes behind the house." Thinking of Lilah, Mrs. Fellowes, and the children being in danger made him anxious. His whole life he'd looked out for someone. First his ma, then Maria and Emma. Now it was the head-strong young woman, the housekeeper, and the other people who lived at the ranch.

"We'll all be watchin' for him." Buster mounted his horse and headed him back the way they came.

Brody searched the direction the man disappeared and then glanced back the way he must have come. Dust in the distance caught his attention. "Someone's coming."

Buster pulled his rifle from the leather cover hanging on his saddle and laid it across his lap.

"Aren't we going to meet them?" he asked.

"They're headed our direction. We'll just wait."

As the men drew closer, Buster replaced the rifle. "It's Sandy and Angel." Buster dug his heels into his horse's side and rode off in the direction of the men.

He followed and pulled to a stop as Buster started talking.

"Are you still following the trail of the person who killed the cow?"

Sandy nodded to Brody. "Yeah, the no-account's been runnin' us in circles."

"He is a man who has run before," said the younger man, he figured was Angel.

"Lilah ran into him here at the watering hole. That's why we're out here. Thought we might see who he was. Now we know." Buster turned his horse. "He headed up the ridge. You might as well come in and get a meal and sleep in your bed. He's on the ranch. We'll find him sooner or later."

"Sounds good. I can only stomach hard tack and jerk for so long." Sandy rubbed his belly.

Brody rode alongside Angel.

"Who are you?" Angel asked.

"Brody Yates."

"Angel Ortiz. Are you a new hire for hay harvest?" The young hand was dressed differently than the others. Buttons adorned the sides of his pant legs. He wore a short jacket and his hat had a wider brim than the hats of the other men.

"You could say that. Why are you dressed different?" He also noticed the man had a bit of an accent that was similar to Maria's.

"I am a vaquero. My family owned land in Mexico. Land that is now Texas."

He didn't miss the bitterness in the man's tone. "If your family has land why are you working for Judge Radley?"

"I also have two older brothers. They will inherit the ranch. I must use my cattle experience for others. Or until I acquire a ranch of my own." There was a gleam to the man's eyes that he'd seen before.

He dropped back from the vaquero and followed behind. He had a feeling Angel wouldn't be happy discovering his relationship to the judge.

***

Lilah changed into a clean dress and brushed her hair until it shined. She was curious to see what Buster and Brody found out, especially when she'd spotted

Angel and Sandy ride back with them.

"Put these rolls on the table and make sure there is water in the glasses," Mrs. Fellowes said, handing her a bowl of yeasty smelling rolls.

They always ate supper in the dining room, except when Judge Radley was away. Tonight she'd set the table for three. What would the conversation be like? She knew so little about Brody. She hoped the judge questioned him about his past during the meal and not afterwards. She had the garden to weed. It was either then or not help Mrs. Fellowes with breakfast and go out early in the morning.

The sound of men's voices in the Judge's office drew her out of the dining room.

"The man who scared Lilah is still on the ranch. Sandy said he's been taking them in circles." Brody's voice was low, urgent sounding. "Tell the women not to go anywhere alone and the kids need to always have a grownup with them."

"I think you're taking this too seriously. I'm sure it's a drifter who believes he can hide out on the ranch without being found." Judge Radley's voice was strong and confident. "We'll find him before he can cause any more trouble."

"I don't think so. If he's the one who violated your prize cow and is still hanging around…he has a reason." Brody wasn't backing down to his grandfather.

"Lilah, finish putting food on the table," Mrs. Fellowes called from the kitchen.

She scurried away from the office door and into the kitchen. Her heart galloped in her chest as if she'd been caught doing something dishonest.

"Why were you listening at the Judge's office?" Mrs. Fellowes asked, handing her a bowl of potatoes.

"I heard Brody and the judge talking and wondered what it was about. I'd hoped they were mending their relationship but it sounds like the opposite." That knowledge brought her heart to a complete stop. She wanted the judge to have the solace of his family when he passed, not regrets.

"Get that on the table and go call the men to supper." Mrs. Fellowes followed her with a large beef roast that still sizzled from the oven.

Lilah placed the potatoes on the table and headed to the office. She tapped on the door this time. The silence as she opened the door told her they were still disagreeing about the trespasser.

"Supper is on the table," she said cheerfully and noted the younger man had changed into his clean clothes for dinner. It pleased her to see he had manners. From the little bit of his past the judge had told her about, she'd expected someone with less manners and more distrust.

Judge Radley stood and moved to the door. Brody rose after the older man. The judge put his arm out to escort her to the dining room as had become their ritual from the first meal she'd ate with him ten years ago. She smiled, patted his hand, and walked into the dining room with him.

She glanced at Brody to motion to the chair he was to take and caught him brooding. His eyebrows nearly touched and his brow wrinkled. His lips weren't curved in a smile but rather in a straight line. Her gaze lifted to his and she felt stung. What was he thinking?

"Sit," Judge Radley commanded.

They all sat. He glanced at his grandson. "We say a short blessing. I'd be pleased if you joined us, but if you're not inclined, I understand as well."

Judge Radley held his hand out to her, and she reached across the table to Brody. He took her hand and held his grandfather's outstretched hand, but she witnessed his reluctance.

His hand was warm, rough, and cradled hers gently. Her cheeks heated, and she didn't hear a word of the blessing. Judge Radley released her hand. The hand still in Brody's tingled, making her glance up.

"The blessing is over."

Lilah pulled her hand back and glanced at the disapproving glower on the judge's face.

She swallowed her embarrassment and picked up the bowl of potatoes, passing them across the table. Judge Radley picked up the carving knife and went to work on the roast.

When the meal was finished, Judge Radley told Mrs. Fellowes, "We'll have coffee in the sitting room, please."

Lilah stood, unsure if she was invited to the sitting room. Before Brody arrived, she'd helped Mrs. Fellowes with the dishes and then joined the judge in the sitting room. He would read while she did needlework. Tonight, she itched to be in with the men. She had a great desire to know all she could about the judge's grandson.

When an invitation wasn't offered, she reluctantly picked up the dishes and started clearing the table. In the kitchen, she worked faster than usual.

"I'd think you'd like to be in the sitting room about now the way you're washing those dishes as if you were expecting a beau." Mrs. Fellowes smiled and dried the plate, stacking it with the others.

"What do you know about Brody?" she asked the housekeeper.

"Same as you. And I figure the same as the judge until the boy decides to open up. I'd bet you a week's worth of dishes, he won't tell anyone until he feels comfortable here, and I don't think that will happen with him staying in the bunkhouse." The older woman packed the plates to the pantry and placed them on a shelf.

What do the men in the bunkhouse think of the judge's grandson living with them? Lilah bet there were lots of questions and possibly trouble brewing. Worry had her drying her hands and hurrying into the sitting room. She needed to have a word with the judge about him banning his grandson to the bunkhouse.

Chapter Eleven

Brody sat in the sitting room enduring the silence and the judge staring at him as if he were waiting for him to tell his life story. It wasn't going to happen. He wasn't here because he felt anyone owed him anything. He was here because it was better than living in prison. The only thing that irritated him was that he liked it here. Liked most of the people and enjoyed learning about the ranch. He was curious about the relationship between the judge and his ward. He could have sworn when they held hands for the blessing, Lilah's cheeks had heated and he'd felt her hand tremble. It gave him the feeling she was a bit smitten with him. His heart had picked up and his lower regions had warmed at the thought of someone like her seeing something in him she liked.

Lilah entered the room, her skirts rustling, her cheeks flushed. "It's awful quiet in here." She glanced from him to the judge.

"Not much to say, I guess," he offered.

"I'd have thought Judge Radley would be quizzing you?" She glanced at the judge and her cheeks darkened in color.

Judge Radley scowled at her. He opened his mouth then clamped it shut.

What had he been about to say? Was he going to admonish her for speaking her mind? That was one of the things he liked about Lilah. She told you what she thought and asked you what she wanted to know.

Brody laughed and stared at the judge. "No, he thinks by not asking, I'll spill my life story. I'll let you both know. I won't have your pity, and I don't need your help. I'm staying because I'm curious about my ma and why she'd run away with my father." He stared pointedly at the judge. "And I'm curious about ranching. Those are the reasons I haven't left."

Judge Radley sat straighter in his chair and narrowed his eyes. "That worthless bastard talked about New York the whole time he was in this house. He had my little girl so enamored with him and that city I couldn't talk sense into her. But I thought she'd at least say good-bye before running off with the man. He saw the potential of this ranch. I thought he took her hoping I'd pay to get her back."

Brody shook his head. "They loved one another. That was plain. But my father couldn't make anything he tried work. Not acting, selling, or even factory work. He died a drunk in a gutter." His voice drifted off as indifferent as he felt toward the man who fathered him. A man who came home telling his wife he'd spent their last ten dollars on a get-rich-quick scheme.

He stood. "I'm beat." He walked to the kitchen, grabbed his cap from the peg by the door, and left the house. It felt strange to walk to the bunkhouse after having had supper in the house and slept there the night before. What were the others going to think when he waltzed into the bunkhouse, plopped on his bunk, and ignored them all?

Approaching the bunkhouse he heard voices.

"What do you say, he is Judge Radley's grandson?" Angel asked.

"That's what Buster told me. That Judge Radley's grandson was coming, and they hadn't seen one another before," Sandy said.

So the judge had only told Buster who he really was. Why? With him eating supper at the house every night it was going to cause the hands to wonder.

He opened the door to the bunkhouse. Eight faces turned his direction, even the men sprawled on their bunks.

"I put my things on that bunk. Is it already taken?" he asked, walking over to the bunk near the door.

"Nope. No one likes that one because of the drafty door," Sandy said. "You can have it."

"Thanks." He sat on the bunk, placed his cap on the peg in the wall above the head of the bed, and unlaced his boots.

"I ain't never seen boots like them before," said a hand about his age. He was long and lanky with blond hair, narrow eyes, and a long nose. "I'm Sy. Best roper in this here bunkhouse."

"Brody Yates. These boots are for working the

docks. I was a dock hand before coming out here." He placed the boots at the end of the bed, took off his shirt and pants, and lay down on the bunk in his long drawers and socks. He plucked the hat from the peg and placed it over his face to block out the lantern glowing from the rafter over the small table several were gathered round playing cards.

"You want to meet everyone before you go to sleep?" Sandy asked.

He lay there a minute thinking it through. He didn't have to make friends with them, but it would be in his interest to know the men he'd be working with. Sweeping the cap from his face, he spun his legs and sat up on the side of the bed. "Might as well."

"I'm Sandy, this here's Angel."

Brody nodded and received the glare he expected.

"This is Stubbs. He was with me when we stopped the wagon."

He nodded to the short, squat man. With his hat off his hairless head shone in the lantern light.

"Sy just introduced himself. Then there's Clem and Roy."

Clem was of average build, hair the color and texture of straw that stuck out over his big ears. Roy was built like Clem, dark short hair and bucked teeth. He nodded to them.

"You've met Smithy and Gus," Sandy said, waving his hand to the two men on their bunks.

"I did." He moved to lay back down.

"Why are you sleeping in the bunkhouse?" Angel asked.

He'd known this was coming after hearing their

conversation before he entered the bunkhouse.

"Because I'm a hired hand." He stared at Angel, daring the man to continue.

Seemed the vaquero didn't have a lick of sense.

"You are not a hired hand. You are the boss's grandson." Angel waved his hand. "We all know. What are you doing here?"

"It was this or prison for stealing food for the neighbor woman and her child." This time he lie back, put the cap over his face, and ignored the silence.

***

The sound of the others rising brought Brody out of a sound sleep. He scrubbed his hands over his face, noticed he needed to shave, and sat up. Everyone was dressed and walking into the kitchen/dining area. That was everyone but Angel.

He groaned and pulled his shirt on.

"Do you not feel ashamed to come to your family?" Angel stood at the end of the bed glaring at him.

"I didn't come to them. The judge sent a U.S. Marshal to bring me here." He dressed as the other man continued to glare.

"Stay away from Lilah. Your kind should not even speak to her." Angel spun on his boot heel and his fancy silver spurs jingled as he marched into the kitchen.

He smiled. He'd been right about his assumption Angel hoped to get this ranch by marrying Lilah. This made sticking around a whole lot more interesting. There had to be a way to find out her feelings for the vaquero and show he only wanted her for the ranch. He didn't want to hurt her, but if the man was only after the ranch, she had a right to know.

The thought of eating in the room with all the other hands wasn't appealing, but he couldn't go begging from Mrs. Fellowes. There was a reason the judge put him out here in the bunkhouse, and it wasn't just for Lilah's reputation.

He laced up his boots, wondering how he could get a pair like the others wore. He'd noticed while riding that Buster's narrow-toed boots slid into the stirrups easily while he had to force his boots to fit.

Crossing the bunkhouse, he entered the back kitchen/dining area. The cook, Sourdough, removed an empty platter and replaced it with a platter full of hotcakes.

There were two empty chairs. He took the one between Sandy and Gus. He had a good feeling about these two. Now the two across the table glaring at him were another thing. Angel wasn't hiding his animosity toward him one bit. But he was surprised to see Sy giving him an angry stare. He'd only met the man last night.

He piled hotcakes on his plate and scooped runny eggs on top. Working at the ranch was giving him more to eat than he could remember. Eggs, the cookies the day before yesterday, and the meat last night. Back in the tenements he'd bring home bones that Maria made into soup for the three of them. On payday he brought her vegetables and they ate bread purchased from the bakery. Meat, eggs, and sweets had been rare.

The bunkhouse door closed and footsteps approached. Buster walked through the kitchen door and took the last chair. He looked tired. Without a word he dished food onto his plate, picked up his eating utensils, then peered around the table.

"Men, we have an intruder on the ranch. Lilah ran into him yesterday at the willow watering hole." Buster motioned toward him. "Me and Brody went out there and he was gone. Angel and Sandy came along following the trail of the person responsible for killing Judge Radley's best cow. He's one and the same. He headed up the South Ridge." Buster put his utensils down and took a big swallow of the coffee Sourdough placed in front of him. "I'm thinking he's up to no good and we need to find him. When you're out checking fences and cattle, keep an eye out for him. It's been suggested the women and children stay close to the buildings unless with someone. If you see Lilah out alone escort her back to the ranch."

Brody glanced at Angel and Sy. They both sat taller and a glint of determination lit their eyes. That was why they didn't like him. He was competition for Lilah. The thought made him smile.

The men all continued eating as Buster picked up his utensils and started shoveling food in his mouth.

Gus shoved his plate to the center of the table. "Come on Brody, we've got chores to do."

He rolled up the last hotcake on his plate and stood. There was no way he'd slack with all these men waiting and watching, hoping he'd fail.

Following Gus to the barn, he glanced at the ranch house. The kitchen lights were on. The sun was barely casting a golden glow over the ranch.

"Why is it necessary to do these chores so early?" he asked the other man as they entered the barn.

"These are daily chores. Best to keep the animals on a regular schedule. These chores have to be done so we can take care of the work given us for the day." Gus scooped grain from a barrel.

Brody plucked the stool and bucket from the pegs on the beam. The grain was poured in the stanchion and Daisy stuck her head through. He pulled the pin and the board moved over. He replaced the pin holding the board so she couldn't back out.

He placed the stool and sat, slipping the bucket under the udder. Today he didn't hesitate to tuck his head into her side, and grab the teats. Before long the bucket was full. He patted the cow's side, picked up the bucket and stool, and moved to the hog pen.

The hungry animals slurped the milk as he scooped the manure out to the outside pen.

He tossed grain to the chickens and grabbed the buckets to get water.

All the time he did the chores Gus whittled a piece of wood.

Returning with the water, he stopped next to Gus. "What are you making?"

"A toy for Buddy." He held up a half carved horse.

"You do good work." Brody poured the water. The night before when he did the chores, watering took three trips. He noted they didn't drink as much overnight as during the hot days.

"Let's head back to the bunkhouse and find out what Buster has for us to do today." Gus stuck the carving in his pocket and headed out of the barn.

Crossing between the buildings, Buster met them halfway. "Gus, you can ride fence with Stubbs today.

Brody, you're with me. We're going to pull out the harvesting equipment and get it ready to use next week."

Gus headed to the horse barn.

Buster glanced over at his cabin.

"Things getting worse for your wife?" he asked.

"I don't see how she can get a baby out of her when she can't do a half a days housework." Buster's fear and worry oozed off him.

"Mind if I visit with her? There was an old woman in the tenement where I lived who cured the people in the neighborhood because we couldn't afford a doctor. I spent lots of time helping her mix things and was paid a penny to deliver the mixtures to the people. I might be able to figure out something that would help."

Buster studied him. "At this point anything will do. She's against having a doctor come look at her."

At that moment, Lilah exited the ranch house, headed for the cabin.

I'll visit with her while Lilah's there." He strode across the area and caught up to the young woman. "Buster said I could visit with his wife. She'd feel more comfortable if you were there with me."

Lilah stopped and stared at Brody. "Why would Buster give you permission to visit with his wife? You don't even know her?" She placed her hand on her hips, waiting. Was this a way for him to avoid work? How would he know anything about a woman's needs?

"I told him I've helped a woman in our tenement who healed people who couldn't afford a doctor. He said she refuses to see a doctor."

"Yes. I suggested yesterday that I could bring one

here knowing the trip would be too much for her. She refused a doctor." She was worried about Agnes. She'd become disinterested in anything other than sleep.

"I just want to see her and ask questions. It can't hurt." He continued toward the cabin.

She followed, wondering what else this man knew. She knocked on the door and entered.

"Agnes, it's Lilah." She turned to Brody. "Wait here until I see if she's properly covered."

He nodded and took a seat at the small table.

Entering the bedroom, She immediately went to the window and opened the curtains. No one could feel interested in the world when they sat in darkness all day.

"Good morning, Agnes." She walked to the bed and noted the woman had gray bags of skin under her eyes. "Did you have a good night?"

The woman stared at her. "I don't feel like getting out of bed today. Could you bring me a cup of tea?"

"I have a visitor. Judge Radley's grandson, Brody." She plumped up the pillows and helped Agnes sit up.

"I don't want visitors," Agnes said.

"He thinks he can help you. You want to get better don't you? For the children and Buster?" Lilah studied the woman. There were days when she didn't think the woman cared about anything but sleep.

"Yes. The children, Buster." Tears streamed down her cheeks.

"Then what can it hurt to have Brody talk to you?" She didn't understand how he could help, but he wanted to and that was what mattered to her. No one else on the ranch besides she and Buster seemed to care what happened to the woman. She knew the judge was worried in his own way, but he said she was Buster's wife and his responsibility. That was one of the things she and the judge argued about. He should take a more active interest in his ranch hands, not just that they did their jobs but know them on a friendlier level. He believed they were his employees and he should not build a friendship because employees came and went.

"Let's fix your hair, and I'll bring him in to visit." She brushed the dull brown hair, pinning the limp strands up away from Agnes' face. "There. I'll get Brody and bring you some tea and toast."

"Thank you." Agnes grasped Lilah's wrist. "You've been so good to me. Buster is thankful as well."

"Don't you worry. This is what you do for friends." She eased out of the woman's grip and stood.

In the other room, she found the kettle steaming and three cups set on a tray.

"You've been busy." She smiled at Brody. The man surprised her each day with his thoughtfulness and knowledge.

"I figured you came here to fix her breakfast and tidy up the place. What have you been feeding her?" His comment also surprised her.

"All she says she can tolerate is tea and toast."

He shook his head. "She needs more than that. Is she ready for me to come in?"

"Yes. I'll take you in and come back for the tea." She led him to the door, knocked, and entered with him beside her.

"Agnes, this is Brody Yates. Brody, this is Agnes

Malone, Buster's wife." She led him up to the bed.

"Mrs. Malone. I heard you've been feeling tired and thought I might be able to figure it out. I helped a healing woman when I was growing up and learned a few things." He glanced around the room and pulled the only chair in the room up to the side of the bed.

Agnes studied him then smiled at her. "He's a handsome young man."

Her cheeks burned knowing what the woman was implying.

"Thank you, Mrs. Malone. Compliments have been few and far between growing up." He smiled at the woman.

Lilah's limbs melted at the sight.

"Could I see your hand?" he asked.

Agnes nodded.

He raised her hand in his, studying the fingers and palm. He glanced up at Lilah. "Hold your hand next to hers."

She did.

"See how pale her finger nails are." He nodded to Agnes' face. "And her skin is pale and no color to her lips."

"Do you know what is wrong?" Her heart raced, hoping he did know what was wrong and praying he had knowledge of what would help.

"Mrs. Malone, I see you're tired. Are you weak and do you get dizzy?"

"Yes. How did you know?" Her eyes widened as she stared at him.

"I believe she needs to eat meat at every meal."

"I can't." Agnes turned her head away from them.

"Mrs. Malone. It is the only way you'll get better and have a healthy child." The urgency in his words, revealed he cared about the woman even though they'd just met.

"Agnes. We'll start with some beef broth this morning. Mrs. Fellowes has some she made for soup."

"Beef stock with tiny bits of meat in it would be a good thing for her at each meal until she has the strength to chew the meat." He stood. "Something else the healing woman suggested were greens."

Lilah grinned. "I have greens in the garden." Excitement welled in her chest. She could help Agnes get well. She'd felt like a failure watching the women get weaker and weaker and not knowing what to do.

"Mrs. Malone, you must force yourself to eat. It's the only thing that will save both you and the baby." He walked to the bedroom door. "I have to get to work. Your husband is expecting me to work with him today."

Lilah followed him into the other room. At the door, she stepped out onto the porch and touched his sleeve. "Do you think making her eat meat and greens will help?" She hoped he hadn't just said that to give the woman and herself hope.

"Yes. The healing woman would have me take broth she made and greens to women who were suffering like Mrs. Malone. The baby's taking what Mrs. Malone's body needs for strength. If she starts eating, especially meat, she'll get her strength back." He placed his cap on his head. "I've work to do."

She nodded and watched him walk across the area between the cabin and the horse barn. Buster had two horses harnessed up. He walked over to Brody and they started talking.

She smiled and started across the area between the cabin and house.

"Miss Lilah!"

Chapter Twelve

Brody swung his attention to Angel who called out to Lilah. The young woman's welcoming smile as the vaquero rode up to her added to his dislike of the man. Angel dismounted and started an animated conversation, touching her more than was necessary.

"I thought he had a job to do," he said, nodding his head in the direction of the vaquero and young woman.

"He does. He also makes it a point to speak to Lilah every day before he heads out." Buster handed the driving reins to him. "I've seen the way he tries to find out about the ranch. He's got his sights set on marrying her and getting the Double R." Buster slapped his back. "You might want to watch your back around him. If he thinks you're a threat to getting what he wants…"

"I'm sure she's smart enough to see what he's after." He held the reins in his hands and slapped the horses' rumps, hoping he looked like he knew what he was doing.

Buster shook his head. "You ever drive a team of horses?"

"Not really. I worked the hoists at the dock, which required making the horses walk forward, but we held onto their headstalls, leading them." He knew nothing about any of this life he'd been dragged into. He was, however, developing an appreciation for it.

The foreman took the reins from him and showed him how to hold them and make the horses pull the equipment out of the barn. By noon they had the equipment lined up outside and had taken apart one of the rakes to have Smithy fix a broken spline.

Sourdough stepped out of the bunkhouse kitchen and hollered at them.

Buster wiped his arm across his forehead and glanced at the cabin.

Lilah was carrying a pot across the porch.

"Think I'll go check on Agnes," Buster said.

"I'm sure she'd like that." He wanted to follow the man to his cabin and ask Lilah what she and Angel had laughed about, but that would make her think he cared about what she did. He didn't. He did care about Angel's intentions. She deserved a man who loved her and wanted her, not the ranch.

He washed up at the bucket outside the bunkhouse door. Sy and Stubbs were sitting at the table.

"Sit on down. You three and Buster are the only ones I'm spectin' this meal." Sourdough set a platter of beef sandwiches on the table.

Brody took a bite and was pleasantly surprised by the fluffiness of the bread. "This bread's good," he said to Sourdough when he set coffee cups and a pot of coffee on the table.

"Mrs. Fellowes bakes it. Any pies and cakes you get are from her kitchen." Sourdough sat down at the end of the table and picked up a sandwich. The man appeared to be older than the rest of the people in the bunkhouse. He had short gray hair, a round face and belly. He stood as tall as Buster but had stooped shoulders.

"After a meal at the house, I believe her baking would be a treat." He took a bite of the sandwich and noticed Sy set his food down.

"Why would that be that you get to eat at the house, but you're put up in the bunkhouse?" Sy asked.

He shrugged. "Ask the judge. He sure as heck won't tell me a thing."

"Could be he don't trust ya." Sy grinned and a malicious glint lit up his eyes.

Was that true? He doesn't trust me. He sort of understood the judge's reasoning that it was for Lilah's reputation but was that the excuse he used because he didn't trust me? Hell, he doesn't even know me. And I don't know him. He could be a crook for all I know.

He picked up his sandwich and wandered outside. The sunshine, fresh air, and solitude was better than sitting in there being judged and getting ideas put in his head.

A chair sat at the end of the porch. He walked down to sit on it and spotted Lilah in the garden behind the cabin. Finishing his sandwich, he headed over to the garden.

She was bent, her backside poked up in the air

toward him as he approached.

"Getting some greens?" he asked.

"Oh!" she cried and tossed the greens in the air.

"I'm sorry. I should have made noise walking up." Brody started collecting the green leaves spread about two rows of vegetables. "This is a big garden. Do you take care of it yourself?"

She also bent to pick up the greens, placing them in a basket in front of her. "Sourdough helps too."

"That's good. It looks like a lot of work for one person." He placed the greens he'd picked up into the basket.

"We need enough to feed everyone not only during the growing season but the winter as well. Mrs. Fellowes and I put up enough to get all of us through to the next harvest." She stuffed wayward strands of her hair under the wide-brimmed hat she wore.

He noted she had on a split skirt. "You aren't going riding by yourself are you?"

Her cheeks deepened in color. "No. Angel is going for a ride with me this afternoon."

That was what the vaquero was up to this morning.

"You and him go on many rides alone?" He hadn't planned for his question to sound like an accusation but that's how it came out.

"What are you insinuating?" She shoved her fisted hands on her hips and glared at him.

He took his time finding the right words so as not to make her any more upset. "If I can't sleep in the house because it might ruin your reputation, how is you riding off alone with a young man not putting your reputation at risk?"

Anger no longer pursed her lips or narrowed her eyes. She stood gaping at him as if at a loss for words.

"Does Judge Radley know you go on rides alone with Angel?"

Her cheeks darkened, and her gaze dropped to her hands clutched in front of her. "I've never asked if I could go. I just go."

He raised her gaze to his by placing a finger under her chin. "Do you tell him afterward that you've been riding with Angel?"

Her emerald colored eyes widened. "No."

He couldn't deny the brief flicker of fear he saw in her eyes. "Why not, if you think it is respectable?"

"I-I living on this ranch around all these older people. I just like to have some fun, no rules, no one watching my every move." Her eyes turned rebellious. She stepped back, taking her chin from his touch. "Angel understands. He was the youngest on his family's ranch. He wasn't allowed the same privileges as his brothers. That's why he set out to find a place of his own."

Brody liked the spirit he saw in her. He didn't like the way she stood up for Angel. "I think he's found that place."

Her brow furrowed and she stared at him as if he were dim-witted. "What are you talking about?"

"Until I showed up, I have no doubt he thought you would inherit the ranch. Why else would he take you out on compromising rides if not in hopes of becoming your husband and one day the owner of the Double R Ranch?"

Her hand shot out and slapped him before he could

react.

"How dare you say something so mean. You don't know Angel. He's sweet and considerate. That's more than I can say for you right now." She picked up the basket of greens and stomped out of the garden and into the cabin.

Good. She wouldn't be in the house while he told the judge his thoughts on Angel.

***

Lilah stormed into the cabin, her dander stirred up hotter than a tea kettle. The nerve of him, telling her she'd been risking her reputation by riding off alone with Angel. He wasn't the only hired hand she'd gone out riding with. How many times had she accompanied Buster or Sandy? Her mind slammed to the one time she'd agreed to go with Sy. He'd shown his colors that day putting his hands on her and trying to kiss her. She'd told Buster and had made certain she was never alone with him again. But Angel. He'd always been a gentleman. He only touched her to help her off and on her horse. He said to steady her and make sure she didn't hurt herself. They had good talks. About the ranch…

I think he's found that place. Brody's words slipped through her mind.

Buster came out of the bedroom. "I think she has a little more color today."

The hopefulness in his voice tugged at her heart and drew her away from her troubles.

"Brody seemed to know what he was talking about. I'm sure it will take her body a while to get the strength up, but she does seem a bit better." Lilah picked up a green. "I'm going to see if I can get her to eat some of these in between meals. If I can get her to eat small portions it will take less energy for her to eat."

"That's a good idea. That Brody. I wasn't too sure if Judge Radley knew what he was doing bringing him out here, but he doesn't mind working and learning new things. I think this might just work." Buster put his hat on and left the cabin.

Lilah stared at the closed door. She wouldn't admit it to anyone, but she had to agree with the foreman. The judge saving his grandson from prison could be the best thing to happen to the Double R Ranch and the people living here.

Chapter Thirteen

Brody entered through the front door. He hoped to slip into the judge's office without Mrs. Fellowes seeing. He didn't need the housekeeper telling Lilah she saw him talking to the judge.

Pulling his hat from his head, he opened the office door and walked in without knocking. Judge Radley slumped in his chair, sleeping. He smiled. This was the image he had of the man when he'd learned he had a grandfather. Not the stubborn, authoritative man who met him at the stage.

He cleared his throat and waited.

Slowly, the older man opened his eyes, blinked twice, and then straightened his body in the chair. "What are you doing sneaking in here?"

"I wasn't sneaking. Well, I was. I didn't want Mrs. Fellowes to see me because I didn't want Lilah to know I came to talk to you." He sat down in the seat across from the judge.

"I see. Why didn't you want Lilah to know?" Judge Radley rested his forearms on the desk top and leaned toward him.

"Do you know Angel is trying to get this ranch by sweet-talking her?" Might as well come to the point of why he came here.

Judge Radley nodded. "Buster has mentioned it to me a time or two. Why are you concerned? Afraid you might not get the ranch when I die?"

He glared at the man. "No. I didn't know this place existed a month ago, and I had no problem seeing a future. I don't want her to get hurt. A man who is only after her for the ranch won't be a good husband for her."

The older man peered at him for a long time. "Why are you worried about Lilah's happiness?"

He squirmed in the chair. The judge had told him to stay away from his ward, but it was hard to do when he met her several times a day while they both did their chores. "I think she deserves better."

"Are you the better man?"

His gaze locked onto the eyes the same color as his own, just a bit faded. "I might be if you give me the chance to show you."

Judge Radley leaned back. "Why do you think you're here? I want you to prove to me you deserve this ranch. As for Lilah. That's her decision. But I won't have you ruining her reputation. You'll remain in the bunkhouse."

Brody shook his head. "I don't mind staying in the bunkhouse. But Angel started a rumor that I'm there because you don't trust me since I was going to prison when you found me." He leaned forward. "And Lilah taking rides alone with Angel is compromising her more than me staying in a house with you and Mrs. Fellowes as chaperones."

A smile tugged at the old man's lips and his eyes lit up. "I put you in that bunkhouse to show those men your character and prove to them you are up to the job of being the boss one day." He placed his hands on the desk and stood. "Tonight after dinner I want you to tell me how you survived after your father died."

He understood the judge was telling him it was time to go. Yet he hadn't said what he planned to do about the two riding off alone. "What about Lilah?"

"She's a smart girl. She'll figure it out." Judge Radley walked to the door. "Get back to work."

He left the house feeling like he'd accomplished a little. At least he knew it wasn't that the judge didn't trust him, he wanted him to gain the hired hands trust. It appeared he'd already gained Buster's trust. The man had allowed him to look at his wife.

As he strode across the area between the house and the horse barn, Buddy came running out of the smaller barn, a dog at his heels.

Brody stopped him. "Hey, where's your sister?"

"She's helpin' Miss Lilah." The boy squirmed out of his hold and headed to the horse barn, the two dogs running behind him their tongues wagging.

He was going to be one handful when he grew up. Shaking his head, he followed Buddy's trail of drug heel tracks. The boy's boots were too big for his feet.

In the barn he found Smithy handing Buster the

repaired spline.

"Just in time." Buster raised the spline. "I need your help."

The sound of hurrying hooves sifted into the barn.

"Who do you think that is?" Brody asked, starting for the door.

"They went on to the house. It's none of our business." Buster nodded for him to open the barn door so he could carry the spline out to the rake.

He glanced toward the house. Two horses were tied to the hitching post out front.

Buster followed his gaze. "Looks like Reinwold and Leighton. They're in charge of the Cattleman's Association in these parts."

Knowing the men were on business and not here to cause trouble, he turned his attention to the rake repairs.

***

Lilah heard the horses and peeked out of the foreman's house. She'd planned to help Mrs. Fellowes with the laundry today, but had ended up making and canning soup and broth for Agnes. It was the best way to have a ready supply without making soup every day. Little Betsy had watched her cutting up the vegetables and asked to help. She'd given the small child the job of pulling the tops off the carrots and tearing the greens into pieces.

She wiped at the perspiration dripping down her temples with the corner of her apron and heard the approach of two horses. Peeking out the window. She saw two men from the Cattleman's Association enter the house. This was nothing new. However, it reminded her that Angel would be coming soon for their ride.

At the bedroom door, she peeked in. "Agnes. I have the soup canned. I'm going to check on Mrs. Fellowes."

"I'll never be able to repay you for all your kindness." The woman gained color in her face with each cup of broth she drank.

"You having a healthy baby is the only repayment I need."

Lilah headed to the outside door, plucking Betsy off the chair. "You need to find your brother and play with him."

Out on the porch she set Betsy down. The girl ran off in the direction of the horse barn where her father and Brody were fixing the haying equipment. Angel appeared on the road, trotting his horse. The two cattlemen and Judge Radley stepped out of the house.

Her gaze flew to Brody, who stood up, his gaze fixed on Angel. The vaquero rode past him grinning, the nose of his horse pointed her direction. She glanced over to the house. Mr. Rienwold, Mr. Leighton, and Judge Radley were all staring at Angel as he approached her.

Her thoughts jumped to Brody's comment about riding alone with Angel. Her chest constricted as the vaquero dismounted with a flourish and stood in front of her.

When she didn't respond with a greeting, he stepped closer. Like someone she was intimate with. Panic raced her heart. She glanced toward the house. The three men weren't talking, they were watching. A glance at the barn found Brody and Buster also watching.

She swallowed the lump in her throat and took a step back. "I can't go riding today. Please get on your horse and go back to work." Her gaze flicked toward the barn.

Angel followed and his face darkened. "Is this because of something the newcomer said?"

"No, it's because seeing the men with Judge Radley watching us, I realized it is inappropriate for me to go on rides with you unchaperoned." She took another step backwards.

"I do not believe you." He took a step toward her. "Someone has said something."

Before she could reply a shadow appeared to her right, and Brody stepped up beside them.

"The lady is backing away from you. To me that means she doesn't want you following her." His voice was low and only for them to hear.

She glanced toward the house. The men were talking but watching. What were they talking about? Would the judge tell them one of the men with her was his grandson?

"I was only trying to stay close to talk to her quietly." Angel picked up his foot to move toward her again.

She took another step backwards and behind Brody.

He stuck his arm out stopping Angel. "It's pretty clear she is through talking."

Angel spat words she didn't understand and mounted his horse. "This is not over gringo," he said, spurring his horse into a lope.

Brody spun around. "Are you all right?"

"I'm fine. You didn't have to step in. He wouldn't hurt me." Even as she said the words, she wasn't so sure. She'd never seen that depth of anger in his eyes before.

"If you believe that why were you backing up?"

She peered into his light blue eyes and shook her head. "Because while I believe he wouldn't hurt me, his actions were different."

"Brody." Buster called.

"Coming." He called back and continued to study her. "Are you going to go riding with Angel later?"

"No. That's why he was upset."

He smiled. "Good." He trotted back to the foreman and the equipment.

While Brody was happy, she had a feeling her saying no to Angel may have made him a target of the vaquero's anger.

Chapter Fourteen

Brody was glad the hired hands hadn't made it back when he cleaned up and headed to the house for dinner. While he understood partially why the judge wanted him to stay in the bunkhouse, he wondered at the hands being jealous he had an invitation to the house for dinner even though they all knew he was family.

He entered the kitchen door and inhaled the delicious aromas. "Mrs. Fellowes, you might be the first person to put more meat on my bones."

The housekeeper giggled and shooed him out of the kitchen.

Lilah stepped out of the dining room, running into him. He put his hands on her waist to steady her.

"Are you all right?" he asked, peering down into her wide green eyes.

"Y-yes. I was preoccupied." Her breathy reply

fueled the heat already racing to his lower regions.

"Lilah!" Mrs. Fellowes called.

He pulled his hands from her person and stepped to the side, making room for her to pass. She disappeared into the kitchen. His hands tingled, remembering the feel of her firm, trim body.

"There you are. Come into the office with me. You saw I had visitors today." The judge stood beside his door.

His cheeks heated. Had the older man witnessed him holding her? Ducking his head, he entered the room and sat in the chair.

Judge Radley took his seat behind the desk. "My visitors were other cattle ranchers who are concerned with rumors they heard about Texas Fever heading this way."

"Texas Fever, what's that?" Brody sat up straight in his chair. He'd never heard of such a thing, but he knew of other fevers that killed many people.

"It's a disease brought by Texas long horn cattle to other cattle. Rienwold heard a Texas rancher planned to purchase land in Idaho. He's fearing the man will bring his fever infested cows up here." Judge Radley shook his head. "The Texas rancher would have to be crazy to think he could bring cattle from down there. I read all about the way Kansas stopped them from driving the longhorns through there and now the animals have to be quarantined before they can be moved anywhere other than Texas."

"So Texas Fever is bad for cattle, not people?" That eased his initial fears.

"Yes. Kills any animal not from Texas. Once a

longhorn has been put with other cattle they soon become sick and die." The judge picked up a magazine. "There's an article in the Stockman's Journal about a couple of scientists trying to figure it out." He handed the magazine to Brody.

"Is this for me to read?" he asked, glancing over the headlines on the front.

"Yes. I have a stack of them over there." The older man pointed to a table in the corner of the room. "You can read any of them you want."

"Your meal's ready," Lilah said from behind him.

"Thank you, dear." Judge Radley stood. "If I'm not mistaken, I believe Mrs. Fellowes made her spice cake for dessert."

She laughed. "You are not mistaken."

Brody followed the two down the short hallway to the dining room. The more he learned about both Lilah and Judge Radley, the more he wanted to make sure he didn't do something to lose their confidence in him. Today, his talk with the judge about the young woman and now being updated on the other men's visit, he felt like he was part of the family and not an outsider.

Taking his place at the table, he smiled at both Lilah and the judge, his grandfather. This was the family he'd dreamed of for so long.

Grandfather and Lilah told him more about the history of the ranch during the meal. It wasn't until they'd retired to the sitting room that the older man turned a serious face his direction.

"Tell me about your life. And don't make it pretty. I read enough of the Pinkerton report to know you had a poor one."

Brody couldn't sit. He stood and walked over to the cold, empty fireplace. The hot August weather made it unnecessary for a fire. "I don't know what you read, but Ma made sure I was fed, clothed, and got an education while she was alive." He didn't know why he felt defensive. She had done the best she could. Better than some mothers. He'd had a friend who didn't attend school because he worked. His clothes were always dirty and tattered. He'd been killed in a factory accident.

"I knew my Mary would be a good mother. She was always bringing the baby animals into the house." The wistfulness in his grandfather's voice and the faraway look in his eyes showed his love of his daughter.

"She told me, she wanted to have lots of children but realized after I was born that my father would never be able to support a big family." Now as an adult, he wondered how love could make a person forgive so many faults. His father had more faults than strengths. And yet his mother had never once said a thing against her husband. Until the day he'd drank himself to death. That day she'd cried, then wiped the tears, and said, "I will never forgive him for leaving us with nothing."

"How did you two survive after your father's death?"

"I continued school and Mother cleaned hotel rooms until she became too sick." He'd noticed her lack of energy and had brought the old healing woman up to look at her. The minute the woman's chin trembled, he knew there was nothing she could do for his mother.

Tears trickled down the judge's cheek. "What did

she die from?"

"I don't know. She became weaker and weaker and then the pain set in. The old woman in the tenement who helped others couldn't do anything except give me something for her pain." His heart ached remembering the final hours. Even the liquid hadn't eased her pain. She'd died clutching his hand and crying.

"I'm so sorry, Mary. If only I could have found you sooner." Grandfather sat back in the chair and stared at the dead fireplace.

Lilah entered the room. Her gaze shot from Brody to his grandfather. Seeing the older man's tears, she hurried across the room and sank to the floor beside the man. "Are you feeling ill?" she asked, her chest squeezing in worry.

"I'm grieving." He put a hand on her head. "I think I'll go to bed now." He stood.

"I'm sorry. I didn't mean—" Brody stood as if reaching out to his grandfather.

"It's not your fault, son. I've wondered about Mary for over twenty years. Knowing her end, I can grieve." Judge Radley stood. "You two should go to bed soon too. We're going to Burns tomorrow." He left the room.

Lilah started to push herself up off the floor. Brody was beside her in a flash. His hands under her arms, raising her to her feet. She looked up and found him studying her face. The heat from where his hands still rested on her body registered.

This was exactly why the judge wanted him to sleep in the bunkhouse. She peered into his light blue eyes. They'd softened since their first meeting. And his attempt to help his grandfather tonight…there was a caring man underneath his insolent behavior. She had a notion it was a survival trait he'd learned while growing up.

"I need to go," he said, stepping backwards. His gaze stayed riveted to hers, but his body continued the retreating movement.

"You don't have to go so soon. I'd enjoy hearing what the east is like." She took a step towards him, then turned and sat on the chair Judge Radley had vacated.

"You heard what he said. We're going to Burns tomorrow. I need to get back to the bunkhouse and let you get your rest." He spun around and headed to the kitchen.

She smiled. After tomorrow, he'd no longer wear that boyish looking cap. His grandfather planned to purchase clothes for him that would make him fit in better.

The back door closed and she sat a few more moments before heading up to bed.

*＊＊

In the bunkhouse Brody ignored the verbal jabs Sy and Angel made toward him. He understood Angel's grudge but he couldn't figure out Sy's.

Sandy left the card game. He sat on the bunk across from him and stared at the cup of coffee in his hands. In a low voice he said, "I don't know what you did that riled Angel up, but you'd best watch yourself if you're alone with him."

He rolled to his side and studied Sandy's face. "You really think he'd try to do something to me?" He'd figured out Angel had a temper. He wasn't scared of the man, but he didn't want it unleashed on Lilah.

Sandy took a sip of coffee and nodded. He moved on back to the card game.

Brody rolled onto his back and turned his head enough to study the men in the bunkhouse. Sandy had shown his loyalty. He could tell Gus, Smithy, Clem, and Roy were loyal to the Double R. But Stubbs, Sy, and Angel were off to themselves, heads bent together, talking low. He'd bet anything they were hashing out a way to get back at him.

Chapter Fifteen

The town of Burns came into view. While the buggy was easier traveling than the wagon, Brody was ready to get out and stretch his legs. They'd started out as soon as breakfast was over, stopping once to stretch their legs and eat the sandwiches Mrs. Fellowes had sent along. As the buggy rolled along the dirt-packed main street, stores were closing.

Judge Radley had allowed both him and Lilah to drive the horses. When his grandfather sat in the back seat of the buggy and they were alone in the front, it had been hard to not keep his body from touching her. They'd talked about New York. He'd answered her questions if they weren't directed at his life.

Grandfather took the reins as they entered town, stopping the horses and buggy in front of the livery. "Brody, get the horses bedded for the night and meet us at the Hopkins House."

"Yes, sir." He jumped out of the buggy and helped Lilah down. The judge moved stiffly, grabbing the two carpet bags that he expected carried their night clothes. No one told him it would be an overnight stay, all he had with him were the clothes he wore.

The two set off toward what he judged to be Main Street. Some buildings were two-story brick and the fronts of the buildings had big windows, inviting the passerby to take a look at the wares inside.

He tied the horses to the hitching post and went in search of the livery man.

***

Lilah stood in the small hotel room fussing with her hair. She didn't know why, but her stomach had the flutters thinking about dining with Brody. It didn't make sense. She had supper with him every night at the ranch, but she couldn't shake her excitement. "It has to be because the judge took him to get new clothes." What would he look like dressed like a ranch hand rather than a dock worker?

The mercantile had been closed when they walked to Hopkins House but Judge Radley had rapped on the door and told the owner he'd be back in twenty minutes to purchase clothing. When Brody arrived at the hotel, he'd been hauled back out by his grandfather.

A soft knock on her door sent her scurrying across the room. Her breath caught at the sight of Brody holding a ranch hat in his hand. He had on a brown suit coat, white shirt, tan suspenders, and brown work pants tucked into the tops of tall pointed-toed riding boots. She'd thought he was handsome in the clothes he'd arrived in, but wearing the clothing she'd grown up seeing every day, he made her heart stutter in her chest.

"Judge asked me to bring you down to the restaurant. He's having a meeting with someone from the Cattleman's Association." He held out his arm.

She tucked her hand through the crook of his arm and pulled the door closed behind her. Her heart fluttered in her chest so fast she couldn't store up enough air to say a word. She smiled and nodded.

This was the best hotel in town but it still lacked the amenities of the hotels she'd stayed at in Denver. The narrow stairs were made for one person at a time. He slid his arm, capturing her hand and leading her down the stairs behind him. She used her free hand to hold up the front of her skirt to keep from tripping.

At the bottom of the stairs, he tucked her hand back on his arm and led her out onto the board walkway. The Hopkins House had a fancy bar which served food, but only men were allowed in the bar.

The restaurant where they usually took their meals while in town stood two blocks down. She'd eaten there many times with Judge Radley and her friend Edna. Which made her realize if her friend found out she'd been to town and not visited, she'd be upset. She'd go see her friend tomorrow morning.

At the restaurant, he held the door and allowed her to walk in first.

Mrs. Shoopman hurried forward. "It's so good to see you again. Does Edna know you're in town?"

"No, this was an unexpected trip." Lilah started to say more but her mind couldn't get her tongue working when Brody placed his hand on her back, escorting her by the woman and over to the table where his grandfather sat.

Judge Radley stood, and Brody pulled out a chair, holding it for her. All this attention had her dizzy. She could still feel his hand imprinted on her back. He pushed in the chair as she sat and took the seat across from his grandfather.

"I heard Mrs. Shoopman. I suppose you want to see her niece Edna at some point on this trip," the judge said.

"I could meet her for breakfast tomorrow and join you at the mercantile to pick up the items Mrs. Fellowes wanted," Lilah said, placing the cloth napkin in her lap.

He nodded. "That will work. Brody and I have a meeting with the sheriff in the morning. I want to make sure he knows there's a cattle killer running about."

She shivered mentally, visualizing the man at the pond. "Do you want me to give you a description?"

Brody leaned toward her. "If you could write it down tonight, we'll take it to the sheriff. There's no need for you to miss your friend."

She knew better than to look into his eyes, but she did. And became locked on the caring she saw in their depths.

"Ahem." The judge cleared his throat.

Lilah jerked her gaze from Brody and turned her attention to the older man. She didn't want to get the grandson in trouble, because each day she saw or learned something new about him that made her like him even more.

They ordered and started a conversation about the town, its growth, and the loss of Fort Harney in 1880.

"Would any of you care for pie?" Mrs. Shoopman asked as she cleared the plates.

A glint in Brody's eye told her he wouldn't turn down a piece. "What kind do you have today?" she asked.

"Apple or peach. Fresh peaches came in from Kimberley yesterday. We're lucky they planted fruit trees there."

"I'll have a piece of peach. Would either of you gentlemen like pie?" Lilah asked, including both men in her smile.

"I'll have apple. Mrs. Fellowes can't bake an apple pie like yours, Mrs. Shoopman." Judge Radley tipped his cup to the woman like a salute.

"I've never had a peach pie. I'll try that." Brody leaned back in his chair and stretched an arm out to pick up his coffee cup.

When the woman left, Lilah turned to him. "You've never had a peach pie? Don't they have peaches in New York?"

"They have them, but they are more expensive than apples. Ma only made pie before Father died. After that we couldn't afford enough fruit for a pie." Brody scowled. He didn't like talking about how they lived. Not to anyone but the judge. Yet, Lilah seemed to pull that information out of him without even trying.

"Then you're sure to enjoy your pie." She patted his hand and smiled.

The touch of her hand on his brought back the warm sensations he'd experienced while escorting her to the restaurant. He'd never escorted a woman before today. He'd watched other men dressed in suits and tucked away all their actions for when he would have the chance. From the way Lilah had smiled at him, he'd remembered well.

"Here you go, folks." Mrs. Shoopman returned with the pie.

Lilah jerked her hand back. He noted the way the older woman watched them both. This was why Grandfather had him living in the bunkhouse. To keep her reputation in good standing.

He picked up a fork and dug into the pie, giving it his full attention. His mouth hummed with joy at the flavorful bite. He'd never tasted anything so sweet and satisfying. Thinking his mind was playing tricks on him, he took another bite. It was even better than the last. He didn't look up until he'd cleaned up every crumb on his plate.

Patting his belly, he asked, "Can Mrs. Fellowes make peach pie?"

His grandfather laughed. "Yes, she can, but I would have to say Lilah's pies are better than Mrs. Fellowes."

He turned his gaze on the young blushing woman. She would make someone a wonderful wife. The thought warmed his body. Those kinds of thoughts would get him stuck in the bunkhouse until she married. His mind went to Angel. That twisted his emotions from content to angry. He'd make sure that didn't happen. The man only wanted the ranch.

"What's wrong?" Lilah asked.

"Nothing. Think I'll go for a walk before heading back to the hotel." He nodded at her and then his grandfather.

"Why don't you take Lilah back to the hotel first? I

want to have a word with the man who just entered the restaurant." Judge Radley stood and sauntered over to a well-dressed man, about the judge's age, seating a woman dressed in an outfit he would have seen on the influential streets of New York City.

Before he moved to help her up, she was standing next to the table.

"Who is that?" he asked.

"Dexter Brightly. He's Judge Radley's attorney." She tucked her hand around his arm. "You know, I wouldn't mind taking the long way back to the hotel."

He sighed. She was part of the reason he needed the long walk, but he also wouldn't disagree with keeping her company. At the door of the restaurant, they turned the opposite direction from the hotel.

"Tell me about the friend you want to see in the morning." He planned to keep her talking about herself so she couldn't ask him questions.

"Edna and I became friends when I moved in with Judge Radley ten years ago. She lived on the other side of Venator and went to school with me. Then I was sent off to finishing school and she used money she'd inherited to start a business here."

He'd caught a reluctance in her tone when she mentioned finishing school. "What's a finishing school and why didn't you want to go?"

She stopped and stared at him. "How did you know I didn't want to go?"

He smiled and started moving again. "I heard it in your voice."

"Well, I didn't want to go but Judge Radley said he promised my parents I would get all the schooling they requested. I guess finishing school was part of that, though I have a sneaky suspicion he sent me thinking he hadn't taught me well enough how to be a lady."

"That's what the school is for? To teach you to be a lady? I'd think that would come natural to any woman. I've never heard of school to teach a man to be a man."

She laughed. "Not how to be a woman but how to know the etiquette for speaking with people, attending social gatherings, writing letters, and how to be proper while at a dinner party or meal."

He shook his head. "That seems like a lot of nonsense. I would think helping the judge entertain guests would have taught you all of that."

"I agree and that was my argument to not go. But he insisted." She stopped as they ran out of board walkways and buildings.

Brody led her across the street and they walked the opposite direction. Across dirt alleys and up onto board walkways in front of businesses. The evening sun was slowly slipping away, leaving a rosy glow in the sky.

"There were girls there who needed the guidance and the cooking lessons. We not only learned how to behave in society, we also learned how to take care of a home. Cooking, laundry, grocery lists."

He thought about what she'd said. A school to teach a girl how to be a wife was what it came down to.

The noise coming from a saloon, intrigued him. He'd never been in a western saloon, only the pubs along the waterfront. Even though he was curious, he couldn't drag Lilah into one. If they were anything like the pubs, the women in those places weren't treated kindly.

Instead, he hurried on by. She kept up the pace with him and slowed when they were two buildings away from the hotel.

Only a few people walked the boardwalks or rode in the street. He'd never witnessed such a quiet street at this time of night. "Is it always this quiet?"

"Every time I've been here it has, but I've heard stories of brawls and shoot-outs."

The hotel was directly across from them. If he took her to her room, he could come back out and explore the saloon. He led her across the street and into the hotel. He could tell by her slow steps as they climbed the stairs she wasn't ready to go to her room. He wouldn't mind spending more time with her, but his grandfather had made it clear he was to stay away from Lilah.

Putting distance between them, especially tonight when she sparkled like a shiny gem, would be the best. He'd caught himself wanting to touch her several times tonight. His grandfather's watchful gaze and knowing he could lose family, he'd keep his distance.

After depositing Lilah at her room, he headed back out to check out the town and keep his mind off her.

Chapter Sixteen

Brody woke with a hammer pounding in his head.

"Boy, open this door!" Judge Radley hollered.

He slipped off the bed, noting he wore the new clothes purchased the day night before. His footsteps added to the banging in his head. Thinking it was the boots, he tiptoed and realized he wasn't wearing any.

He twisted the key in the lock. The door shoved him backwards.

"What is wrong with you?" His grandfather slammed the door closed and stood over him in an angry, towering stance.

"I had a little too much whiskey." Last night he'd found the atmosphere in the saloon exciting. He'd stood at the bar watching and drinking until someone called him over to a card game. His gaze dropped to his feet. Damn! How was he going to explain losing his new boots in a card game?

"I heard. I also heard Sheriff Davies has already met you." Judge Radley put a hand on his shoulder turning him to the bed. "Get your boots and coat on, we have a meeting with the sheriff."

Brody blinked and stumbled to the bed. He shoved his arms into the suitcoat and found his new wide-brimmed hat on the bed post. Gently setting that on his pounding head, he walked to the chair where his old clothes were piled on top of his dock boots.

"Not those boots. The new ones," the old man barked.

"I lost them in a card game last night. This is all I have." He knew last night he'd broken one of the judge's rules. Knowing this, he wasn't sure what would happen. If his grandfather would send him back to face his prison sentence or find some other way to punish him.

"Put those on. After our meeting with the sheriff, I'll purchase another pair of boots. The clothes I purchased yesterday were a gift. The boots today come off your wages." Judge Radley held the door open, waiting for him to tie his boots and get out into the hall.

"Judge, may I walk with you to Edna's?" Lilah asked.

Brody felt like he'd sucked on a sock all night. His tongue was thick and dry as toast.

"Yes." Judge Radley held out his arm, and she tucked her hand in the crook.

She glanced over her shoulder at him. He forced a smile and closed his eyes a moment to stop the thundering of drums going on in his head.

"Good morning, Brody," she said, smiling.

"Morning," was all he could get out before the pounding urged him to close his eyes again.

"Come on, boy," the judge called.

Leaning a shoulder against the wall of the stairwell, he worked his way, one step at a time, down the stairs. The old man and Lilah were out on the street by the time he touched the floor at the bottom of the stairs.

They both glanced back at him and smiled.

He pushed off the wall and walked to the doors. Out in the street the fresh air was welcome. He drew in long breaths and slowly his legs moved smoothly and his head didn't jar as much. His stomach grumbled. In a block, he caught up to the two. At the entrance of a bakery, Lilah left the judge and opened the door. She smiled and entered the building.

Catching up to his grandfather, he asked, "Is that where her friend works?"

"Yes." The old man didn't look at him.

"Will she get her friend in trouble for talking with her at work?" They had strict rules on the dock that no one other than workers were allowed on the docks and no talking other than doing your job.

"Not likely. Edna owns the bakery." Judge Radley crossed the street. He dodged a couple of wagons, making his way toward the sheriff's office.

Brody had to jog to catch up. The action started the hammers in his head. He growled and worked at ignoring the pain and noise.

At the sheriff's, his grandfather opened the door and ushered Brody in ahead of him.

"Morning, Judge." A tall, thin man with a thin brown mustache and short-cropped brown hair held his hand out to the judge.

"Morning, Delbert." His grandfather, motioned to him. "This is Brody, my grandson."

The sheriff's full eyebrows raised. "Grandson. We met last night. He didn't mention you were related." He held out his hand. "Pleased to meet you, Brody."

He shook Sheriff Davies' hand and nodded. He didn't remember meeting the man last night. He'd never in his life had enough to drink to forget things. He wasn't going to be like his father.

"You staying long?" the sheriff asked.

"That depends on my grandfather," he said, glancing over at the older man.

"Doesn't depend on me. Depends on you, son." Grandfather put a hand on his shoulder and squeezed. "Last night makes me wonder."

Guilt added to the unease already churning in his gut. He'd have to ask the man if he'd ever done things when he was younger that at the time were exciting but later he regretted. Most of all he regretted that this incident would make the judge think he was like his father, a drunkard who didn't give a whistle about his family.

Sheriff Davies glanced between the two and finally took his seat behind an old wooden desk that had seen better days. "What can I do for you?"

Grandfather took the one chair in the room besides the one the sheriff sat in and left him standing.

He leaned against the wall next to a couple of wanted posters.

"Four days ago someone killed and skinned one of my prized shorthorns. The man was later seen near the pond a mile and a half from the house. After being told to get off the ranch property, he traveled deeper into our property. We think he's staying up in the trees on the southeast ridge. I've told my hands to chase him off if they come across him."

Sheriff Davies leaned forward. "That's all he did was kill the cow?"

"Yes."

Brody glanced at his grandfather. The man's eyes glistened with unshed tears.

"Why would he kill and skin a cow? It doesn't make sense. You said someone saw him. Did they get close enough to get a description?" The sheriff held a pencil over a pad of paper.

Judge Radley pulled a paper out of his vest pocket. "This is Lilah's description. She's the one who saw him. He shook her up pretty good. You might look through those wanted posters. From what she said, he could be a wanted man."

"I'll do that. You might want to keep that little gal close to the house. This man sounds like trouble." Sheriff Davies unfolded the paper and scanned the page. "Good description."

"Wanted you to be aware of the man causing trouble." Judge Radley stood.

Brody shoved away from the wall and headed for the door.

"Interesting boots you have there," the sheriff said.

"We're going to remedy that right now. Thank you, Sheriff." Grandfather motioned for him to open the door. The old man walked out and he followed.

"We'll get you another pair of boots, then pick up

Lilah and head back to the ranch. I don't like being gone very long." The older man led him down the street and into the mercantile where they purchased another pair of boots.

Back out on the street, instead of walking toward the bakery to gather Lilah, the judge turned into a saloon. Not the one he'd sat in the night before. This one had shiny, thick wood tables and a big mirror behind the bar.

Grandfather sat down at a table and motioned for him to sit. "We're going to have a man to man talk here, away from the ranch."

"Hey Judge. What'll you have?" called the bartender from behind the polished wood counter.

"A beer for me and water for the boy."

Brody frowned at the old man sitting across from him. "I'm not a boy. I've been working like a man since I was thirteen."

"You may have been working like a man, but a man doesn't lose his boots in a card game and then drink himself sick." Grandfather handed the man a silver dollar as he set the drinks on the table.

The bartender grinned. "Thanks. Anything else you need?"

"We're fine. Thank you." The judge sipped his beer, sighed, and set the glass down. "This is the first beer I've had since my last trip away from the ranch. Each trip I allow myself one drink." He leaned back in his chair and took another sip. "Tell me what happened last night."

He repeated how he was interested in seeing if a saloon was anything like a pub. He'd thought he'd only had two drinks. He was asked to join a card game and lost his boots.

"Does that happen often?"

"Losing my boots? No. I'm usually fairly good at cards. It was the drink." He wanted to make sure the man knew this rarely happened to him.

"No. The drinking. I said that was one of my rules, no drinking." Judge Radley placed his emptied glass on the table. "A man that doesn't know his limits, isn't worth his salt."

"I know my limits. I didn't realize I'd drank that much." The more he thought about it, he'd only purchased two drinks, but his glass had always seemed full. "I only paid for two drinks."

Grandfather eyed him up and down. "You are this ill from two drinks?"

"No. Two drinks is always my limit. I swear. I think the bartender was filling my glass when I wasn't looking. It was always full." He vaguely remembered the woman in the scanty dress had been sitting on the card dealer's lap before she walked over to the bar, smiled at him and said something to the man behind the bar. "I think I was set up. With the new clothes they probably thought I had money."

The older man nodded. "Which saloon?"

"The one just down the street from the hotel." He couldn't remember the name on the sign.

"That's Dodger's place. He was probably the one dealing the cards and making sure you lost as well as were drunk." Grandfather stood. "Come on. We'll collect Lilah and head home."

***

Lilah sat in the back of her friend's bakery, sampling the cookies. "These are delicious, Edna."

"Thank you. I've been trying different spices to see which ones are tastier." Edna was plump, rosy cheeked, and always had a smile on her face. She complained about her head of dark curls and kept them covered in a nightcap while working in the bakery. She sat down. "You need to tell me more about the judge's grandson. Your eyes light up when you talk about him."

Biting a point off the star in her hand, she stalled the conversation. Edna was her best friend, but she wanted to keep her feelings about Brody to herself until she'd completely sorted them out. She swallowed the cookie and took a sip of her tea.

"Come on. What's he look like?"

"A young version of Judge Radley." She smiled. While she saw the resemblance there were other things about him she liked more than he reminded her of the judge.

"Ugh! You sure you want to know what he'll look like as he ages."

She laughed. "I find the judge to be a handsome older man."

"I guess so. There are a lot of worse looking older men around here." Edna scrunched her small nose.

"You are naughty the way you talk." And she loved Edna because she spoke exactly what she thought.

"You're avoiding my question." Edna poured more tea into her cup and waited.

"He has light blue eyes. A reddish tint to his whiskers when they have a few days growth. His face is lean and his mouth and nose are the right size for his face. He's taller than me and is stronger than he looks."

"He sounds like a hero in a dime novel." Edna clasped her hands in front of her ample bosom and closed her eyes.

Lilah laughed. "He has many flaws, but he also is generous and knowledgeable."

"Like helping Agnes. Oh, I hope what he told you works. For Agnes and for his sake."

She stared at her friend. "Why do you say for his sake?"

"What do you think it would be like for him to stay at the ranch if you, the judge, and Mr. Malone were mad at him?" Edna sipped her tea and peered at her over the cup with sympathetic eyes.

"I hadn't thought of that. Getting her to eat can't be bad. And she is eating and she's stronger. I helped her out to the table yesterday. She sat there sipping broth and talking to Betsy. She hasn't done that in months." Her heart swelled, remembering the interaction between Agnes and her daughter. The sight had brought pain when she first witnessed it. Reminding her of the mother she had and lost. Now she thought only of the daughter she would one day have. With that thought, the vision of Brody came to mind, heating her cheeks.

"There you are, thinking of him aren't you?" Edna chortled and stood. "I have sweets to bake. Say hello to everyone for me." She picked up a small tin. "These are for the children."

Lilah stood and hugged her friend. "Thank you. They'll love whatever is in here."

The bell over the front door jingled. She followed Edna out of the kitchen area.

"Judge, it's good to see you." Edna plowed forward, extending her hand. "And you must be Brody." She grasped his hand and glanced over her shoulder at Lilah and winked.

Her cheeks flamed from embarrassment as she caught Judge Radley watching her.

How was she to keep her thoughts and feelings hidden when all she had to do was look at the man and her body reacted?

Chapter Seventeen

Brody was glad to be back at the ranch and working. The long ride to and from town had been hard to take. He wasn't a sitter. He liked to be moving and accomplishing something. Today, he finished his chores and found Buster waiting for him.

"Judge says we're going to start cutting hay today. Gus, me, and Lilah will be doing the cutting. You'll be in charge of bringing buckets of water out for us to drink and the horses to drink. Also the noonday meal. If a horse throws a shoe, you'll bring a new horse and take the other one to Smithy. We have a breakdown, you'll bring Smithy and a tool box out. We'll work 'til dark."

They walked to the barn. Three pair of horses were hitched up to the cutting machines. He didn't like the idea of Lilah driving such a wicked looking machine. Her smile and straight back told him he'd get nowhere arguing about it. She was determined to do this job.

Buster climbed up onto the seat of his mowing machine and clucked at the horses. He moved out followed but Gus and then Lilah.

Not sure what he was to do until they needed water or something happened, he filled two buckets and followed along behind to watch. Barking dogs behind him said he wasn't the only curious person. He glanced over his shoulder. Buddy ran down the road after them, followed by the two noisy dogs.

He stopped long enough for the boy to catch up. "You like watching them cut hay?"

"Yeah! I want to make machines like those when I'm big." Buddy skipped alongside of him as they continued.

"That's a good plan. Machines are going to become more and more useful." He'd seen major advancements in the factories and knew the people who had the imagination and skills could make a name for themselves helping move industry forward.

He and the boy sat in the grass near the gate half the morning before the foreman waved for him to bring water. The first bucket had a dipper, Buster, Gus, and Lilah drank from that one, while he watered the horses, making several trips from the stream running along the edge of the field.

The thought of sitting around for several more hours before they needed food seemed ridiculous.

"Buster, how about I go back to the ranch and do something. Buddy can come get me if you need more than water. I'll grab the noon meal and bring it down when it's time." Brody wanted to be busy.

"You can see if Smithy needs help," said the

foreman.

Lilah smiled. "The garden always needs weeded."

"There's a pile of headstalls that need oiled in the bucket by the chair in the tack area," Gus added.

"That all sounds better than sitting here watching you three going around the field." He patted the boy on the head and headed back to the ranch buildings.

As he walked up the road, he stared at the hills behind the gully where the buildings sat. A few trees dotted the upper area of the hill. A flash caught his eyes. He stared harder and swore. He'd bet his boots there was someone up there watching things.

He ran the rest of the way to the barn.

"Which horse can I use?" he asked between gulps of air.

Smithy studied him. "Why?"

"I think there's someone on the hill. I want to ride up and see." He strode past the man toward the corrals.

"Bein' a greenhorn, I'd suggest, the dark brown one." Smithy pointed out the horse standing with his head over the corral fence about twenty feet from the barn.

He nodded, grabbed a rope, and entered the corral. Others shuffled away or around him as he made his way to the brown horse. He placed the rope around the animal's neck and led it into the barn. Once the horse was saddled and bridled, he headed out of the barn and straight up the gully, following the stream.

This was new country to him. So far he'd only been down on the flat areas of the ranch. The stream meandered along the bottom of the crevice. Water spilled down a short waterfall, spilling out of a small lake. He assumed it collected the rain and snow melt. At the lake, he headed up the side of the ridge where he'd spotted the flash of light and a man.

Near the top of the ridge, the ground became steeper and his horse blew air with every step.

Fearful the person he was after might hear his approach, Brody slipped off the horse. He rolled a big rock onto the ends of the reins and started climbing the hill with his hands and feet.

If this ridge had been like others in the area with small rocks covering the sides, he would have never made it this far. Grasping a large rock, he pulled himself up to see the top of the ridge. The trees he'd spotted below, were fifty feet to his left. A saddled horse grazed under the tree closest to him.

Trying not to startle the horse, he crouched and crept along the edge of the ridge, hoping to get a look at the person with the horse.

He looked around a boulder as the grazing horse's head came up. Its ears pointed straight up as it stared down the ridge line. The sound of an approaching horse riveted his attention to who would be meeting with the man up here. The horse and rider stopped.

His gut tightened as Angel dismounted and approached the trees. A man, he'd never seen in person but would know from Lilah's description, stepped out of the trees, greeting Angel with a handshake and a pat on the back.

He couldn't get any closer without being seen. They both wore holsters and had rifles in the scabbards on their saddles. To try and approach them was foolish. The only thing he could do was creep back to his horse, get to the ranch, and tell the judge what he'd seen.

As he made his way back to his horse, his thoughts raced in scattered directions. Lilah needed to know Angel was consorting with the man who killed the cow. Grandfather needed to know his hired hand was suspicious. And he had to make a decision—to learn to shoot. He'd noticed the hired hands, all but Angel and Sy only carried a rifle in the scabbard on their saddles. Buster told him for protection from predators. Even Lilah carried a rifle when out riding. He'd get lessons on shooting a rifle starting today and ask his grandfather for a rifle to carry with him.

***

Lilah was surprised when Judge Radley appeared with their noon meal. She'd expected Brody. But after he'd asked to go find work, they hadn't seen him the rest of the morning or into the afternoon. When she'd asked the judge, he'd shrugged and said something about Smithy.

Her back ached and bottom throbbed from the bouncing machine she rode. Her arms ached from holding the reins and operating the sickle bar lift. Even though her body was sore from head to toe, she took pride in seeing the grass cut and spread across the ground. They'd made good time, getting this field cut an hour before dark.

At the barn she crawled off the metal seat and winced as her muscles cried out.

"You don't have to drive that machine tomorrow. There's several others who can run it," Buster said, taking the reins from her hands.

"I know. But it makes me feel like I'm part of the

146

ranch by helping out." She shoved her hat down her back and let the evening breeze cool her perspiring head.

"You are a part of the ranch. Taking care of the garden, helping Mrs. Fellowes and my Agnes. You don't have to prove anything to any of us." Buster put a hand on her shoulder. "Don't come out here tomorrow. I'll have Stubbs drive this machine."

"But—"

"No. I'm not allowing you to drive this anymore. Take care of Agnes or go for a ride with the judge."

She winced at the thought of sitting in a saddle on a rocking horse.

He laughed. "Maybe riding a horse isn't a good thing."

"We'll see how I feel tomorrow." She turned and headed to the house, looking forward to the hot bath she knew Mrs. Fellowes would have waiting for her. The woman knew when a hot bath was needed and always had the wherewithal to make it happen.

Boom! The sound of a rifle behind the house had her picking up her skirts and running past the house and up the gully.

She stopped at the sight of Judge Radley showing his grandson how to shoot. Now why would Brody want to shoot a rifle and where had he been all day?

He raised the butt of the weapon to his shoulder, leaned his head to site in the target—a white handkerchief on a tree.

Her body tensed as if she were the one aiming for the cloth. Boom! She jumped and peered at the cloth. He'd hit the square. The elation she felt for him made her giddy. She knew the excitement of hitting the target when first learning and even now when she competed in shooting events. There was a rush when you put a bullet in the target. While sadness also claimed her when she killed animals, she only did so for protection or for food. In the ten years she'd been here, she'd shot a deer, an antelope, and a cougar that had cornered her and her horse in a canyon.

Her thoughts went to the man she'd encountered at the pond. He'd scared her enough that if he cornered her and she had her rifle, she wouldn't hesitate to pull the trigger.

Boom!

She jumped and spun about. Best get cleaned up before Mrs. Fellowes put supper on the table.

Chapter Eighteen

Brody entered the dining room for supper and encountered Lilah. She walked slowly into the room, her smile a whisper of her usually curved lips. She reminded him of a wilting rose. He hurried to her side, pulling her chair back and waiting for her to sit before taking his seat. After he'd returned from his ride up the gully, he'd headed straight to his grandfather and told him what had taken him away and what he'd witnessed. They'd both decided to keep it between them until they could catch the man and find out what was going on. Grandfather had, however, dispatched Sandy and Clem to see if the man was still there and to apprehend him if he was.

"Where did you disappear to today?" Lilah asked, once the food had been passed around.

He didn't like lying but it was for her own good. "Smithy found things to keep me busy."

"So busy you couldn't bring out the noon meal?" She stared at him as if she knew he lied.

"I offered to take out the meal so I could see the progress." His grandfather smiled. "You three are a good team. You managed to cut that whole field in one day."

She wearily curved her lips into a smile. "We didn't have anything break and the horses all behaved. It was a good day." She winced and tipped from side to side. "But I don't remember being this sore last year."

Brody studied her. He didn't like seeing her so tired and obviously hurting. "There must be someone else who could take over for you tomorrow."

"That's what Buster said." She frowned. "But I like to finish what I start."

He studied her before directing his attention to the man sitting at the head of the table. "I think her cutting the hay in a field is finishing what she started."

His grandfather nodded. "Lilah, my dear, there is no need for you to get on the mowing machine tomorrow. We have hired hands that are capable of doing that."

She started to nod, when racing horse hooves and a shout carried through the open windows.

Both he and his grandfather shot to their feet and headed to the front door.

Sandy sat atop his horse. A body lay over the horse he was leading.

"Judge! Judge! Me and Clem found that man hiding in the trees. He shot Clem and raced off down the side of the ridge."

Brody hurried to the man slumped over his saddle.

Clem was breathing but blood trickled down his neck and side of his face. "Help me." He grabbed the unconscious man under the arms and dragged him off the horse.

"Put him on the kitchen table," Grandfather said.

The men in the bunkhouse all ran up at the same time. Brody scolded himself to not look at Angel. The man would see the accusation in his eyes. He and Sandy carried the wounded man into the kitchen and placed him on the empty table.

"Get back. I need to see the injuries." Mrs. Fellowes shooed them out the back door as Lilah appeared in the kitchen doorway with an armful of bandages.

He glanced at her weary face. She was tired but she was determined. This man would live if the two women, peeling off his shirt, had anything to say about it.

Stepping off the porch, he heard the men all talking at once.

"Listen!" Grandfather stood on the front porch commanding their attention.

They all closed their mouths and turned to the older man.

"Everyone. And I mean everyone, who is out riding the fences and checking cattle will go in pairs. This man, for whatever reason, has holed up on Double R property and it's become obvious he isn't afraid to shoot and kill people." Worry etched the lines on the judge's face deeper.

The men started talking again.

Brody whistled and took a spot on the porch next

to his grandfather. "Listen to Judge Radley. You have to go in pairs." He hoped this would prevent Angel from meeting with the man.

"But Sandy and Clem were together and looked what happened," said Roy.

The others agreed with him.

"That's because we seen the man and I told Clem to go around behind him. When I showed myself, the killer took off straight where I'd sent him. His getting shot is my fault." Sandy pointed his face to the ground. His wide-brimmed hat covering his emotions.

"It's not your fault. This man is a killer, and he's not wanting anyone to catch him," Brody said, trying as hard as he could to not stare daggers at Angel. The man was in cahoots with the killer, and yet, he stood there quietly watching everything. He wanted to mention the sheriff was checking to find out who the man was but that information could get to the killer through Angel.

"Men, go to the bunkhouse and get a good night's rest. We have more hay to cut and a ranch to run. Now that we know this man is quick to pull a trigger, we'll be more watchful." Judge Radley waved for them to go back to the bunkhouse.

"Buster," his grandfather called to the foreman.

Buster spun around and came back to the porch.

"We need a word with you. Come on inside." Grandfather led the way into the house and straight to his office. Once Brody and Buster were in the room, he closed the door.

The foreman swung his gaze from him to his grandfather. "What do you two know?"

Grandfather nodded to him.

He repeated what he'd told his grandfather that led to Sandy and Clem confronting the killer.

"And you say Angel met this man?" Buster asked.

"Yes. I'd like to volunteer to ride with Angel. I don't want anyone else to get hurt." The hired hand wasn't going to like having the greenhorn along but he'd deal with it.

Buster glanced at the judge. "Are you all right with him riding with the vaquero?"

"No. But it's the only way to keep Angel's involvement with this person between us and not get an innocent person hurt." His grandfather stared at him a moment and resumed his conversation with the foreman. "Send the three pairs out tomorrow to ride fence and check on cattle. Send Angel and Brody the direction we know the man was last seen. Keep the others away from the killer if we can."

"I don't think it's a good idea to send Brody alone. That crazy vaquero already has a grudge against him." The foreman glanced toward him.

"I know he doesn't like me and why. If he knew I was the one who saw him with the killer that would definitely get me a bullet in my back. When you tell everyone their jobs tomorrow, if he balks, tell him I'm a greenhorn and you need the most experienced cattleman with me. That will fulfill his need to be the best." He'd worked with men like the vaquero on the docks. They required someone telling them how good they were to get them to do the work many others did without the praise.

"I will, but this means I can't let Lilah rest tomorrow. She's going to have to drive a mowing machine." The regret in Buster's voice showed his affection for the young woman.

"She'll understand," said Judge Radley. "But there's to be no mention to her of Angel or the man. Is that clear?"

"Yes," they both said at the same time.

"Let's go check on Clem. He's in good hands with Mrs. Fellowes and Lilah, but I'm sure the boys in the bunkhouse would like to know how he is." Judge Radley opened the office door and they filed down the hall to the kitchen.

Chapter Nineteen

Lilah sat on the mowing machine watching Brody and Angel ride to the south while all the other hands headed north. She glanced to the top of the ridge where Clem was shot. A niggling in her belly said the two young men were headed into danger. After helping Mrs. Fellowes with the hired hand's bullet wound, it squeezed her chest with fear to think of either man on the kitchen table having a bullet pulled from their body.

Her gaze landed on the foreman driving the lead mowing machine. Why would he send them in the opposite direction of everyone else? At the end of the row, she grabbed the take-up bar and raised the sickle bar using every bit of muscle in her arm. The horses knew the routine, making a wide turn and stepping into the row Gus's mowing machine had just cut. She dropped the sickle bar and rubbed her arm. She'd brought a quilt out to sit on for cushion on the metal seat but there wasn't anything that could relieve the burning muscle in her arm from raising the sickle bar on every pass.

This was one time she wished she hadn't pushed so hard to learn how to help with the hay harvest. But she was needed. With Clem injured, but recovering due to Mrs. Fellowes knowledge of bullet wounds, she had to operate the mowing machine. Three machines made the cutting go faster. While the country was known for its hot dry summers, a rain storm could show up without notice.

At the first water break, Lilah maneuvered Buster away from Gus.

"Why did you send Angel and Brody off in the direction of the man who shot Clem?" She studied the man. She'd grown up watching and following the foreman. If he lied, she'd know.

"Just following orders." He sipped from the dipper, avoiding eye contact.

"Judge Radley told you to send them looking for the killer?" She couldn't believe the judge would do something to put his grandson in danger.

"He told me to pair up the hands and send them off to check fences and cattle. That's what I did." He dropped the dipper in the bucket, sloshing water over the sides and walked over to Gus.

His irritation suggested he hadn't liked sending them south either.

Why would the judge make such an order?

***

Brody rode out beside Angel. After trying to start up a conversation twice and meeting silence, he'd dropped back. He glanced down at the rifle Buster had slipped into his scabbard as he'd saddled the horse.

"In case," the foreman had said in a low voice.

He'd nodded, understanding what the man meant. He might need it if they saw the killer or he might need it to protect himself from Angel.

After two hours, they stopped at a four strand barb wire fence.

"This is the south border of the ranch," Angel said. He nodded east. "That way there are many meadows and gullies where the cattle stay." The vaquero turned his horse west.

"If the cattle are east, why are you going west?" he asked, holding his horse from following.

"If the man who shot Clem trespassed from this side, he would have to cut the fence. The west is closer to any roads he might have left while being chased." The arrogant man dug his spurs into his horse's sides and headed west along the fence.

He had no choice but to follow. Why would the vaquero search for the hole where his friend came through? It didn't make sense, but it was opposite the last known place of the stranger. Which meant he'd only have to be wary of Angel's actions.

Again, he rode behind the vaquero. Better to keep him in front where he didn't have a chance to put a bullet in my back.

This section of fence covered flat ground dotted with sagebrush and a smaller bush with yellow flowers. He'd have to ask Lilah what those plants were. Brown bunch grass had been eaten down to stubby bumps between the brush.

"When were the cows down here?" he asked, curious about the lack of fences on the property, yet the cattle seemed to stay together in certain areas.

"This is the first spring feed. They were here April and May. This grass comes on first. As the snow melts higher up and the grass grows, they move up the hills."

That made sense.

"So there's no chance cows may have went through the hole the stranger might have cut in the fence?" He didn't like the idea cattle could be lost because of the trespasser's behavior.

"There are no cattle here. They are all on higher ground." Angel dug his heels into his horse. They shot forward through the sagebrush.

Brody urged his horse to follow. He wasn't sure what the man was up to, but he had a feeling he wasn't just looking for the hole in the fence.

All of a sudden the horse and rider in front of him disappeared as if they'd fallen into a hole.

He pulled back on his horse to slow the animal's pace and then yanked back hard on the reins. The horse stopped, sitting back. He almost toppled off the side of the gelding's neck. An eight-foot jagged rock drop-off was inches from the horse's hooves.

The sound of hooves on rock caught his attention. He spotted Angel and his horse walking along the bottom of the rocky crack in the earth.

His mind tried to fathom how the two could have leaped down into the crack without the horse being injured.

"Are you coming?" the vaquero called.

Brody scanned the edge of the crack and spotted

what appeared to be a trail. He reined his horse to the trail, and the animal walked down without any problems. His best guess, Angel and his horse were enough ahead of him he hadn't see them veer this direction and take the path. The vaquero had attempted to get him hurt or killed. That answered his question about why the man hadn't appeared upset this morning when they were paired together.

They followed the crack in the ground for half an hour before a trail appeared on the opposite side. Angel's horse climbed up out of the rocky cavern, knocking rocks back down the trail.

With the falling rocks, he held his horse at the bottom, hoping one didn't bounce and strike them. His horse started fidgeting.

"Whoa, it's okay those rocks can't get you." He soothed the horse the best he knew how.

The gelding snorted and danced.

As Angel topped the side, a sound he'd never heard before, like steam releasing from machinery, had him peering around. On the ground not far from the horse, a snake was coiled. The creature shook its tail, and he realized that was the sound he heard.

The horse snorted again.

"Go!" Brody said, leaning forward and giving the horse rein.

The animal lunged up the trail. He wasn't ready and slid off the back of the horse, landing in the rocks.

Everything was a blur except for the pain in his right shoulder blade. His head lay beside a rock. He thanked the heavens he hadn't struck his head. Would Angel come back for him? Not likely. The man wanted him dead. The others would come looking for him but it was a lot of ground to cover.

He pushed up with the arm that wasn't attached to his throbbing shoulder blade.

The steam sound was close. Before he had time to find the snake, its fangs sunk into his arm.

"Aaahhhh!" He yelled in surprise and pain. He grabbed the snake behind the head and flung it as far as he could.

Damn! This was worse than just a shoulder injured. He had to get out of this snake pit. A noise at the top of the crack gave him hope. Angel did come back.

He scanned the edge and saw his horse. All I have to do is get to the horse. He'll take me home.

Pushing to his feet, he clutched his aching arm. Dizziness struck. He stopped, waited for that to pass enough he could move. His mind flashed to a dime novel Maria had read out loud while he was teaching her to read and speak English. The hero in the book had been bitten by a rattler. He'd tied a bandana tight around his leg to keep the poison from spreading so fast.

He didn't have a bandana. He did have a suspender. Unbuttoning the strap, he used one hand and his teeth to tie the suspender tightly around his upper arm. Dizziness claimed him again. Waiting it out, he heard the horse moving up above.

"Wait. I'm coming." He pushed forward, using the arm with the bruised shoulder blade to help get up the incline. At the top he sat a moment. The horse sniffed him and he captured the dangling rein.

He stood, pulled himself onto the saddle, and made

the horse go back through the crack. Angel wouldn't come looking for him. He needed to get as close to the ranch as he could so whoever did come looking for him could find him. Hopefully before he died.

***

Lilah was bone tired as she drove the mowing machine to the barn. They had three-quarters of the second field done, but it was getting dark. Smithy came out and took the reins from her. He even lifted her down off the machine.

"You look tired," he said.

"I am. I don't think I can lift food to my mouth." It was an effort to smile, but she did.

Walking by the bunkhouse toward the house, she spotted Angel out in the corral working a horse. One good thing this evening would be seeing Brody at supper.

She washed up at the pan outside the kitchen and entered, inhaling the wonderful aromas. Her stomach growled.

Mrs. Fellowes turned from the stove. "I've been keeping you and Brody's dinners warm."

The woman received her full attention. "What do you mean you're keeping Brody's dinner warm?"

"He hasn't come in." Mrs. Fellowes held a plate heaped with food.

"Where's Judge Radley?" Her weary legs took on new energy as she headed out of the kitchen.

"His office."

She pushed the door open. "Brody isn't back yet," she said, standing in the doorway.

"He and Angel went to check the fences to the

161

south." The judge waved her off.

"But Angel is out working horses in the corral."

Judge Radley's attention left his papers and his gaze speared her. "What did you say?"

"I saw Angel out in the corrals working the horses. If he's back, why isn't Brody?" She didn't like the knot of fear forming in her belly.

The judge pushed out of his chair and past her. "I'll go talk with Buster and Angel. Eat your dinner."

The knot in her belly wouldn't let her eat. She followed the older man out of the house and over to the bunkhouse. When they both burst through the door, every head turned their way.

"Where's Buster?" Judge Radley asked.

"He's at his house," Sandy said.

"Any of you know where Brody is?" The judge stared at each hand.

"Angel said he took off on a trail he thought was made by the guy who shot Clem after they found the hole in the fence where the man came through," Sy said, leaning back on a bunk.

"He wouldn't do that. He's smart enough to know that's an old trail." Lilah glared at Sy.

"Go get Angel," the judge ordered and motioned to Roy.

The hand jumped up and headed for the door.

"Round up Buster, too," added Judge Radley.

She stood beside the judge, studying each of the hands. All appeared upset but Sy. He had a smile on his lips. He knew something.

The door opened and Angel walked in. The second he saw the judge and her, his eyes held wariness.

"Angel take a seat at the table," Judge Radley said, pointing to the small table where Sy and Stubbs were sitting.

"Want us to move?" Stubbs asked.

"If you don't mind." The ranch owner took a seat and folded his hands in front of him on the table. He watched Angel.

Lilah moved to stand behind the judge. She wanted to see everything he did.

The door opened. Buster and Roy walked in.

"Have a seat, Buster," Judge Radley said.

"What's this about, Judge?" Buster asked, taking a seat and seeing Angel across from him. His gaze immediately scanned the room. "Where's Brody?"

"That's what I want to ask Angel." The older man leaned forward. "Angel, where's Brody? We all saw you ride out with him this morning."

Chapter Twenty

Brody body rocked back and forth with the rhythm of the horse under him, but he couldn't remember why he was on a horse. His arm throbbed, his shoulder blade was on fire, and he was thirsty. But he'd dropped his canteen the last time he took a drink. His chest constricted making it hard to breathe. He forced his eyes open and found he was surrounded in blurry darkness.

The snake bite reminded him of why he felt the way he did. Angel had left him out here to die. That only made him more determined to discover the man's connection to the stranger and make sure the vaquero was never alone with Lilah again. That is if he survived the snake bite. Right now, he had to focus on breathing and keeping the horse moving.

"Over there!" shouted a familiar voice.

The call roused him momentarily before his body

slumped to the side and he hit the ground, blacking out.

***

"He fell!" Lilah jabbed her heels into Dusty's sides, running straight to the horse she'd spotted before Brody fell. She pulled back on the reins, sitting Dusty on her haunches. The horse hadn't finishing sliding when her feet hit the ground and she ran to Brody.

She dropped to her knees as the pounding of hooves brought Judge Radley and Sandy closer, rolling dust over her.

"He's barely breathing and fevered," she said, looking up at the two men.

"Bring that lantern closer," ordered the judge.

"He's been bit," Sandy said, as the light illuminated the stretched cloth of one of his sleeves, a suspender tied around the arm, and two small bloody spots on the sleeve.

"Why would he leave Angel?" she asked. Her chest constricted, realizing if they hadn't found him when they did, he would never have lived. Even though she hadn't known him a very long time, she'd come to think of him as more than Judge Radley's grandson.

The judge shook his head and pulled out a knife, slicing the sleeve on his grandson's shirt. "Sandy, bring me the snake bite remedy."

When Sandy was out of hearing the judge whispered to her, "There is no way this boy would have rode off on his own."

Lilah stroked Brody's fevered cheek and stared at Judge Radley. "You think Angel left him after he was bit?"

Sandy's approaching steps had the judge clamping

his mouth closed, but he nodded slightly.

What weren't they telling her? She cradled his head in her lap as his grandfather used a knife to make a cut from fang mark to fang mark and poured whiskey over the wound.

"Arggh!" Brody raised his arm, but his grandfather held it down.

"You have to keep this arm as immobile as possible to keep the poison from spreading," the older man said close to his grandson's ear. "We'll get you home, son. Mrs. Fellowes will take over."

"Sandy, we'll put him in your saddle. You can ride behind him to keep him upright." Judge Radley slipped an arm under his grandson's arm, and with Sandy on the other side, they managed to get him on Sandy's horse.

The hired hand swung up behind him.

Lilah gathered the reins to Brody's horse and mounted Dusty. Judge Radley swung up into his saddle. He held the lit lantern, leading the way back to the ranch at a fast walk.

They'd found Brody two miles from the house. He'd been headed back. She couldn't believe their luck in finding him so soon. Her mind had raced to so many bad outcomes that she'd nearly made herself crazy with the thoughts. When he'd fallen to the ground, she'd thought he'd died. Her heart had lodged in her throat. Touching him, seeing he was still alive, had revived her soul. Knowing he was out there alone and not knowing the land, she'd feared for his safety.

Even though she'd wanted to believe Angel's story about Brody going off on his own, deep down she'd known he wouldn't do something that reckless. Judge Radley knew something about Angel. Something that led to the vaquero leaving Brody alone with a snake bite. Hadn't the hand realized they would go looking for him?

She urged her horse to move up alongside the judge.

He didn't acknowledge her arrival.

"How did you know Brody wouldn't have gone off looking for the stranger?"

"I know his mind. He knows better than that. The man has killed a cow and wounded Clem. He knows how to use a gun. Brody doesn't." The older man's face was illuminated by the lantern he carried. Worry sagged his jowls and wrinkled his brow. "He's smart enough to know he'd be outmatched. And he doesn't know this country well enough to know if he'd get back home on his own."

"If he didn't go off on his own, why would Angel say so?" She had a soft spot for Angel. On their rides, he'd talked about his family and said sweet things to her. But his touch never made her skin tingle and peering into his eyes had never held her like Brody's did. Her heart squeezed thinking they could lose Brody before ever really getting to know him.

"There are things you don't know. Leave it at that." Judge Radley handed her the lantern. "I'm going to ride ahead and tell Mrs. Fellowes to gather what she needs for a snake bite." He took off into the darkness. But they were close enough she could see the square glow of light from the windows in both the house and the bunkhouse.

***

Pain shot up his arm. He heard voices. Whispers. He forced his eyes to open. Two blurred objects hovered over the arm that ached.

"The arm has to stay down, no movement. We'll use bandages to tie it to his body," Mrs. Fellowes said.

"That's all?"

"Water." Lilah's fearful voice made him force out the word.

She jumped and put a hand on his forehead. "I'll get it." Her cool hand disappeared as well as her blurry form.

"Once the arm is secured, I'll put a poultice of egg, salt, and gunpowder on the wound. It should suck the poison out." Mrs. Fellowes rolled him to the side with the bruised shoulder.

"Ow!" His eyes watered from the pain.

"Sorry! Are you hurt besides the bite?" the housekeeper asked.

"Left shoulder. Hit rock. Horse dumped me."

Lilah raised his head, pressing a cool glass to his lips.

He drank all the water, ignoring the pull on his shoulder. "Thank you."

"You're welcome." She brushed a hand across his forehead again.

"Help me get this bandage wrapped around him."

"I can sit up if you help me," he offered, knowing it would worsen his dizziness.

"We can get it. You stay down." Mrs. Fellowes rolled him again. This time toward his swollen arm. "Grab the end of the bandage."

"I have it." Lilah's cold fingers touched his back where the pain centered in his shoulder. "Oh! He has a nasty bruise back here."

"If it's just a bruise, it will heal. The rattler bite is our concern."

He wanted to stay awake as it seemed to relieve Lilah, but he felt himself slipping into darkness. He hoped it was to sleep and not die. He'd finally found the best reason to live. He had family again.

Panic squeezed her chest. "His eyes are closed!" she said, leaning down to feel his breath on her cheek. When short puffs tickled her skin, she drew in a relieved breath herself. "He's still alive."

"He'll remain that way if we get this poultice on." The housekeeper spread a nasty looking mash onto Brody's arm, covering the open wound Judge Radley had made when they found him. She lay a cloth over the poultice and the arm. "All we can do now is wait. You go on and get your dinner. I'll sit with him."

Lilah didn't want to leave him, but her stomach gnawed on itself. "I'll sit with him when I finish eating."

The older woman nodded as she sat in the chair next to the bed.

She'd been surprised and happy when Judge Radley and Sandy carried Brody up to the bed he'd occupied the first night at the ranch. She'd feared the judge would make them take care of him out at the bunkhouse.

In the kitchen, she pulled her dinner out of the warming oven and sat at the table. Even though she was hungry, her mind and stomach were at war. One wanted fed, the other was preoccupied.

"Eat. You put in a hard day's work." Judge Radley walked into the kitchen, poured a cup of coffee, and sat at the table.

"I'm almost too tired and worried to eat," she admitted.

He placed a large hand over hers. "He'll be fine. I've seen men with a weaker will survive a snake bite."

She nodded. The judge was right but that didn't keep her from worrying. "Why did Angel leave him out there alone?"

Judge Radley picked up his coffee cup, took a sip, and set it on the table. "Eat and I'll tell you what I know."

She stuck her fork into a potato and lifted it to her mouth. "Why would you tell me now and not before?"

"Because I believe you are in danger now, too."

The potato stuck in her throat. She gagged and coughed.

The older man pumped her a glass of water and handed it to her.

She swallowed, forcing the potato down. "Why?"

"I should have stopped your rides with Angel from the beginning. But you and he got along well and he was close to your age." Judge Radley raised his cup and peered at her over the rim. "He was given false ideas by my not intervening."

"I don't understand?" She stared at him. He motioned for her to keep eating. She shoved her fork into a piece of meat.

"By my allowing Angel to ride with you unchaperoned, he had the impression I thought you two were a good match. And until Brody arrived, he thought you would inherit the ranch."

Her mind flashed through the conversations Angel had shared with her on those outings. "I'm as much to blame as you. I enjoyed his company and listened, giving him the idea I was interested in him more than just as friends." She blushed. He'd kissed her on the last ride they'd taken together. While it had been pleasant, she hadn't dwelled on it for days as she'd heard girls at the finishing school do after their beaus had kissed them.

Judge Radley's bushy gray eyebrows rose. "How much interest did you show him?"

Her cheeks heated. Would he think less of her? For that fact, what would Brody think of her knowing she'd kissed Angel. "Not that much. We kissed once."

He slammed a hand down on the table. "That's the reason I shouldn't have allowed you to ride alone with him. I should have had my grandson's good sense." He narrowed his eyes. "You are not to ride alone with any one man anymore. You're of an age we must be careful."

"You said I could give Brody riding lessons after the haying." He and Buster were the only men she'd consider riding with alone.

"He is proving to not need lessons." Judge Radley glanced at her plate. "Eat. I'm going to check on the boy. When I get back I expect to find that plate clean."

Hurried footsteps on the porch and a loud rapping on the door, sent the judge to the back door.

He opened the door to Sandy. The hired hands face was animated, his breathing sounded like he'd ran to the house.

"What's wrong?" Judge Radley asked.

"Angel packed up his things and took off on the horse he rode in on." Sandy's gaze landed on her. "Sorry to intrude, Miss Wells."

"There's a reason you're upset about him heading out. What is it?" The judge asked, drawing the hand's attention back to him.

"He didn't head down the road. He headed for the ridge where Clem was shot."

Chapter Twenty-one

Lilah tried to sleep in her bed, but she had nightmares about Angel and Brody. She ended up in the chair in Brody's room. Being near him eased her mind.

Sunlight filtered through the lace curtains as she opened her eyes and realized she slept with her head on his chest. His unrestricted arm lay across her back. She eased off of him and out of his embrace.

"Don't go," he whispered. His eyes were closed, but his lips were parted as he drew in breaths.

"I have to get breakfast and get on that mowing machine." The thought of another day on the machine made her backside ache.

"Get. Someone. Else," he said, between intakes of breath.

"There is no one else. Angel left last night." She reached over and grabbed the glass of water she'd offered him during the night when he asked.

"Good. He. Lured. Me. And. Left. Me."

"Shhh. We figured it out. Here's a drink." She placed her hand behind his head, helping him raise up to drink. As happened the night before, her hand had its own mind and brushed across his forehead. She wanted to touch more than his forehead but refrained, knowing it was inappropriate for her to have slept on his chest.

A quick knock and the door opened. She pulled her hand back as if she'd been caught stealing.

Judge Radley walked in. His gaze swept over her nightdress and cover. "You should be dressed and eating breakfast."

"I was just headed that way." She scurried around him and out the door. From the frown on his face, she had a feeling he'd be sitting in this room tonight.

Brody's bitten arm ached and tingled. He'd enjoyed the weight and feel of Lilah sleeping on his chest. It gave him something to think about other than his arm. He had trouble breathing, but her weight had made him feel as if someone cared. As much as he hated to admit it, the woman was working her way into his heart.

"How are you feeling this morning?" Grandfather asked.

He tried hard to open his eyes. Since being bit, they had become as heavy as an anvil. He gave up. "Hard. Breathe. Arm. Aches. Dizzy."

"Thought as much. I'm surprised you aren't fevered to point of unconsciousness."

One more thing to look forward to. "No. Thirsty."

A larger, warmer hand held his head and the cool glass touched his lips. He drank again.

When his head rested back on the pillow, he heard the chair beside him creak.

"Angel left during the night. Makes me think the story he told us is a lie."

"What. He. Say?" It was getting harder and harder to speak and draw in air.

"He told us that you rode off alone following the killer's trail." He heard the disbelief in his grandfather's voice.

"He. Led. Crevice. Rocks. Snake." He sucked in air.

"Don't talk. We've figured out the truth."

The silence told him something else was wrong.

"Worried."

"When Angel left, he didn't leave the ranch. Sandy saw him head for the ridge. Buster and I think he's meeting up with the killer."

"Lilah."

"She'll remain at the ranch. Best place for her is out in the field with Buster and Gus cutting the hay."

"Tired."

"I'll leave you be."

"No. Lilah. Tired."

"I know she is. But she's safer out there."

"House."

Grandfather chuckled. "I don't think that's safer. She'd be up here with you." A hand squeezed his shoulder. "I'll check on you throughout the day."

He would rather have Lilah check on him. As the morning progressed, his body heated and the dizziness turned into vomiting. The incessant pain in his arm made him wish he'd struck his head and died in the rocky crack in the earth.

***

Lilah didn't know how she'd stayed on the mowing machine the last hour. Her body ached and her mind had gone to sleep even though she still drove the horses and worked the lever. Walking to the house was more effort than her legs wanted to manage. The step up onto the porch required grabbing the porch post and pulling with her arms. She washed up and entered the kitchen, plopping down in a chair.

"How is Brody?" she asked, before downing a glass of milk. Either, the judge, Mrs. Fellowes or herself, had kept an eye on him the past four days.

"As to be expected. He's burning up with fever, delirious, and finally stopped vomiting." The housekeeper set a plate of food in front of her.

She stood. "How can you be so calm? He's gone days without food and his arm…" She didn't want to think about how nasty it had looked when Mrs. Fellowes replaced the poultice that morning.

Mrs. Fellowes put her hands on Lilah's shoulders, pressing her back into the chair. "The judge is with him right now. There is nothing that can be done. We keep him cool, change the poultice, and wait for the poison to leave his body. We'll know he's on the mend when he asks for food."

Lilah melted back down into the chair, mainly because she didn't have the strength to resist the housekeeper's pressure.

"Eat. I have a tub of water waiting for you in my room." Mrs. Fellowes sat down at the end of the table. "You are a strong young woman. Not many could have helped like you have the last few days."

"Don't tell the men, but I'm glad the cutting is done. I don't think I could have sat on that machine another day." She dug into the stew on her plate and picked up the thick slice of bread slathered in butter.

Judge Radley wandered into the kitchen. "I need more water." He held the pitcher from Brody's room.

"How's he doing?" she asked, watching the older man's weary face.

"I think the fever's broke and the arm seems less swollen." He walked to the hand pump and filled the pitcher.

"I'll take over as soon as I get a bath," she offered.

"I'd appreciate that. I need to visit with Buster and see how things are going." He set the pitcher on the table and took a seat. "Did you finish the south field today?"

"Yes. All the hay fields are cut." A sense of pride filled her as Judge Radley smiled.

He patted her hand. "I won't forget how hard you've worked. I'll send along a large allowance when you go to the university."

She swallowed the bite of stew in her mouth. "At the first of the year. I'll have stories that will curl the other girls' hair." She turned her attention to the housekeeper. "How is Agnes doing? I haven't had the time to check on her."

"She's getting up and puttering around the house a few hours each day and eating more and more. I think that young man knew exactly what he was talking about." Mrs. Fellowes flashed a bright smile. She picked up the water pitcher. "I'll go change his poultice and check on him. Come up when you're done bathing. Judge, go talk to Buster."

The older man smiled and shook his head. "She's been here long enough she thinks she can boss me around."

Lilah smiled. "And you enjoy it."

His light blue gaze stared into hers. "You really want to stay here until Agnes has the baby? You'll miss out on the beginning of the year classes. You could learn so much and perhaps bring a young man home for Christmas."

Now she knew the real reason he pushed this so much. "I'm not going to the university to meet young men. I'm going to learn more and perhaps someday make a difference for women and children." She put her hand on his arm.

"You will one day want to marry. You aren't going to find someone at this ranch. A pretty thing like you should have someone who loves you in your life." He continued to stare into her eyes.

She swallowed and voiced the thought that had been building in her mind since the first night she slept on Brody's chest. "I may have found him."

He pulled his arm out from under her hand. "Brody."

"Yes."

Judge Radley stood. "What has he said?"

"Nothing. I don't know how he feels about me. I saw flashes of caring in his eyes before he was bit. I won't be looking for a husband while I'm at school. I'll be learning how I can be of help with the books here, at the ranch." She stood, picking up her empty dishes.

He nodded, took his hat from the peg by the back door, and left.

She stared at the door wondering if her voicing her feelings would get Brody sent back to the bunkhouse when he healed.

Chapter Twenty-two

Brody woke with a gnawing ache in his belly. His eyes no longer felt weighted, air filled his lungs with ease, and best of all—his arm didn't throb.

He glanced down and smiled. Even when he didn't know whether he'd come out of this alive, he knew when it was night. Lilah spent every night using his chest as a pillow while she slept, sitting in the chair by the bed.

Her brown hair spread across his chest and down his side. He placed his unrestricted hand on her head, feeling the silky strands.

Soft murmurs escaped her and her head turned, bringing her face into view. He stared into her sleepy, half-open eyes.

"Good morning," he said, taking in her partly-opened, full lips and widening eyes.

"You're feeling better." She pushed off him, sitting

back in the chair. Her long hair cascaded around her shoulders. Her beautiful green eyes sparkled with happiness.

"I do feel much better." His stomach made noises.

"And you're hungry!" She leaned forward and kissed his cheek.

He wanted to turn and kiss her, but he'd spent most of his time in this bed vomiting. Besides the putrid smell of his arm, his mouth had to be just as bad.

"I'm glad my being hungry makes you happy," he said, reaching up and touching her hair one more time.

"Mrs. Fellowes said when you were hungry you would be on the mend." She reached up, grasping his hand, and holding it between hers. "I'm glad you recovered."

He'd learned to read people while growing up and avoiding jail. He could tell by the shine in her eyes and the flush on her cheeks she had feelings for him. Part of him rejoiced that she could be interested in a dock rat like him. The other part of him didn't feel worthy.

His stomach growled. "Could you see what Mrs. Fellowes recommends for me to eat? My belly is getting angry."

"Yes." She released his hand and hurried from the room.

Damn! He'd give anything to reap the joys of Lilah's love, but he had nothing to give her. Just because he was the last living relative of Judge Radley didn't mean he'd get the ranch. And until he knew he had a future, he couldn't give her any hopes there was one with him.

Mrs. Fellowes entered the room carrying a tray.

He'd expected her to be smiling. The frown on her face made him wary.

"Heard you're hungry." She set the tray on the table by the bed.

The aroma of beef broth started his stomach talking. "Yes, I am."

"You feel like sitting up?"

"I'd like to try." He rolled to the side of his unrestricted arm and swung his legs over the side of the bed while pushing up with his arm. His head whooshed and his sight blurred a moment before everything settled.

"Can you slide closer to the table? That way you can rest the cup of broth on the table when you need to." Mrs. Fellowes helped him slide over and handed him a cup of broth.

"Thank you." He eased the cup to his lips and sipped. After all the vomiting he'd done, he wasn't sure how steady his belly would be. But the liquid soothed his stomach and he continued drinking.

"I'll have Gus drag the bathing tub up here so we can get you cleaned up," Mrs. Fellowes said, slipping scissors between his side and the injured arm. She cut the cloths binding his arm to his side. The arm above his elbow was normal size and color.

He made sure the liquid was all down before she removed the poultice from his arm. The sight nearly had him losing the broth. An area the size of his fist around the bite was purplish black, and had white ooze. His lower arm was still swollen.

"How long until my arm is back the way it was?" he asked, trying to flex his fingers. They didn't flex and pain centered on the bite area.

"Hard to say. Some never quite get the full use of their limbs." Mrs. Fellowes picked up a bowl of water and a rag. "This is going to hurt but we have to get that wound cleaned up." She dunked the rag in the water and scrubbed at his arm with the bowl underneath.

As much as the scrubbing hurt, it also felt better seeing the nastiness of the wound disappearing. Once she deemed the wound clean enough, she tied a bandage around the site.

"After your bath, I'll put salve and a better bandage on the wound." She placed everything on the tray. "Do you need anything else before I send Gus up?"

"You could save him the trouble and let me take my bath out in the lean-to."

"You feel you could walk down there and back up?" Her skeptical expression made him wonder.

"If I'm too tired to come back up right away I can rest in the sitting room."

She watched him a bit. "I'll have the judge come help you downstairs." She disappeared out the door.

A few minutes later his grandfather entered the room. His smile lit up his eyes. "It's good to see you up and about. Hear you're wanting a bath in the lean-to."

"I think I smell worse than the boar." His heart danced with happiness seeing the relief and joy in his grandfather's eyes.

"This room has started to reek." His grandfather stepped up to the bed. "You might be a bit wobbly after being in bed for a week."

"A week? That's how long it's been since I was bit?" He stared at the older man. "Have you caught the stranger or Angel?"

"No. If they're still here, they're hiding well. No one has seen them." Grandfather put an arm under his good one and helped him stand.

He wobbled a bit but put one foot in front of the other and was soon standing at the door. At the doorway, he leaned, resting.

"You sure you want to go all the way downstairs?" his grandfather asked.

"Yes. I need out of the room." He pushed away and started for the stairway. One step at a time he moved closer to the bottom. At the bottom, grandfather stepped into the dining room and brought out a chair.

"Sit. I'll go see if the water is ready."

He nodded and sat, relieving his shaking legs.

"What are you doing down here?" Lilah asked, walking in the front door.

"Heading to the lean-to for a bath." He straightened his spine. She didn't need to know how much this trip was wearing him out.

"You're awful white. Are you sure?" She placed a cool hand on his forehead.

He leaned into the touch. Forgetting he should keep his distance from her for both their sakes, he said, "I might be too weak to wash myself."

Her cheeks flashed bright red and her hand shot back to her side.

Before she could comment, Grandfather returned.

"The water is ready. Come on, you can rest in the tub with water washing away the stench of sickness." He ducked under Brody's arm, taking more of the weight.

"I can make it on my own," he protested, but the older man didn't budge.

Out in the lean-to, he stripped with the help of his grandfather, and settled into the warm tub of water. This was his second warm bath since childhood. He slid down in the water, bending his knees to soak his shoulders and head. Unsure if he should get the injured arm wet he asked his grandfather to put the question to Mrs. Fellowes.

In the quiet solitude of the lean-to he thought about the day he was bit. A week ago. He knew Angel had taken him to that crack in the ground hoping to either get him injured by his running the horse over the edge or a snake bite. How did the man think he could get away with it? And why would he meet up with the stranger who killed a cow and shot Clem. Why would they hide out on this ranch? Something was up. They had a reason. And how were they living?

Racing hooves and shouts made their way to the lean-to. Something had happened. He struggled to push up out of the water. He hadn't scrubbed yet, but matters of the ranch came first.

Chapter Twenty-three

Lilah rushed out of the garden as Judge Radley came around the side of the main house.

"Judge! Judge!" Roy yanked his horse up short of the small flower bed in front of the house and porch.

"What's wrong?" the judge asked, taking hold of the headstall on Roy's horse.

"Me and Stubbs found three cows shot. One was partly skinned and looked like someone hacked off some meat." He pointed to the east. "Out on that knobby hill just afore the fence line."

Judge Radley's face turned the color of her favorite red blouse. "Round up everyone! We're going to hunt those murderers down." He released the head stall. "Tell Smithy to get my horse ready." The older man spun around and strode into the house.

A flicker of white at the corner of the house caught her attention. Brody stood leaning against the house, a towel wrapped around his lower half.

"What are you doing up and…like this?" She ran over putting an arm around his bare waist. She'd never touched a man's skin other than a hand, or in the case of Brody, his face. Her body heated when she pulled his long, lean body against her side to maneuver him to the kitchen door.

"Did I hear right? More cattle were killed?" he asked, his bare feet shuffling along the porch.

"Yes. Stop talking and put effort into moving your feet," she said, trying to keep her mind from chasing the thoughts that made her body warm.

"I need to dress and go with them." His steps became less dragging.

"No, you don't. Well, you need to dress. But you aren't going with them. You wouldn't be able to sit in a saddle for more than an hour."

They were at the kitchen's screen door. "Mrs. Fellowes!" she called out.

The housekeeper poked her head out of the pantry. "Oh dear!" She scurried to the door and opened it. "Set him in a chair and go upstairs and fetch him some clothes."

Lilah settled him in a chair. She was reluctant to release him but felt Mrs. Fellowes watchful gaze. "Sit tight."

She hurried out of the kitchen, up the stairs, and into his room. She hadn't realized how it smelled until now. It would need cleaning before he came back up. The window was already raised. She walked to the wardrobe and opened the doors. His bag had been brought over from the bunkhouse when it was evident he'd be in the house for a while.

She opened the bag and found a photograph of a woman and a small boy. The woman had the judge's and Brody's light-colored eyes that made them look as if they had sight-less eyes in photographs. Judge Radley had shown her a photograph of his daughter. This woman resembled her, only years older. The boy had an adoring smile on his lips. His face was tipped up toward the woman. The scene showed how close he was with his mother. Her heart went out to the young man who lost his mother and had to battle to keep alive.

She pushed the photo aside and dug deeper into the bag for clothing. She hesitated as she pulled out a clean pair of underdrawers. She'd helped Mrs. Fellowes with the wash and had folded the judge's underdrawers, but touching Brody's heated her body as much as when she held his bare waist. Quickly, without thinking of what she touched, she pulled out a cotton shirt and duck cloth pants. Socks could wait.

Back downstairs, she heard him arguing with the judge.

"Boy, I don't have time for this. You will stay here. You're in no shape to be riding hard. And there will only be Smithy here to see to things. Another man around here would be good, considering we don't know where the men we're looking for could be." Judge Radley motioned her forward. "Give him his clothes and go in the other room. Mrs. Fellowes will see he gets dressed."

Judge Radley strode to the door dressed in his work clothes, making him look like one of the hired hands rather than the ranch owner. He turned. "I don't want anyone leaving here for any reason." His gaze bore into her. "Is that clear?"

"Yes." She glanced at Brody. It was going to be hard to keep him here when he clearly wanted to be with the other men.

"Good. I don't know when we'll be back. Could be tonight, could be a couple of days." He shoved the screen door open and disappeared.

Lilah placed the clothing on the table next to Brody. Her first thought was it might be best to not give him clothes. That would keep him from going too far from the house. But that would make getting things done a whole lot harder. Her gaze fell on his chest and the sprinkling of reddish blond hairs. Below that muscles rippled across his belly. Muscle she'd felt while helping him into the house. Her fingers tingled remembering the firmness.

"Shoo!" Mrs. Fellowes waved her apron at her like she chased away chickens.

She walked down the hall and stared out the front window watching the men mount up and head out, following Sandy. Even Clem, who had recovered quickly from his bullet wound, was riding out. She hoped they found Angel and the other man. There was hay to harvest and the men didn't need to fear for their lives while out checking the cattle.

***

Brody felt like a little kid again with Mrs. Fellowes helping him dress. She'd held the towel out so she couldn't see while he pulled on his drawers one-handed. Once he was covered, she helped him put on the pants and the shirt. The sleeve didn't fit over his swollen arm.

"I'm not going to ruin a good shirt. I'll put salve on the wound and bandage up that arm. You can hold it against your body, and we'll button it inside your shirt." She walked over to him with a small square tin and bandages.

"That will make me one-handed. Lilah could go up and get one of my old shirts and we can cut the sleeve off," he offered.

"I'd rather you keep that arm still as long as possible." She spread the salve and wrapped the bandage around the wound.

The woman was bossy. But she knew more about caring for snake bites than he did. He grudgingly allowed her to button his arm into his shirt.

"I'll get you more broth and some bread." The housekeeper made herself busy by the stove.

Lilah returned to the kitchen. She took a seat at the table across from him. "Looks like we're stuck here," she said, her cheeks deepening in color.

He wondered what she was thinking about that had her cheeks coloring. Could be her arm wrapped around his waist. He'd enjoyed feeling her body pressed to his as she helped him into the kitchen. The only thing that would have made it better would have been if they were skin to skin. The thought shot heat to his man parts. Good thing he was dressed and wasn't wearing only a towel.

"I have a score to settle with Angel." Anger replaced the lust. The man had purposely left him to die.

"Why do you think he left you out there?" Lilah

leaned forward on the table. Her beautiful eyes searched his.

"He wanted this ranch."

"How? He is a hired hand. How did he plan to get the ranch?" She sat back as if he were talking foolish.

"You know how. We talked about it before." He leaned forward. "He plans to get rid of me and sweet talk you."

She leaned back and crossed her arms. "He will never get me. After what he did to you, I don't care if I ever see him again."

He felt sorry for Angel if Lilah had a gun when she saw him. That was the depth of anger he saw swirling in her eyes.

A knock at the front door startled both of them.

"I'll see who it is," Mrs. Fellowes said, marching out of the kitchen.

She returned with Sheriff Davies.

"Brody, Miss Lilah, I'm looking for Judge Radley. Mrs. Fellowes says you've had more trouble." Sheriff Davies sat in a chair and the housekeeper placed a cup of coffee and plate of cookies in front of him.

"Yes. Sandy rode in saying they found more dead cattle. My grandfather rounded everyone up to go see if they can catch the man responsible." Brody smiled at Mrs. Fellowes when she placed a glass of milk in front of him.

"You sittin' here because of that bum arm?" The sheriff waved a cookie toward the bulge under Brody's shirt.

"Yes. My grandfather thought it was too soon for me to ride."

"He was bit by a rattlesnake a week ago. This is the first time he's been out of bed," Lilah said, plucking a cookie from the plate.

"How'd you come to get bit? They don't generally hang around buildings with this much activity." The man raised a cookie to his mouth.

"I was out riding, checking fences, and my horse dumped me." He wasn't one to share his business with the law.

"He's lucky we found him when we did," Lilah added.

"You were out riding alone?" The sheriff studied him.

He stared back at the man.

"No! Angel left him there to die." There was the anger. Her face darkened and her eyes narrowed and glared at the sheriff. "Sandy thinks he's with the man who's killing the cattle."

"I always thought there was something a little off about that vaquero." Sheriff Davies pulled a folded paper from inside his vest. "This came in the mail yesterday. The man fits your description." He unfolded and spread the paper on the table.

Lilah studied it and nodded. "That's him."

Brody turned the paper to look at the man and read his name. William Talbot. Wanted for escaping prison.

"What did he do to get put in prison?" he asked.

"Killed three men." Sheriff Davies tapped a finger on the paper. "This one is dangerous."

"He shot Clem," she said, staring at the paper.

"Why is he staying on this ranch?" He glanced at the sheriff, then Lilah and Mrs. Fellowes who stood beside Lilah's chair.

"It was Judge Radley who put him in prison ten years ago. From what I gather, this Talbot was the last man the judge sentenced before retiring." Sheriff Davies stood. "Make sure the judge gets this." He stopped at the door. "And let me know if you need any help."

"I will." Brody pulled the paper closer to get a good look at the man.

"I'll show you out." Mrs. Fellowes escorted the sheriff back to the front door.

"Do you think he's here to take revenge on Judge Radley?" Lilah asked.

He didn't want to say anything, but she brought it up. "I think that is exactly what he is doing here. Why else would he continue to kill cattle?"

Chapter Twenty-four

Brody spent the rest of the day sitting around the house and taking short walks to the privy. He needed to get his strength back, and the use of his arm, quickly. There was a murderer lurking on the ranch. And his actions proved he was hell bent on revenge.

He sat on the porch watching the horses in the corral. He'd decided which three he wanted. Now he had to cut them from the rest and start working with them with some guidance from Sy.

Lilah came around the corner of the house, a basket over her arm.

"Where are you going?" he asked.

She stopped next to the porch. "Taking bread to Sourdough. Then I thought I'd check on Agnes. With Buster gone, I don't want her overdoing."

He nodded. "I take it Agnes is doing better?"

Her face lit up. "Yes! Your advice has her out of

bed and slowly getting back to taking care of her family." She sat down on the top step and peered up at him. "I would enjoy hearing all you learned while working for that healing woman."

"I don't know that much. I delivered healing herbs more than I helped her. It was how I made extra money to help my mother." Remembering how little they had, he was grateful to his grandfather for reaching out to him. Just the meals alone made him feel like a wealthy man.

"I'm sorry you and your mother struggled. I wish I could say I knew what it was like, but I don't. My parents were professors at a college. I always had clothes and food." She placed a hand on his bare foot. "I know the judge would have helped you had he been able to find you both sooner."

He nodded and ignored the heat swirling up his leg from her touch.

"Go tend to your errands." He waved his good hand toward the bunkhouse.

She rose, smiled, and headed across the dirt and grass toward the bunkhouse. He enjoyed the sway of her hips and the sweeping motion of her skirt. His grandfather had said he wasn't to dally with Lilah but the more he was around her, he could see growing old with her.

Mrs. Fellowes banged through the doorway, swinging the screen door wide with the tray she carried. "I need to check your bandage and put more salve on that bite."

"How many times a day are you going to check this?" he asked. She'd taken to tending his wound every hour. He figured she only used it as an excuse to make sure he hadn't headed off after the rest of the men.

"Until I'm positive the wound is clear of infection."

Using the one hand, he unbuttoned his shirt and slipped his swollen arm out.

Her small, chubby fingers untied the bandage. He glanced down and wished he hadn't. The flesh around the gaping wound looked like raw meat. A dark blue to black streak ran almost to his elbow.

"You're lucky. I've had a few snake bites where the arm had to come off to stop the infection. You're healing nicely." She washed the wound with amber liquid.

"Ouch! What is that?" He jerked his arm out of her hand.

"Whiskey. Only thing we have to disinfect."

"Where did you learn all of this?" He needed to take his mind away from the burning pain.

"I was just coming of age when the war broke out. My daddy was an army doctor. I helped him in the surgery." Her hazel eyes dulled. "That war changed so many lives. Mine included. I married one of the patients. He lived longer than my father predicted and we had a wonderful life." She rubbed salve into the wound. "That's how I know so much about caring for gunshots and military type wounds. I couldn't help poor Agnes. Never tended to anyone having a baby and never had one myself."

Brody had a new-found admiration for the housekeeper. She'd been through a lot. He'd heard some of the dockworkers talk about the war.

"How did you get out here to Oregon?"

She wound a new bandage around his arm. "A friend knew Mrs. Radley's cousin and said Mrs. Radley was looking for a housekeeper in Oregon City. After my husband died, I became tired of the sadness and pity on my friends and family's faces. I had a good life with Teddy and I wouldn't change a thing. But I needed a new life. Something different. So I sent a letter to Mrs. Radley, and they paid my passage to Oregon. I've been with the family ever since." She folded and stuffed his arm into his shirt and started buttoning the garment.

"Have you ever gone back to see your family?" He had always yearned to know his family and now that he was here, he wished he'd met them sooner.

"No. I only had the cousins once my parents died. Judge Radley, Lilah, and now you, are my family." She picked up the tray and waddled back into the house, slamming the screen door behind her.

He liked the idea of the housekeeper being family. He had to agree. Family wasn't always the people of your blood, they were the people you surrounded yourself with. Betsy and Buddy ran out of the barn laughing and his thoughts drifted to Maria and her daughter. He wondered how they were doing.

***

Two days passed and the men hadn't returned. Brody grew stronger and his arm was healing well, according to Mrs. Fellowes. He'd taken over the chores of milking, feeding the hogs and chickens, and watering from Smithy. Even though he did most of it one-handed, finding his arm and hand still didn't work as they had before the bite. Keeping busy didn't give him

197

less time to think about what the others might encounter with Talbot and Angel.

He was carrying a bucket of water to the animals when an old horse with a small child on its back came trotting up the road. Dropping the bucket, he hurried over and caught the slobbering horse by the headstall.

"What's wrong?" he asked.

"Need Lilah," the young boy said, staring at the house.

"Come on. I don't think your horse can take another step." He turned to the horse barn. "Smithy!"

The man poked his head out of the barn.

"Come take care of this horse, please." Brody scooped the child up in his good arm and strode to the house.

At the back door he shoved the door open.

"Darrin, what are you doing here?" Lilah asked, setting the dishes in her hand on the table and hurrying across the kitchen.

"Pa's gone again and Mattie, she hurt herself bad tryin' to find us food. I got her home, but…" Tears welled up in the small boy's eyes.

"The others? Your brothers and sisters?" She took the boy from Brody's arm and placed him at the table.

Mrs. Fellowes placed a glass of milk in front of him.

"They's hungry and scared, but I told them not to go nowhere. They had to stay with Mattie and help her." He gulped the milk.

"Mrs. Fellowes, put together a basket of food for the Lund children and I'll get my riding skirt on." Lilah headed to the doorway.

Brody caught her arm. "You're not supposed to leave the ranch."

She glared at him. "Didn't you hear? There's an injured child and three others who are hungry. I'll not forsake them to keep myself safe." She shook off his hand and marched out of the room.

He turned to the boy. "How many kids are in your family?"

"Five."

"How old?" He had a feeling this family had a father like he'd had.

"Mattie is the oldest. She's twelve. I'm—"

"I'll figure it out on the way." Brody went into the office and found the pistol and holster his grandfather said he'd worn when riding around the country as a circuit judge. He pulled the holster around his hips and buckled the leather. He'd never shot a pistol, but he had a feeling it would come naturally, just like when he shot the rifle.

He strode through the kitchen. "I'll help Smithy saddle up the horses."

At the barn, he encountered more objections than he had from Mrs. Fellowes.

"The boss said no one was to leave the ranch while he was gone." Smithy stood in front of the gate leading out to the horses in the corral.

"We aren't going after them. If I don't go with Lilah, she's going to find a way to sneak out of here and help these children. What would you do if Buddy or Betsy were hurt? You'd disregard the judge's orders and get them help wouldn't you?" He had to find a way to the soft spot in Smithy's heart.

"Mrs. Fellowes could help them."

He could see the big man was softening. "She only knows about gunshot wounds and snake bites. She wouldn't know how to help a child who was sick."

"I don't believe you." Smithy crossed his arms.

"Get out of the way. We have an injured child and younger children who are hungry." Lilah walked up to Smithy and shoved him out of the way. "Get the horses," she ordered Brody.

He hurried by the big man. Smithy's arms were crossed as he stared at her. The woman stared right back, her eyes narrowed and her lips in a firm line. He caught the horse he usually rode and Lilah's mare. The boy could ride behind one of them and leave his poor, tired horse here.

Lilah grabbed her saddle and slung it over Dusty's back. No one was going to keep her from helping the Lund children. If she'd known their no-good father had left them again, she would have ridden out to see them earlier. She'd told him on numerous occasions to let her know when he was off looking for work and she'd keep an eye on the children.

Anger had given her the courage and strength to make Smithy move. She didn't think the big man would have physically kept Brody from getting the horses, but she didn't want him injuring his arm.

Once they were saddled up, they rode over to the house. Brody dismounted and handed Darrin up to sit behind her. Mrs. Fellowes handed him a bulging set of canvas saddlebags. He slung them over the rump of his mount. The housekeeper tied the rawhide holding the saddlebags on and he mounted.

Lilah kept the pace at a steady trot. She knew it was the first time back on a horse for Brody in a while, but she worried they would get to Mattie too late.

"What is Mattie's injury?" she asked.

"She was tryin' to trap a rabbit. When none would go into the trap on their own, she tried to chase one in and while runnin' after it she caught her foot in a crack in the rocks. She fell and heard her leg snap. I found her and dragged her home. I couldn't get her on old gray. She kept fallin' ta sleep."

Fear for the girl had her nudging her horse into a faster pace. "Hold on tight," she said putting a hand over the small hands clasped against her belly. The thin arms circled her and his head rested against her back. They had to get to the child in time.

Chapter Twenty-five

Brody followed Lilah. They'd ridden an hour when he spotted what looked like the front of a shack against a wall of rock.

Three small children ran out the rickety door as they approached.

"Lilah!" one of them cried out and launched herself at the woman the minute her feet touched the ground.

"Amelia, I'm happy to see you, too. But we must hurry to Mattie. How is she?"

"She mutters and feels hot." A boy smaller than Darrin stood halfway between them and the door.

Lilah set the child on the ground and grabbed the bag she'd hung from her saddle horn. "Brody, would you bring the food in. Darrin, tie up the horses."

He had to smile at the way she took charge. It was an admirable trait. He untied the rawhide and pulled the saddlebags off his horse.

Darrin collected the reins from both horses and led them over to a grassy spot.

Unsure what he'd find inside, he ducked through the low doorway. It was dark but for one oil lantern. There were two sets of three bunks against the rock wall in the back. A rickety table and stools took up the middle of the room. A small cookstove stood against the front wall with the stove pipe sticking out the wooden partition.

Lilah knelt next to a blanket-covered form on the floor. "Dooley, give each of your siblings a sandwich from the food we brought."

The boy moved to take the saddlebags. Brody placed them on the small table where the lantern sat.

"Brody, we'll need to move Mattie outside so I can see what needs done." Lilah grasped the corners on the bottom end of a blanket that appeared to be underneath the girl.

He stepped cautiously through the dimly lit room and clutched the other two corners of the blanket by the girl's head.

"One, two, three, lift."

They lifted the blanket. The child was lighter than she should be for her age. Dooley moved to the door, opening it for them to carry his sister outside.

Lilah led the way to a shady spot along the rock wall. When she was satisfied, she nodded, and they lowered the child to the ground. Before he could ask if he could help, she knelt, assessing the injury.

"Oh my!" she exclaimed then caught herself.

He dropped to his knees beside her. "What's wrong?"

"I don't know if I can help her by myself. I need Mrs. Fellowes to help."

He stared down at the child's swollen leg and booted foot that leaned at an odd angle to the placement of her knee.

She turned her face to him. Tears glistened in her eyes. "How could someone so little endure such pain," she whispered and placed a hand over her mouth stifling a sob.

He pulled Lilah against his side with an arm and whispered into her ear. "You couldn't have prevented this. Her broken leg is on her father."

"I know. If he'd just told me they were here alone." She sniffed, gathered herself together, and pushed away from him. "We're going to need the wagon to move her and take the children to the ranch."

"We can ride back and get the wagon," he said, hoping she'd see it as the wisest choice.

"No. I'll stay here with the children." Her pink lips held a firm resolve.

"I don't like leaving you alone here." He stared into her eyes. The determination staring back at him, told him he had no choice. She wouldn't leave the children. Going against his better judgement, he said, "I'll only do this if you promise to stay inside so anyone passing by doesn't know you're here, and Darrin needs to hide your horse."

"Take my horse with you." She reached out, placing a hand on the girl's leg. "We need to get the swelling down. Darrin!"

"I won't take your horse. You may need it." He didn't want to leave her here, but he saw no choice. The girl needed attention and short of tying Lilah up, he knew he'd never get her away from the child.

Darrin appeared by their sides. "Yes, Miss Lilah?"

"I need rags and water to try and get the swelling down on her leg." Lilah saw the worry in the boy's eyes. "Brody is going to go back to the ranch and get the wagon. We'll take all of you back with us until your sister is well or your father returns."

Brody stood, but didn't walk away. "I'll help you get her back in the shack."

She nodded and they carried Mattie back in, this time placing her closer to the open door, giving more light to better doctor her leg.

"You should go now." She straightened and peered through the dim light at Brody.

He stood in the open doorway. His hesitation told her he was having a hard time leaving her here.

"You'll only be a couple of hours." She held out a hand.

He grasped it.

She squeezed. "We'll be fine."

"I don't like this." His gruff voice was filled with emotion.

She smiled. "I know you don't. But this is the only choice. Go. The sooner you leave, the sooner we'll all be back safe at the ranch."

He nodded and strode over to his horse. He mounted and reined the horse to face her. "Remember to have Darrin hide your horse."

"I will. Go." She waved her hand, and he spun the horse around, heading off at a lope.

The brave front she'd put on while he was here,

sloughed off like a snake shedding skin. Alone with the children and Mattie with a fever and a dangerous break, she didn't know what to say to the children.

Darrin held out a metal bowl and rag to her. She dipped the rag in the water. It wasn't as cold as it should be but they had no way to keep anything cold, even the water they hauled up from the creek a quarter mile from the shack wasn't cold.

She pressed the wet rag to the girl's forehead.

"Is Mattie goin' to live?" Amelia asked.

Lilah's heart squeezed. Amelia had been the one to find their mother when she'd collapsed.

"Yes. Mattie won't die. Brody will bring the wagon, and we'll all go to the Double R. Mrs. Fellowes knows more about fixing broken bones than I do." The housekeeper knew more about surgical procedures than the doctor in Burns.

"Good. We need Mattie," said the matter-of-fact Dooley.

"You need parents. Not a father who goes off and leaves small children alone." Her anger took hold and she spoke before she'd meant to. "I'm sorry. I shouldn't talk ill of your father."

"It's the truth," Darrin said.

She could see his anger and resentment in his eyes. He was old enough to know, he and Mattie were the grown-ups in this family. They had taken on all the burdens that came with taking care of siblings. "You all go sit down and eat. I'll tend Mattie." At that moment she remembered Brody telling her to have Darrin put her horse out of sight. She didn't want to burden the boy. "I'll be right back." She stood and walked out into the bright sunlight.

Her anger at Mr. Lund made her hands shake as she captured Dusty's dangling reins. She kicked at the rock on the end of the reins and stubbed her toe. The pain only fueled her anger at the man. She led Dusty around the side of the rock cave following the worn path to the privy and the small creek beyond.

Something caught her attention on the far hill. Land that was part of the Double R.

***

Brody pushed the horse harder than he should, but he wasn't going to leave Lilah by herself any longer than necessary. When the horse started breathing heavy, he walked the animal until he seemed rested and then took up the faster pace. The thundering sound of the running horse's hooves brought Smithy out of the lean-to with the forge and the children running out of the animal barn.

He slid the horse to a stop and dismounted. "I need horses hitched up to the wagon. The oldest girl has a bad leg. Lilah needs help fixing it. I'm going to get Mrs. Fellowes." He strode straight for the house.

Mrs. Fellowes opened the front door. "Where's Lilah?"

"She wouldn't leave the girl. She told me to come get a wagon and you. We have to bring the children and the girl here. Lilah said she can't fix the leg by herself." His stomach squeezed with fear for the girl.

"I'll get my bag and come back with you. There are some things we can do before we lay her in a wagon." The housekeeper's wide backside hustled through the house.

Brody remained on the porch, waiting. He had no reason to go inside. He wandered around to the back and drank a dipper full of water. His gaze went to the two doors in the mound of dirt. Ice would help cool the girl's swollen leg. Crossing the space between the house and the cellar, he pulled on the door to the ice house. Using an axe, he chopped off a chunk and wrapped it in burlap that sat by the door.

Outside, he carried the ice to the wagon. Mrs. Fellowes met him there with a satchel. She glanced at the parcel but said nothing.

He took her bag, put it in the back of the wagon and helped her onto the seat.

Climbing onto the wagon, he said to Smithy, "We'll be back with the children. See that the four who are well have bunks to sleep in and let Sourdough know he'll have children at the meals."

He slapped the horses' rumps with the reins and the wagon lurched forward. He set the horses at a trot even though the ride was a bit rough bumping down the road that fast.

Chapter Twenty-six

Lilah stared at the spot on the hill. Nothing moved. The movement she thought she saw must have been her eyes getting accustom to the bright sunlight after the dark interior of the shack. She removed the saddle from Dusty, placing it on the ground upside down. Taking the rope from her saddle, she secured a loop around the horse's neck and tied her to a big rock where she could nibble on the grass.

She pulled her rifle from the scabbard and headed back to the children. Rounding the rock outcropping a shiver slithered up her spine. She spun around and stared at the hill, but she didn't see anything move.

In the shack, she placed her rifle by the door. Darrin stood up from where he'd been tending the rag on Mattie's leg. He glanced at the rifle then at Lilah.

"There's some bad men running around on the Double R. I want to be prepared in case they come down this way." She wouldn't have revealed the scary truth to any other child. But the Lund children had been through more in their short lives than most grown-ups. Having them vigilant would be good for everyone.

Her stomach grumbled as she sat on the floor beside Mattie.

A tap on her shoulder had her peering into the wide eyes of Rosie, the smallest child. She was three. Their mother had died shortly after the youngster was born. The girl held out a half-eaten sandwich toward her.

"Thank you, Rosie. You can finish the sandwich." She smiled at the tiny thing. All the children were much too thin. She could go without lunch today and let the children eat their fill.

"Here, Miss Lilah." Amelia held a sandwich out to her.

"Thank you. It was kind of you to make a sandwich for me." She took the offered food. "Would one of you like to read a book out loud to help us pass the time?" she asked, hoping it would take the children's thoughts off their injured sister.

"The only book we have is the Bible and the words are too confusing for me," Darrin said.

"Where are the books I brought you the last time your father left?" She'd brought half a dozen children's books to the family the last time she'd checked on them. Mattie and Darrin had learned to read and do numbers from their mother and were teaching the others.

"Our pa said we don't take charity and tossed them in the stove." Dooley's angry tone bothered her. But so did their father taking books away from them.

"Why would he say that? It wasn't charity, it was a gift from me to you children." She'd made up her mind when Darrin had ridden into the ranch looking for help that she would do whatever it took to take these children in and raise them as they deserved.

Dusty nickered. The horse could only see someone who approached from the backside of the property. The side where she'd witnessed something moving on the hill.

"Amelia and Rose, go hide on the top bunk and don't come down until I tell you," she whispered and grabbed Dooley's arm as he started for the door. "You grab a frying pan."

While the boy picked up the frying pan, she placed a stool behind the door. "Stand up there. If a man comes through the door, let him have it with the pan."

Dooley scrambled up on the stool, grinning.

"What about me?" Darrin asked.

"Do you know how to shoot a rifle?" she asked.

"Yes, but Pa never leaves us a gun. Says no one is going to hurt children." The disgust in the boy's voice, further settled her mind about the children.

"Take my rifle. If a man comes through the door and your brother misses with the pan, you shoot him." Lilah handed the rifle to the boy. She pulled Mattie out of the way of the door and any falling bodies. There was no sense in pretending she wasn't here if the person coming had seen her tethering out her horse. She had a pretty good idea who it was. Angel would know she wouldn't leave her horse here, even for the children. And if he'd been watching, he knew that Brody had ridden off without her.

The slow footsteps of a horse approaching cautiously, made her grin. He had enough sense to know she wouldn't hesitate to put a bullet through him, knowing he left Brody to die from the snake bite.

But what about the man everyone believed Angel had taken up with? Was he also out there?

"Lilah, it is I, Angel."

His caution gave her strength. "What do you want?" She remained hidden in the shadows inside the shack.

"I wanted to say I am sorry for losing your trust in me." The creak of leather and jingling spurs proved he'd dismounted and walked toward the shack.

"Don't come in here. The children have a fever, it's not safe."

"Is that why the judge's thieving grandson left you here alone? Is he not so big a man if he is scared of a little fever?" The animosity and arrogance in his tone nearly had her stepping out and confronting him.

Her good sense caught hold before she did. He was baiting her. Seeing where her loyalties lie. Should she say Brody was returning or let that be a surprise to the vaquero?

"Come out and talk to me," he crooned in a heavier accent than he usually used.

She'd told him once how much she liked his accent. In fact, it was the one time they'd kissed. Was he trying to draw her out of the shack for a reason?

"I can't. I need to tend to the children." She wasn't stepping out of the shack. There had to be a reason he had come to her when she was alone. Knowing the other man hiding out on the ranch wanted revenge against the judge, she didn't want to get caught up in their differences.

"Surely you would like fresh air and sunshine for a few minutes while you talk with me." He sighed loudly. "We had such wonderful conversations while on rides. Do you remember, *Novia*?"

Sweetheart.

He'd called her *novia* the second time they'd ridden out together. When she'd asked him what it meant, he'd told her sweetheart. And he'd used the endearment with her only when they were alone.

"I'm not your sweetheart. And as I recall, you asked me questions about the ranch, the cattle, if the judge had relatives. You talked very little about me." Steam of anger began to build in her mind. Brody had been right. The young vaquero had been digging for information about the ranch and how he could come by it.

"You put a dagger through my heart with your talk," he said. His voice sounded closer to the shack.

Dooley raised the frying pan.

"I'd like nothing better than to put a dagger in you after you left Brody to die of a snake bite." She started for the door. Her anger consumed her. How had she fallen for this man's proposed friendship?

A small hand grabbed her sleeve, pulling her away from the door.

"Brody is no better than a horse thief. He deserves to suffer." Angel stepped into the doorway.

The sun silhouetted him. She couldn't see his eyes, but she knew when he spied Darrin holding the rifle.

"Give me that," he demanded, taking another step

into the shack.

Whack! The frying pan hit him square on the head, knocking Angel to his knees. Both boys jumped on him, shoving his face into the dirt floor.

"Amelia, bring the rope we use to hang the wash," Darrin said, clearly taking control of the situation.

Before Lilah had a chance to fully comprehend Angel wasn't a threat, the boys had him trussed up and had dragged him outside using his own horse.

She stepped out of the shack and found Angel propped up against the rocks. His hands and feet tied together and his own silk bandana shoved in his mouth. His dark eyes sparked with rage. She and the children had made an enemy of the vaquero.

To avoid the man's accusing glare, she stepped back into the shack and tended Mattie.

***

Fear had Brody pushing the horses and wagon faster than he should. To her credit, Mrs. Fellowes didn't say a word. She clung to the seat with white knuckles.

Approaching the shack, his fear turned to rage. He spotted Angel's horse standing near the shack, saddled and eating grass. Where was the vaquero?

Something moved in the shadow of the rocks. He handed the reins to Mrs. Fellowes and picked up the rifle Smithy had set under the wagon seat. The butt of the gun touched his shoulder at the same time he recognized a small form with a rifle standing over a man sitting on the ground.

As soon as Mrs. Fellowes stopped the wagon at the shack, he covered the ground between the wagon and the trussed up vaquero. He patted Darrin on the back. "Good job. Where's Lilah?"

The boy's chest puffed out from his compliment. "She's inside tendin' Mattie."

"We'll sling him over his horse after we get your sister loaded." He strode to the shack, entering behind Mrs. Fellowes.

Small arms wrapped around his legs. He looked down at the two small girls. He patted their heads as his gaze sought Lilah.

"Get Mattie out into the wagon," Mrs. Fellowes ordered before he could ask Lilah if Angel had hurt her.

He grabbed the blanket at the girl's head and Lilah grasped the corners at her feet. They carried the child to the back of the wagon. He heard Mrs. Fellowes inside giving the children orders. With the woman and children occupied, he stepped up to her.

"Did he hurt you?" he asked, placing a hand on her arm.

Her grin stole the breath from his chest.

"No. He didn't have a chance. Dooley stood on a stool behind the door. When Angel entered he hit him on the head with a frying pan. Then the two boys tied him up and dragged him outside." She glanced over at Darrin. "I don't want the children to come back here again. I don't care if their father comes back, it isn't right leaving children alone."

"I agree. We'll see what we can do. Grandfather should know what legal steps to take."

Lilah threw her arms around his neck. "I knew you'd understand."

Not letting his chance get away, he lowered his

head and pressed his lips to hers. He hadn't expected to feel more than any other kiss he'd had with a woman, but her soft lips churned his heart and made him forget there was anyone else. Shifting his mouth, he captured hers completely. She sighed and pressed closer.

He'd dreamed of kissing her like this since their first disagreement. But he'd held back knowing it would displease his grandfather. Having tasted her lips, he didn't care what his grandfather thought. Lilah was the woman he wanted.

Giggling filtered through his thoughts.

She pulled out of his arms. "Oh my!" Pressing fingers to her lips, she stared at him with glistening eyes.

"Miss Lilah kissed a man!" sung Amelia.

"Children load up into the wagon and be careful you don't disturb your sister." Mrs. Fellowes hustled by them, capturing Lilah's arm. "You'll drive the wagon."

Brody shook off the kiss. "Where's your horse?" he asked, hoping his voice didn't sound as confused as he felt.

"Behind the rocks." Lilah stepped to the front of the wagon.

"Darrin, go get Miss Lilah's horse, please." He stepped up behind Lilah and grasped her waist, lifting her up onto the wagon wheel. She gripped the wagon seat and pulled herself the rest of the way up. When she looked down at him, her lips were tipped in a smile.

He couldn't help grinning back like a fool.

Darrin arrived with the mare.

"You want to ride in the wagon or behind me on this horse?" Brody asked the boy.

His young gaze traveled over the wagon full of his siblings and then to the man on the ground. "I better stick with you and keep an eye on the bad guy."

"I like the idea of having a helper." He put a hand on the boy's shoulder and raised his face to Lilah. "You head on out. Me and the boy will load Angel on his horse and catch up."

She nodded and slapped the reins on the horses' rumps, turning them and heading toward the ranch.

"Come on. We'll tie him over the saddle like a newborn calf." He didn't feel any remorse for Angel when they had him laying over the saddle on his belly. To keep the man from falling off, they tied his hands to one stirrup and one of his legs to the other one. After this man had left him for dead, Angel was lucky they didn't drag him all the way back to the ranch.

Brody mounted Lilah's horse and pulled Darrin up behind him. They set out at a trot and soon caught up to the wagon. The trip back to the ranch would be slower than the trip out. Lilah kept the horses at an easy even pace as Mrs. Fellowes sat in the back of the wagon tending to Mattie.

Chapter Twenty-seven

Lilah spent most of the trip back to the ranch thinking about that kiss. When Brody hopped out of the wagon and ran straight to Angel, her heart had thundered in her chest, unsure what he might do. She understood his need to make sure she hadn't been harmed. When he'd turned to her with worry in his eyes, she couldn't have stopped herself from clinging to him if there had been a rattler between them.

Driving up to the ranch buildings, she was happy to see the hands were back. She hoped they had captured the man looking to seek revenge on the judge.

Buddy and Betsy ran out to greet the wagon. They called up to the children who stood and called back. She drove the wagon straight to the house. Roy and Clem stepped out of the bunkhouse as they drove by. Lilah glanced back over her shoulder and watched as Brody handed the reins to Angel's horse over to Sandy, who'd walked out of the barn. The two men talked, and

Darrin slipped off the back of her horse.

As soon as the wagon stopped at the house, the children jumped out and ran over to Buddy and Betsy. It was a treat for all the children to have someone new to play with.

"Help me get Mattie into my room," Mrs. Fellowes said.

Lilah climbed down off the wagon and helped carry the injured girl in through the front door.

"Smithy said you left the ranch," Judge Radley called out from his office.

"I'm busy," she replied, following Mrs. Fellowes down the hall to the small room off the kitchen. They placed the child on the bed, blanket and all.

"We'll need sticks for splints, lots of bandages, and strength," Mrs. Fellowes said, untying the boot on the child's injured leg.

Lilah hurried out the kitchen door and picked up the axe to split kindling sticks off a log for the splints. It didn't surprise her when a shadow fell across the chopping log.

"Let me do that," Brody said, taking the axe from her hands.

Fearful of throwing her arms around him to enjoy another kiss, she backed away. "Bring that into the kitchen. I need to make bandages." She turned and he grabbed her arm.

"Are you scared of me?"

His soft tone had her spinning toward him. "No. I'm scared of me. We need to get Mattie well and talk to the judge about Talbot, but all I want to do is remain in your arms."

The worry lines smoothed and he smiled. "We'll figure this out later. The children, the man, and the judge."

"The judge?" She didn't know what he meant.

"He told me to keep my hands off you." His hand moved up her arm, drawing her closer. "But after kissing you, there is no way I'll let him keep us apart."

The determination in his eyes and the low almost growl of his words, reminded her of one of the dogs as he guarded a bone. It thrilled and scared her that Brody or any man would feel so strongly about her as to go against his grandfather's wishes.

She swallowed, finding her mouth dry. His lips lowered to hers, and she raised up on her toes to meet him halfway. She'd only had one other kiss from another man and it had never sent the sensations zipping through her body that she had when kissing Brody.

He stepped back, leaving her with raised lips, closed eyes, and a racing heart.

"Get to the house. Like I said, we'll figure it all out later." He turned to the log and raised the axe.

Lilah hurried back into the house and started shredding an old sheet Mrs. Fellowes used for bandages. Her heart raced with anticipation of the next kiss and their talk with the judge.

***

After putting the sticks in the kitchen and sticking his head into Mrs. Fellowes' room to let them know the splints were there, Brody walked into his grandfather's office.

"What is this I hear of you taking Lilah to the

220

Lund's?" His grandfather glared at him over his spectacles the minute he entered the room.

"It was that or she'd go alone. And it's a good thing I did go with her. Mattie may lose her leg. We'll know more after Mrs. Fellowes gets the injury cleaned up." He sat in the chair in front of the old man's desk.

"Did you run into anyone?"

"Angel came to the shack while I was getting the wagon and Mrs. Fellowes."

His grandfather's face reddened. "What? You left her alone?"

He raised a hand. "She was in good hands. The boys, Darrin and Dooley, knocked Angel out and tied him up tight. We brought him back here. I don't know if we'll learn anything from him but Sheriff Davies was here."

Grandfather held up the wanted poster. "That what this is all about?"

"Yes. That's the man Lilah saw by the watering hole. The man who is killing your cattle." He waited for the information to seep in and asked, "Did you find him?"

"No! He's slipperier than any man we've tracked. But we can't continue chasing him around, there's hay to be put up." He slammed the poster on the desk. "We need the hay harvest to make sure we don't lose cattle through the winter."

"We can get started on the harvest tomorrow." The way his grandfather's gaze kept straying to the poster, he could tell he feared the man killing his cattle. "With you and Smithy here at the buildings the women and children should be safe."

Pale blue eyes narrowed on him. "I'm not hiding out here like a woman."

"I didn't say that. I said you and Smithy would protect the women and children. We have more children to protect now."

"What are you talking about?"

He filled his grandfather in on the Lund children and how he and Lilah planned to keep them away from their father. They deserved to be children before becoming adults.

Grandfather sat straighter and took on the stern bearing of a judge. "How do you know their father isn't hurt somewhere?"

"We don't. And if that is the case the children need a place to live and be cared for." He thought of Maria and her daughter. Had anyone stepped in and helped them out? He hoped so. Maria had been a good friend to him.

"I can draw up the papers needed, but you can't keep the children if the father returns and refuses to give you custody of them." The older man peered into his eyes. "By law a parent has rights to their children you can't take away."

He nodded. "But it would seem that with their father always leaving them home alone and not providing for them, he would be happy to have someone else take care of them."

"We'll see. Some men can be hard set on no help. Makes them feel weak."

"I understand, but he has to see that his children are suffering." He couldn't shake the dreariness of the shack and the meager supplies the children had to live.

"Save your arguments for when the father shows up." Grandfather pushed up out of his chair. "Let's have a look at the injured girl and see to the rest of the brood."

He grinned. The judge might appear gruff, but when it came to children, he had a soft spot.

***

Once Brody and his grandfather made sure the children were settled into bunks in the bunkhouse and Sourdough didn't mind having the youngsters around, they went in search of Angel. They found him tied up in a stall in the barn. Roy stood guard over the vaquero.

"Where is Talbot?" the judge asked.

Angel glared at them, his lips firmly pressed together.

"If you don't talk, you don't go free," the judge said.

Brody noticed a flicker in the vaquero's eyes. He hoped his grandfather wouldn't let this man go free. He'd shown every indication he'd planned to kill him and today tried to get Lilah.

"We don't have time to take you to the sheriff. But once the hay is harvested, I'll take you myself. You'll be charged with attempted murder and kidnapping, and consorting with an escaped convict." Judge Radley turned his back on the vaquero and motioned to Roy.

"He's to only have biscuits and water. Put hobbles on his feet but make sure they are tied to something. He can relieve himself in a bucket, but don't untie his hands and keep the children away from him." Once his grandfather had laid out how Angel was to be treated, he headed back to the house.

Brody remained in the barn. The vaquero glared at him. There was something eating at the man. Wondering if he'd spit it out if they were alone, he said, "Roy, why don't you go get yourself a cup of coffee. I can watch him while you're gone."

Roy stared at him. "You ain't gonna kill him for leaving you for dead?"

He shook his head. "No. I think being kept tied up until we get him to the law is worse than almost dying. It eats at a man's dignity." He nodded to the door. "Go on."

Roy handed him the rifle and left the barn.

He sat on an upturned bucket a rifle length away from Angel. He reached out and tugged the scarf, still in the vaquero's mouth, down.

Angel spit at him. He leaned back and the glob landed on the ground between his legs.

"That's not nice. Here I am willing to sit and visit with you and you spit at me." He touched the scarf with the end of the rifle barrel. "I could put that cloth back in your mouth, and I could hit you with this rifle."

The vaquero's eyes narrowed and darkened. "You will not hit me. You are a greenhorn gringo."

The idea the man thought he was soft, didn't bother him. That gave him the upper hand. The vaquero didn't know about all the fights and tussles he'd been in and won while trying to make his way living in the slums and fighting for a better job. There were days it felt like he had to whip every man who walked on the dock just to keep his job. The management didn't care who they paid as long as the cargo moved on and off the dock without complaints from the ships.

"I might be a greenhorn, but I survived a rattler bite and I have you where I know you won't do any harm to anyone."

"I will not stay here. I will not go to the law."

The confidence in his words, sent Brody's thoughts to the man on the wanted poster—Talbot.

"I'd think you'd have some loyalty to Judge Radley and Double R. Talbot is a murderer and a prison escapee. He'd just as soon kill you as have you tell us anything would be my guess."

A flicker of fear dulled the vaquero's eyes for a moment before they turned hard and dark again.

"He can't get you a ranch. Working here and being loyal to the ranch would have earned you cattle and the possibility of the judge carrying a loan for you to get your own land." Brody didn't know if his grandfather did that for his employees, but he would do it if he took over the ranch one day. He'd made note of the men who worked hard and were loyal.

"I would have had the ranch if you had gone to prison." Angel spit again.

This time the glob landed on his chest.

"Guess you made your choice." He put the scarf back in the vaquero's mouth and moved the bucket back where he'd found it. Angel wasn't going to help them find the other man, and he was a threat to everyone on the ranch. He'd have to make sure the children and Lilah stayed out of here. Especially Lilah. He had a feeling she had a soft spot for the vaquero and that could put her in harm.

Roy returned. His gaze went immediately to Angel. While he scrutinized the vaquero, Brody reached down, grabbed a handful of hay and cleaned the spit from his shirt.

"Make sure no one comes near him," he repeated.

Roy nodded. "I will. Sandy's gonna relieve me for supper and then Stubbs is taking a shift."

"Sounds like you have it all figured out." A thought struck him. "What are we going to do with him tomorrow when we're all harvesting the hay?"

The smile on Roy's face, said he was going to like the answer.

"Smithy said he'd put a harness on him and hang him from the lean-to while he worked."

"Maybe we should do that tonight and everyone could get a full night's sleep." Brody left the barn laughing.

Chapter Twenty-eight

Lilah wondered if the judge or Brody had ordered everyone to keep her away from Angel. After two days of driving the stacker horses, even with wearing gloves, her hands had blisters. Buster figured they had at least two to three more days of harvesting before they had all the meadows cleared of the cured grass hay.

Brody drove his sweep rake up to the stacker. The last two times he'd arrived with a load his face had appeared pinched in pain. When he grabbed the levers to lift the sweep rake and shove the hay farther onto the stacker's wooden tines, his right arm, the one that had been bitten by the rattlesnake, dropped to his side.

She ran around his horses and placed a hand on his shoulder. "Mrs. Fellowes said you shouldn't be working that arm so hard so soon."

Pain dulled his eyes as he made a grab for the lever again.

"Stop. You can't do this." She tugged on his sleeve. "Come work the horses on the stacker. I'll run the sweep rake."

"No. You can't run this. The levers are hard to pull."

She had him halfway off the sweep when Buster strolled up.

"Looks to me like you've angered your arm. Get over there and operate the stacker. I'll take over the sweep." Buster winked at her. "Lilah, go help Sy on the stack until Gus and Stubbs finish raking the last field."

Brody slid off the metal seat on the sweep. "Thanks. I didn't want her climbing on there, but I couldn't have made another trip." He held his right arm in his left hand.

"Lilah, show him what to do." The foreman sat on the sweep and finished shoving the hay onto the stacker. Then he backed the horses up, turning them and heading back out into the field.

Sandy headed their way with a full sweep.

"Come on." She grasped Brody's good hand and led him to the horses hitched to the pulleys that pulled the stacker arm, full of hay, upward.

She stood him to the side and picked up the reins. With a cluck and a slap of the reins to the horses' rumps, she moved the two horses forward. The animals pulled the rope attached to the stacker through the pulleys, and the pile of hay was flung over onto the stack that grew with each load Sandy, Roy, and now Buster, hauled over with the sweeps.

"This is the easiest job of all the harvesting," she said, easing the horses backwards and lowering the large wooden tines of the stacker.

Sandy arrived, pushing a pile of hay with his sweep. He expertly shoved and re-shoved the load onto the stacker.

"Let me try this one," Brody said, taking the reins from her hands. He used one hand but managed to urge the horses forward, dump the hay, and ease the horses backwards, returning the wooden forks to the ground.

"I think you can handle this. I'll go help Sy on the stack." She turned to leave as Roy arrived with a full sweep.

Brody grasped her arm. "Be careful up there. It's a long way to fall."

She smiled. "I'll be fine. You just don't use that arm any more than you have to."

He clucked to the horses.

She scurried around the stack to the far side where a ladder stood against the large pile of hay. She climbed the ladder and was surprised and thankful when Sy offered a hand to help her up the last few feet that the ladder didn't reach.

"Thank you." She tugged to pull her hand away from Sy's grasp when he didn't release her.

He clasped her hand tighter and grinned. "I've wanted to hold your hand and be alone with you for some time, but I didn't think it would happen on the top of a hay stack."

"Let go before one of us gets hurt." No sooner had the words escaped her mouth than a pile of hay landed inches from them. Sy released her to get out of the way. She stepped backwards and felt her body tipping.

Swinging her arms and throwing her body forward,

she caught her footing before she toppled over the side of the stack. Angry with Sy for putting them both in danger, she picked up the hay fork and started shoving the pile of hay out across the top of the large stack.

The stack work was constant as the sweeps worked closer and closer to the stack. Sweat dampened her back and trickled down her neck.

A horse and what looked like two riders came across the field. She smiled. Their lunch was coming. Darrin and Buddy rode out to the fields every day with their lunch. The two boys had become inseparable. Darrin was the older of the two, but he treated Buddy like an equal, and the younger boy enjoyed having a boy around. He and Dooley played as well, but Darrin being an older sibling put up with Buddy's constant questions better than Dooley.

"Looks like we can take a break," Sy said, motioning to the sweeps all moving to the stacker and Gus and Stubbs walking through the field from where they had been raking. He stood at the top of the ladder. "I can help you down." His hand reached out toward her.

"You go. I'll follow after you're on the ground." After his actions of helping her off the ladder, she wasn't going to have him behind her as she descended.

By the time Sy touched the ground, Buster stood at the ladder. He waved Sy off and held the wooden footing as she climbed down. Before he released the ladder, she spun and hugged Buster.

"What was that for?" he asked, his face turning as red as the bandana around his neck.

"For being at the bottom of the ladder." She

wrinkled her nose. "Sy has trouble being a gentleman."

"I figured as much the way you were standing up there waiting for him to come down. Actually, it was Brody who sent me over. Well, not really sent me. He was headed this way, but the way he looked, I figured he wouldn't be much help so I told him I'd make sure you climbed down safe." He studied her. "He's been awful attentive to you lately. You two sweet on one another?"

She'd told Agnes about the kisses and thought the woman might have told her husband, but apparently she'd kept Lilah's confidence.

"I'm not sure what you call it. But I like him and he likes me. Brody said we'd talk to the judge after harvest, but I think we need to wait. No sense riling up the judge until that man Talbot is back behind bars." She started walking around the hay stack.

"I'll send Stubbs on the stack after we eat."

She'd always thought of Buster as an uncle. He was living up to her love for him today. "Thank you."

They reached the rest of the haying crew. Brody patted the ground next to him. She sat Indian style. Working in the fields, she wore a riding skirt and riding boots. That meant she didn't have to worry about anyone seeing more than was respectable no matter what job she took on.

Once she was seated, Darrin handed her a cold jar of water and a sandwich.

"Thank you. How are the girls doing?" she asked.

"Mattie was sittin' out on the porch when me and Buddy left. She's not sayin' much." His small face scrunched up as if he would cry. He swallowed and fought to straighten his lips and open his eyes. "She's not happy havin' to sit."

She wanted to pull the boy into her arms and console him, but she knew enough from growing up around men that males don't like to be coddled.

Brody couldn't miss the sadness in the boy's eyes or how hard it was for Lilah to keep from hugging him. He knew Darrin was at the age they didn't think they needed a woman fawning over them, but he also knew while they might act like they didn't like it, they did. He nudged her and motioned toward Darrin who stood in front of her, his face tipped toward the ground.

She set her sandwich and jar on the ground and wrapped her arms around the boy. He didn't hug her back but his body relaxed against her. Tears glistened in her eyes, and she mouthed "thank you" to him.

He had an idea but he'd been waiting to say anything until he could ask Gus if he could do the job. Seeing how worried Darrin was for his sister and knowing the children's fears and worries upset Lilah, he decided to let them both in on his idea.

"Working the docks in New York, I knew several men who'd nearly lost their legs in boating accidents, but they still came to work with the leg all bundled up like Mattie's."

Darrin leaned out of Lilah's hug. He and Buddy stared at Brody.

He glanced around and noted he had everyone's attention, even Gus.

"How'd they work on the docks with a bundled up leg?" Darrin asked.

"They had wooden crutches. They're sticks with a

Y-shape that cradles them under the arms. Those pieces of wood helped them move around and they still had use of their arms and could pull on ropes and work the horses." He locked gazes with Gus. "I've seen the fine work Gus does making toys for Buddy and Betsy, I bet he could whittle out a fine set of crutches for Mattie."

Gus beamed and nodded his head. "I sure could. That little girl will be walking around like she don't have a bum leg."

Darrin ran over to Gus. "You could do that Mr. Gus?"

"I do think I could. Of course, I'd have to work on it in the evenings, this is the busiest time of the year around here. I can't sit around whittling when there are chores to do." Gus bit into his sandwich.

"Me and Dooley could take care of the barn chores. That would give you more time." Darrin's eyes pleaded with Gus.

Seeing how badly the boy wanted the crutches for his sister, Brody piped up. "I'll help you boys with the chores. I can't see either one of you hauling the water to the animals."

"We'd figure out a way," Darrin said, crossing his arms.

"I know you two would." Lilah ruffled Darrin's hair. "The way you two took down Angel and tied him up, I have every confidence you two can tackle anything."

He studied her. She'd tried a couple of times to see Angel. Smithy and Clem had told him when he'd asked. Both men knew she was not to see the vaquero.

"Time to get back to work," Buster said, standing.

"Stubbs, take a turn up on the stack and let Sy rake hay."

Brody and the two men Buster had mentioned stared at the foreman.

"Why do I have to run the rake?" Sy questioned, much like a disobedient child.

"Because that's the job I gave you." Buster's gaze never drifted to Lilah, but he saw her smile at Stubbs.

He'd wondered if having her on the stack with Sy was a good idea, and now he knew what had kept Buster and Lilah at the back of the stack so long. She must have asked for someone else to work with.

He'd also told Smithy and Clem to not allow the children or Sy near Angel. He'd seen the hand and the vaquero with their heads together enough to know they could be working together.

Lilah stood. "Come on, Stubbs. These men will be pushing hay up faster than we can pitch it in a few minutes."

The short, wide man smiled and followed her around to the back of the stack.

Sy was headed across the field with Gus, and the boys had climbed up on the horse they rode to the field.

"Best get to your job," Buster said, his gaze at the top of the stack where Lilah waved.

"Did Sy do something to her?" He couldn't shake his unease about the hired hand.

"Moving the men around is good." Buster slapped him on the back. "Sandy has his hay on the stacker."

Brody walked over and picked up the reins to the horses and went back to work. After the three sweeps had headed back to the field, he had a few minutes to rest. He sat on the side of the stacker and peered up at the hay stack. Lilah was pushing hay around and smoothing out the top like a bird making its nest.

He scanned the hills behind the stack and sat up straighter. A flash and movement on one of the hills caught his attention. Talbot. The man was still watching. What was his plan? When would he move on or attempt whatever he had in mind for the judge?

Chapter Twenty-nine

Four more days and they'd finished the hay harvest. The three fields where his grandfather said they kept the cattle in the winter had large stacks of hay and the middle of the large barn was full for the horses and animals kept close to the buildings.

Brody sat in the kitchen finishing up his morning meal, getting ready to head out and see what his job would be today.

Mrs. Fellowes stood by the sink washing up the dishes, Lilah had just helped Mattie out onto the chair on the porch where she could watch the other children or read a book.

Grandfather entered the kitchen. He was dressed in what Brody had come to know as his grandfather's town clothes.

"Judge, where are you going?" he asked, rising.

"Take that no account Angel to Sheriff Davies."

The judge had a gun belt buckled around his hips.

"I can go with you or you could have Sandy and Roy take him." He didn't like the idea of his grandfather on the road to town alone with the vaquero. If Talbot watched the going's on here as much as he thought, the man could shoot the judge and free Angel.

"I need to go. I know the legal words to make sure the sheriff keeps him behind bars until a hearing." The older man picked up a cloth-wrapped package sitting on the end of the table.

He'd noticed when the housekeeper set the bundle there but hadn't thought much about it.

"I'm not sure it's a good idea for either of you to go," Lilah said, standing between them. "Judge, you have a man looking for revenge after you, and Brody, your arm still isn't back to normal."

"I don't need two hands to make sure the judge and Angel get to town." He didn't want to argue with her, but he wasn't going to let the snake bite keep him from doing things the rest of his life. Mrs. Fellowes kept saying give it time, but he knew there was part of his arm that was dead and would never be the same.

"I think it's better to have others take Angel." Lilah moved to the door and crossed her arms.

"I won't put any of my hired hands lives in jeopardy doing something I can do myself." His grandfather stared at him. "Move this girl and let's get going."

He couldn't stop the grin when her mouth formed a perfect circle and her eyes widened in astonishment. Grasping her upper arms, he lifted the young woman and set her to the side of the door.

Grandfather walked out the door.

He leaned over, kissed her cheek, and whispered, "We'll be fine." Reaching out, he plucked his hat from the peg by the door and followed his grandfather to the barn.

Sy was riding one of the horses Brody had picked as his.

The judge walked over to the corral. "Hand that horse over to Brody."

The hired hand narrowed his eyes, but he dismounted and led the horse to the gate. "Do I have to give him my saddle, too?" The smart-mouthed hand asked.

"No. But after today, this is Brody's horse. Go saddle him, son." Grandfather turned from the corral and headed to where Smithy was hitching horses to the buggy.

"I didn't break this horse for you," Sy said, hauling his saddle off the red roan gelding Brody had told his grandfather was his first pick of the three that were to be his.

"I didn't ask the judge to give me a horse. But this one did catch my eye." He grasped the reins and led the horse to the hitching rail outside the barn.

Smithy carried the saddle he'd been using out to the horse and tossed it on. "You sure the judge taking Angel to the sheriff is a good idea?" he asked in a tone just above a whisper.

"No. But he's determined, so I'm riding along." He tightened the cinch. "Wouldn't mind if a couple of trusted hands decided to head to town about thirty minutes after we do but stay back and not let the judge know."

Smithy winked. "I'll pass that along to Buster."

"Smithy, go get Angel and toss him in the back seat of this buggy," his grandfather ordered.

Brody led his horse up beside the buggy. "You know we could take one or two hands along, give them a break after working so hard on the harvest."

"I told you. This is my business, I won't get a hired hand killed for me." His eyes narrowed as Smithy brought Angel out of the barn.

The vaquero glared at both of them. As he'd requested, the scarf had only been removed from the man's mouth when he ate. He chewed on the cloth as if he wished to lash out at them with words.

"But you're willing to risk my life?" He wasn't sure what to think of his grandfather allowing him to come along now.

"You're family. You can count on family no matter how tough things get." His faded eyes glistened with unshed tears. "I wish your mother would have remembered that."

Smithy had the trussed up vaquero in the back seat of the buggy.

"Hup!" Grandfather said and started the horses trotting down the road.

Brody followed behind the buggy far enough back to not eat dust. The pace remained at a trot all the way to Venator. Every ten to fifteen minutes, he stopped and searched behind and around them scanning the hills for any movement showing that Talbot was interested in saving Angel. From all appearances the murderer didn't care a whit about the vaquero.

The judge stopped at Venator and watered the horses. He also stretched his legs and handed Brody a cookie from the parcel he'd picked up off the table.

They stood by the water trough as they ate the cookies. He kept his eyes on Angel as he spoke low to his grandfather. "I've been keeping an eye on the hills and haven't seen anyone following."

"I didn't think Talbot would care about Angel. I wish he'd understand the murderer was using him. But he won't get past his anger to listen to reason." Grandfather handed him another cookie. "We need to keep moving. I want to hand Angel over to the sheriff and see if we can't get a posse to come out and help find Talbot."

"Having more men looking for him is a good idea." He finished off the sweet and walked his horse away from the buggy to mount.

The buggy headed down the road to Burns at the same pace his grandfather had kept from the Double R.

He glanced around the small community. He didn't harbor the aversion he'd experienced the day he crawled off the stage. The community was a necessity for the ranches in the area. He urged his horse down the road and grinned. The Double R and this country had worked its charm on him. He never wanted to go back to the docks of New York.

They were several miles from Venator when the buggy whipped around. Grandfather's face was red, his eyes narrowed and glaring.

Brody urged his horse alongside the buggy and saw what was wrong. Angel wasn't in the back seat.

"He was there right after I climbed up into the

seat." Grandfather said. "Didn't you see him fall out?"

"No. But I wasn't watching the buggy when I climbed in the saddle." He thought about sitting in the street looking over the town. He hadn't seen the man lying in the street. "Angel must have slipped out right as you took off and rolled behind the trough." He kicked his horse into a lope and raced back to the scattering of buildings. If the man talked someone into letting him loose there was no telling what kind of revenge he'd wage on the ranch.

He slid his horse to a stop when he recognized two hired hands at the water trough in Venator. Sandy and Roy were watering their horses. Angel sat with his back against the end of the trough, glaring.

"Glad I had you follow. He must have rolled out when we stopped to water the horses. Judge Radley noticed he was missing a passenger a couple miles out." Brody slapped Sandy on the back. "Want to hide until I get him loaded into the buggy and we're headed to Burns?"

The tall blond hand grinned. "Judge don't want us following does he?"

"No. He said he didn't want any of you getting hurt. But I figured if we ran into trouble you'd be close enough to come to our rescue." He made eye contact with both men. "I trust both of you to keep the judge safe. And it doesn't hurt my pride to ask when I know I need help."

Both men nodded. They grabbed the reins of their horses and led them to the back of the store.

A cloud of dust heralded the buggy returning. Even in his anger, his grandfather hadn't whipped the horses into anything faster than a trot. He knew better than to mistreat an animal. Brody's admiration of the man grew with each complication his grandfather met head on and proceeded to tackle.

"Good! He didn't get away." Grandfather climbed down from the buggy and helped shove Angel up into the back seat. "This time we'll tie him in."

Using the ropes around the vaquero's wrists, they tied his hands to the steel on the side of the seat. If he tried to roll out he'd be dragged.

The judge climbed back into the buggy, and Brody crawled up on his horse.

Shoving on Angel to get him into the buggy had his arm throbbing. The snake bite had also left a large dark indention in his arm where the flesh had rotted under the poultice. Living with the scar didn't matter. Being able to do all the things needed to keep a ranch running could be a factor of his grandfather believing he deserved the Double R.

Chapter Thirty

Lilah found joy in helping the children but worried about Mattie and how she'd withdrawn from everyday things. She also worried about the smaller girls living in the bunkhouse. Darrin and Dooley were thriving in the bunkhouse and helping with chores. But a building full of men wasn't a good place for two small girls.

Mattie still slept in Mrs. Fellowes room. The housekeeper slept on a cot Gus had made for her. She'd mentioned moving Mattie to the cot, but the older woman would have none of that.

"I think Amelia and Rosie should move into the empty room upstairs," she said as she and Mrs. Fellowes finished up the morning's dishes.

"I've been thinking the same thing after seeing Amelia spitting on the ground like Stubbs and Clem." The housekeeper placed a clean plate on the drain to dry. "This house is getting full. We either need to find those children a family or we need to add on rooms."

The thought of sending them to anyone else saddened her. But she couldn't expect the judge to take in every child who lost parents, as he had with her.

"I'll go make the room ready." She went in the pantry and grabbed the broom and a dusting cloth. Climbing the stairs, she remembered the first night she'd spent in this house. Her parents had been dead a week. Judge Radley had stayed in her family's home while setting all their affairs in order. Then he had women from the local church help pack all of Lilah's things and the items the women thought she would want went she became an adult. She'd forgotten her sadness when she walked into the room she now occupied and it was filled with all her belongings. It was as if she hadn't left home at all.

There had been nothing in the Lund shack to bring for the children. They each had two sets of clothing and one night shirt. Once the room had been aired out, dusted, and swept, she headed to her room. Kneeling in front of the trunk at the foot of her bed, she pulled out the dolls and toys she'd kept. She'd planned on giving them to her children one day, but she could always buy new toys for any children she had, the Lund children needed the toys now.

Back in the last spare bedroom, she placed the well-loved raggedy doll on the bed and the fancy porcelain doll on the bureau. The top and marbles, she put in her apron pocket. She'd give these to the boys to play with. Setting out the toys reminded her of the small doll house with furniture that Judge Radley gave her that first Christmas on the ranch. Mrs. Fellowes would know where it had been stored.

She picked up the broom and dust cloth and headed downstairs. The sight of Mattie sitting in the chair on the porch gave her an idea.

Lilah quickly replaced the broom and shook out the cloth. The housekeeper had started preparations for the next meal.

"Mrs. Fellowes, whatever happened to the doll house I received for Christmas?" She wiggled the marbles in her apron pocket.

"It's in the attic. I can have one of the men get it down." The older woman's eyes twinkled. "Are you setting it up for the children?"

"After I get Mattie interested in helping restore it. I'm sure over the years it's had some damage."

"That's an excellent idea!" Mrs. Fellowes hugged her. "If anything will bring her out of the doldrums its being useful and helping on a project for her sisters."

"That's what I thought." She held up her hand, showing half a dozen marbles. "I'm taking these out to the boys while I gather Amelia and Rosie. I'll send the first hired hand I see over to get the doll house down."

The housekeeper waved her off.

Feeling lighter than she had in weeks, Lilah stepped out the back door and wandered over to the bunkhouse. She didn't believe she'd find the children there. They had full run of the buildings and could be playing in any one of them. But Sourdough usually knew where they were.

Sy was in the corral working a horse. She could tell by the way he treated the animal he was in a foul mood. Since the haystack incident she'd made sure to never be alone with him. As far as she knew, he'd never been in the house and she planned to keep it that way. He might be the first hand she came to, but she'd find someone else to get the doll house down.

At the bunkhouse, she skirted the main door and went to the door leading straight into the lean-to kitchen. She knocked.

"Come in," called Sourdough.

She opened the door and found the cook sitting on a chair at the table, peeling potatoes. Rosie sat on a chair beside him, shoving the peelings into a bucket. Lilah smiled. "I see you have help."

"For a tiny thing she sure does like to work." He smiled at the small girl and put a wide hand on her small head. The child smiled up at Sourdough as if he'd just handed her a huge piece of candy.

"Where are Amelia and the two boys?" she asked, wondering how Sourdough would take the news of moving the girls to the house.

"Those three and Buddy are playing hide-n-seek in the barn." He nodded in the direction of the cabin next door. "Betsy has been hanging onto her momma's apron strings since Mrs. Malone is feelin' more like herself."

"That's good for both of them. I'll check in with Agnes after I've spoken with the others." She held a hand out to Rosie. "Want to help me find the others?"

The little girl peered up at the cook.

"Go on. I've been cooking a long time without your help." He smiled.

The child slid off the chair and walked over to Lilah. "Mrs. Fellowes and I have decided the girls,

Amelia and Rosie, should stay in the house rather than the bunkhouse. I'm gathering their things and showing them their new room."

Sourdough's gaze flew from the child's face to hers. "Will they still eat here?"

She shook her head. "No, they'll take their meals in the house. The boys will be welcome to eat in the house as well, but until we figure out how to make a room for them, they'll sleep out here."

The sadness in Sourdough's eyes tugged at her heart. "Rosie can come out and help you cook any time."

He nodded. "This bunkhouse is no place for girls. I know it. Just going to miss this little one."

"I come see you," the little girl said, releasing her hand and running back to Sourdough.

"I know, little one. You can come see me any time you want." Sourdough patted her head and nodded to Lilah.

She walked over and gathered the child into her arms. "Show me where you and Amelia keep your things." They walked through the door from the kitchen into the bunkhouse.

Sy stood beside a bunk, digging under the straw mattress.

She cleared her throat.

He spun around. His eyes narrowed, then widened and a smile lifted the corners of his lips. It wasn't a genuine smile. His eyes remained cold and calculating. "What are you doing in here?"

"I've come to collect the girls' belongings. We're moving them into the house." She ignored him and asked Rosie. "Where are your things?"

The child pointed to the bunks closest to the kitchen. No doubt Sourdough wanted to keep them close by. She knew a little of his history. He'd been a father for a short time, losing his wife and two children to diphtheria. After wandering about, he'd landed on the Double R as the cook.

She carried the girl to the bunks, placing her on the top one. The child crawled to the top of the bunk and dug her night dress and extra clothes out from under the pillow.

Lilah bent and retrieved Amelia's clothes from under the pillow on the bottom bunk. As she straightened, an arm looped around her waist, pulling her back against a body.

"Let go of me," she said, through clenched teeth.

"I like the way you feel." His free hand wandered up her side and touched her breast.

She stomped trying to land on his toes. But he was quicker and laughed at her attempt to get free.

Most times she preferred to fight her own fights, but she had to think of Rosie, who sat on the top bunk watching, her eyes wide with fear.

"Sourdough!" she yelled.

Sy released her at the same time the large cook came barreling through from the kitchen.

"What's going on in here?" he asked, his gaze landing on Sy and narrowing.

"I'm leaving." Sy backed away from her and strode out the door.

She sunk to the bunk. Her legs shook and her heart thudded in her chest like a run-away horse. That was three times now Sy had pushed the boundaries.

"You all right, Miss Lilah?" Sourdough asked. He stood at the end of the bunks. Rosie crawled to him and climbed down him like a tree, before climbing up into Lilah's lap.

She hugged the child. They had both been scared. "I'm fine. I think it's time I told Judge Radley about Sy. I'm getting tired of fighting him off."

The cook's eyes narrowed. "He's done this before?"

"Yes." She shuddered. If Sourdough hadn't been in the kitchen…she didn't want to think about what could have happened. And with Rosie watching.

She clutched the clothing to her chest with one arm and slid Rosie to her hip as she stood. "Let's go find your sister." As she passed Sourdough she smiled. "Thank you for coming so fast when I called."

"No man has a right to push himself on a woman." Sourdough's face held a wrath she'd never witnessed before. "I'll see to it everyone knows what Sy tried. We'll keep an eye on him until the Judge gets back and sends him down the road."

"It's not necessary to tell everyone. Buster knows about the other times. I'll let him know, and the judge." She had a notion if Brody found out, he'd lay into Sy, and she didn't want him getting hurt on her account.

Outside, she scanned the barnyard for Sy. She didn't see him and proceeded to the large barn.

Clem sat in the tack room cleaning harnesses and counting.

Lilah smiled and waited for him to finish.

"Thirty. Here I come!" he called out and continued

to clean the tack.

Laughing, she sat Rosie on one of the saddles. "Playing hide-n-seek I see."

Clem grinned. "I don't go lookin' for them until one comes and finds me working instead of hunting. That way I get some work done."

"I need to talk to them. So I'll hunt them down." She glanced at the work he was doing. He'd not helped with any of the harvest because of his gun-shot injury. "Any idea where I could find someone to go to the house and get something out of the attic. Mrs. Fellowes knows where it is."

Clem placed a hand on his side. "Is it heavy?"

"No. It's a doll house."

"I can help." He set the harness and rag down and stood. "Mrs. Fellowes hasn't told me I can do any heavy lifting or riding yet. But I can get a doll house out of the attic." He left the barn.

Lilah shifted Rosie back on her hip and started through the barn, methodically checking all the hiding places she remembered as a child. After making her way through all of the barn, she'd found everyone but Dooley.

Darrin, Amelia, and Buddy followed her around snickering.

"She'll never find him," Amelia said.

She'd checked everything ground level. Her gaze rose to the loft above the tack room. Boards were nailed on a post to climb up to the loft.

"Watch your sister." She stood Rosie beside Darrin. "And hold your clothes." She pressed the clothing into Amelia's arms.

Gripping the boards tightly, Lilah climbed up the makeshift ladder and peered into the loft. Even in the darkness, she could see footsteps had displaced the layer of dust. They led around a wooden crate.

"Dooley, you're behind that crate. Come on out." She waited and he didn't appear.

Carefully, she climbed the rest of the way and walked bent over toward the crate. Dooley lay behind the crate, unmoving.

"Dooley? Dooley!" She shoved the crate to the side and bent to pick the boy up. He'd vomited but was listless.

"Go get Sourdough and Mrs. Fellowes! Quick!" She walked to the edge of the loft and found Amelia and Rosie peering up at her, their eyes wide with fear.

Chapter Thirty-one

Brody was glad his grandfather wanted to return to the ranch as soon as he'd made sure Sheriff Davies would hold Angel until the circuit judge arrived. He wasn't in the mood to stay away from the ranch for long. Not with Talbot seeking revenge. The older man had asked him to drive the buggy. He'd tied his horse to the back of the contraption and the judge climbed into the back seat and fell asleep.

He met Sandy and Roy just after the judge had nodded off. He motioned for the two men to ride close to the buggy so he didn't have to stop.

"Go ahead and stay in town tonight and ride out with the posse if the sheriff can round one up. No sense all three of us losing a night's sleep."

Sandy glanced down the road away from Burns. "Aren't you afraid something could happen on the way back to the ranch?"

"If Talbot didn't follow us to save Angel, he's busy getting ready to do something else. I think he wants to make the judge suffer before he strikes." He didn't like the idea of the man coming for his grandfather. That's why he hoped the sheriff felt a need for a posse and they could find Talbot before he did any more harm.

The hands nodded and headed to town. Brody kicked the horses into a trot and headed home. He couldn't wait to see Lilah. He'd hoped to have a discussion with his grandfather on the ride back, but now it looked like he'd have to wait until tomorrow to discuss his feelings and intentions toward the woman.

***

Brody stopped the buggy at the barn and stared at the house. All the lights were on and it was three in the morning. Something was wrong.

"Judge? Judge, wake up. We're home." He shook his grandfather, waking the man from a sound sleep.

"What? What?" The older man sat up and stared at him in the light from the lantern he'd used to guide them home.

Smithy stepped out of the bunkhouse and walked their way. "Thought you'd spend the night."

"No. Needed to get home," the judge said, attempting to climb down from the buggy.

"Why are all the lights on in the house?" Brody asked, jumping out of the buggy and assisting his grandfather.

"One of the boys isn't doing too well. Miss Lilah found him in the barn loft sick." Smithy grasped the horses' headstalls.

"Take care of my horse as well." He took off at a

run for the house. One of the boys. What could have made him sick?

He hit the front door and found Darrin sitting in a chair. He'd fallen asleep with his head on the chair arm.

Brody hurried down the hall to Mrs. Fellowes room. Mattie sat up in bed with her lantern on. She glanced up, hope in her eyes. When she saw him that hope was replaced with worry.

"What's wrong with Dooley? Where is he?" he asked, taking one step inside the room.

"They think he ate something poisonous. Miss Lilah had him put in the girls' room." She wiped at her eyes with the sleeve of her night dress.

"The girls' room? I thought they were sleeping in the bunkhouse?" Gone for one day and things changed.

"Miss Lilah fixed up a room upstairs for the girls. She said when I'm walking, I can sleep in it with them." The girl's tone reflected she didn't see that happening.

"You'll be walking as soon as Gus gets your crutches finished." He wanted to hug the girl, but he'd witnessed her aversion to men and kept his distance. There had been girls and young women in his borough who acted the same. Maria told him what caused them to act the way they did. He didn't wish that on any female and only knew of one man who could have violated her—her father.

"I'll go check on Dooley. Do you need anything before I go?"

She shook her head and slipped down under the covers farther.

He took the stairs two at a time and found light

coming from the room at the end of the hall across from his room. At the door, he stopped. Mrs. Fellowes was asleep in the chair by the bed. Lilah sat on the side of the bed, brushing the hair from Dooley's forehead. Her back was to him.

Brody crossed the room and stood behind her. "How's he doing?" he whispered and put a hand on her shoulder.

She startled then leaned back against him as if needing his strength. "We think he'll pull through. Whatever he ate, we think came up when he vomited."

"You're sure it is something he ate?"

She stood and faced him. "What else could it be?" Her frightened eyes were red-rimmed. She hadn't slept.

He pulled her into his arms. "What was he doing before you found him?"

"The children were playing hide-n-seek in the barn with Clem. I sent him to the house on an errand and took over finding the children. I found everyone but Dooley and decided he was in the loft. I saw his footprints go behind a crate. I found him there, passed out and he'd vomited." She shuddered and he hugged her tighter.

"Shh. We'll figure it out. What did Mrs. Fellowes think?"

She shrugged. "She doesn't know this kind of medicine well. She suggested giving him milk to dilute whatever he ate, but he vomited that up."

"Did you ask him what he ate?"

"He just shakes his head and moans when he isn't sleeping."

"What is going on up here?" Judge Radley's voice

boomed.

Brody kept Lilah against his side as he faced his grandfather. "Quiet. Dooley ate something that has him ill."

The judge glanced at the bed, then back at them. He waved a hand. "I mean this. You hanging onto Lilah."

"I planned to talk about it with you on the trip back tonight but you slept the whole way."

She squirmed at his side, but he kept his arm around her.

"I see."

A moan from the bed captured all their attention. Lilah dropped to sit beside the boy who wriggled with a pain pinched face.

"I'm going to check out the loft." He squeezed her shoulder and headed to the door.

"We'll discuss this in the morning. I want both of you in my office before breakfast." Judge Radley didn't move from the doorway.

"I'll be there," Brody said. He glanced over his shoulder. She nodded her head.

His grandfather moved out of his way and he headed to the barn.

Before leaving the house, he lit a lantern. Out at the barn, he eased the door open and walked over to the ladder leading up to the loft. He couldn't think of anything that could be in the barn that would poison a person.

He climbed the ladder and noticed the disturbed dust. Following the trail, he found the crate. The lid was nailed tight. The boy couldn't have taken anything out of the box. He held the lantern up allowing the glow to shine behind the crate. A broken cobweb shimmered in the light.

A smile came to his lips for the first time today. Dooley wasn't poisoned. He'd known many children and adults who were bitten by a spider that left them sick for several days.

Back down the ladder, he headed for the house. His discovery should relieve everyone. In the sitting room, he picked up Darrin and laid him out on the seat for two, covering the boy with a crocheted blanket Mrs. Fellowes draped over her legs at night while doing needlework. He walked to the kitchen and paused at the door to Mrs. Fellowes room. Mattie was asleep. He tiptoed in and blew out the oil lamp.

His long day and night were wearing on him as he climbed the stairs. He found Lilah lying on the bed beside Dooley, her eyes closed and her breathing even.

Mrs. Fellowes stirred. "Oh my!" She sat up and touched her hair. "When did you get back?" she whispered.

"An hour ago. Go on down to your room. It's almost morning." Pink sky filtered in through the window.

"How's the boy?" Her gaze landed on Dooley and then Lilah.

"He'll be fine. I just came from the barn. I'm pretty sure it was a spider bite. I've never heard of anyone dying from one." He took the chair the housekeeper exited.

She stopped at the door and faced him. "The judge?"

"Should be sleeping in his room."

She nodded and left.

Brody watched Lilah sleep until his eyes grew heavy and he nodded off.

***

Lilah woke and stared at the boy on the bed beside her. His breathing sounded more even, less labored. Snoring came from the chair beyond the bed. She'd never heard Mrs. Fellowes snore like that before. She pushed up on an arm and found Brody sleeping in the chair.

Sunlight caught the red tone in his whiskers making his face appear golden. She smiled and her heart danced in her chest. He'd held her last night and told the judge they would talk with him this morning. What did he plan to say? Did he want to court her?

The thought of courting him sent her body humming. She'd never had an interest in anyone courting her before. Her dreams never included a husband. The thought sunk her elation. Did that mean she really didn't want a husband? She stared at the man sleeping in the chair. Her heart raced, and she wanted him to kiss her again. Only married or engaged couples were to kiss. It must mean I want to be married—to Brody.

He shifted and the light crossed over his eyes. Snorting and his hands moving to cover his eyes caused her to giggle.

That stopped his actions and he slowly opened his eyes. His gaze landed on her.

The intensity of that gaze made her breath hitch and her insides dance.

"Good morning," he said, sliding his body straighter in the chair.

"Good morning," she whispered. "His breathing sounds better this morning."

"It should and by tomorrow he should be back to normal." Brody sat on the edge of the chair, studying the boy.

She sat up and pulled the pins from her falling hair. "How do you know that?"

His light blue gaze connected with hers. "I'm pretty sure he was bitten by a spider. I found a broken cobweb behind the box where you found him."

"Oh!" Her heart raced as he stood and walked around the bed. She'd spent the night wishing he was there to help ease her worry. And here he was, telling her all was well and moving toward her with warmth shimmering in his light blue eyes.

He held out a hand. His lips curved into an inviting smile.

She grasped his outstretched hand. His fingers encasing hers sent heat up her arm and lightness to her heart.

He tugged her to her feet and into his arms. "We're supposed to meet the judge in his office before breakfast."

Her heart thudded against her ribs. "I remember." She licked her lips and peered into his eyes. "What are we going to say?"

His gaze flicked to her lips and back to her eyes. "What do you want to say?"

She swallowed, her mouth too dry to say anything as she stared into his smoldering gaze and his hard body pressed against her.

"Thirsty." Dooley's faint voice was barely heard over her beating heart.

Brody released her and held a glass of water to the boy's lips. It was his actions with the children, the hired hands, and her that nudged her to the edge of falling in love with him. But witnessing the concern and care he gave Dooley just helping him drink water, she tumbled over the brink and knew there was nothing the man could do that would sour her love for him.

When Dooley had drank his fill, Brody replaced the glass on the table by the bed and returned to her.

"You didn't answer my question. What do you want to say about us to Judge Radley?" He didn't pull her into his arms this time. His hand rose, gathering her hair. He sifted the locks through is fingers, his gaze fully on her face.

Heat tingled through her body as if he held her tight. She couldn't ignore the sensations his presence unleashed. She wanted to know more about him and her reactions to his touch and kisses.

"That I would like you to court me." She wasn't going to say she loved him. They'd only known each other a couple of months. She wasn't going to say anything that would make her vulnerable.

Chapter Thirty-two

Brody had never touched anything as silky as Lilah's hair. His fingers moved from the ends, up to her scalp until he held her small head in his hand. "I'd like to court you." He leaned close, his lips hovering over hers. "And show you we could be very good together."

He'd expected her to lean back. Instead, her head moved out of his hand, pressing her lips to his. From their first kiss he knew she wasn't experienced, but her boldness took him by surprise.

Once the initial shock wore off, he deepened the kiss, winding his arms around her and drawing them body to body.

"Ahem."

Not wanting anyone to think what they did was wrong, he slowly drew out of the kiss and turned his attention to the door. Mrs. Fellowes and the youngest Lund children stood in the doorway.

"Dooley will be fine. I believe he suffered a spider bite." Brody drew her to his side. "He was a wake a minute ago."

"Still am," a soft, weak voice said.

The children scurried to the bed.

The housekeeper narrowed her eyes at the two of them. "This behavior will get Brody sent back out to the bunkhouse."

He grinned and hugged Lilah to his side. "She's worth it."

She smacked his chest with her hand. "We need to see Judge Radley."

Holding her hand, he led Lilah down the stairs and to the office door. It was closed so he knocked.

"Yes." The judge's voice was gruff. Not a good sign for this conversation.

Brody opened the door and ushered her in ahead of him. She took the seat in front of the desk, and he stood behind her, one hand on her shoulder.

His grandfather's gaze landed on his hand on her shoulder and then studied her face. "Tell me what's been going on under my roof?"

He shook his head. "It's not like that, Grandfather. Lilah and I have talked and come to see we care about one another."

She scooted closer to the edge of the seat, reaching out to the older man. "We'd like to get to know one another better."

"What about continuing your education?" Judge Radley asked, his hawk-like gaze peering at him.

He was confident that now Lilah knew he wanted to marry her, she would shove the schooling to the side.

"I plan to go. To learn all I can about keeping books and the health of cattle. I told you I wanted to be able to help with the ranch. But I won't leave until after Agnes has the baby. She'll need some help right after." Lilah peered up at him.

He stared back at her, unable to form words. She wanted to continue going to the university. That would make it hard to court and even marry her. He pulled his hand from her shoulder.

Her eyes lost the gleam they'd had moments before. "You don't want me to continue my education."

"You won't need more. You'll be married. To me." Unless she didn't think he was worthy of her.

"And I can help you with the ranch books and the breeding. You know nothing about any of this. With my learning, I can help with that." She stood and faced him.

"Upstairs you said you wanted me to court you. How can I do that if you're not even here?" Her words had boosted his ego and made him think he could love someone and be loved back without losing them. And now, she was ready to leave him.

"You can start now. We can get engaged, and when I come back, we can marry." She turned to his grandfather. "That would be the respectable way to handle this, correct?"

His grandfather sat back in his chair, studying both of them.

Brody started searching his mind for the words that would make his grandfather and Lilah see that her going away wouldn't make them stronger, only give her a chance to find another man who was more learned and sophisticated than himself.

"Five years ago when I discovered I had a grandson, I'd hoped he'd be someone of good character. Someone who would love this ranch and keep it for generations to live on and prosper." The judge leaned forward, his intense stare on him.

What was he thinking? Because of my arrest and not wanting Lilah to go to the university is he going to give the ranch to someone else?

"Grandfather, I explained the stealing and not wanting Lilah—"

The old man raised his hand. "Let me finish." He cleared his throat and leaned back into the high-backed leather chair. "I believe I've found that person. Brody, you have shown your character from the moment we met the stage. I'm impressed with your leadership and your compassion." He set his gaze on Lilah and his face softened. "Girl, you stole this old man's heart the first time I met you and you hugged me around the leg. When I discovered your parents had left me as your guardian, I couldn't have been happier. But I promised them you would be fully educated." He waggled a finger back and forth between them. "I would think that if this is really what you two want, you could finish your education and Brody can tend the ranch until you return. And if you still want each other, I'll not stand in the way."

Brody wasn't sure how long a woman went to university. But he had his grandfather's blessing if he let her go. His gaze landed on Lilah.

Happiness glistened in her eyes once more. "Thank you, Judge." She scurried around the desk and hugged his neck.

Brody shook his head. He wasn't sure what she was so happy about.

She hurried back to his side and slipped her hand in his. Her face tipped up to his. "We can court."

His heart thudded in his chest. Maybe once they started courting she wouldn't want to leave him behind and go off to school. That was his plan. He'd make her so happy that she wouldn't want to leave him.

His grandfather waved his hand. "You may court, but you will move back to the bunkhouse. I know what it's like to have a woman you're randy for just a few doors away. I'll not abide that kind of behavior in this house. I should have been more vigilant with your mother."

The last comment riled. Had he been conceived while his mother still lived at home? His father must have been a guest at one time.

Lilah squeezed his hand, drawing him from his reveries.

"Come on," he said, leading her out of the office. Once they were standing in the kitchen, he faced her. "You'd really leave me to go learn about numbers and cows?"

She didn't smile. "I'll only be gone six months to a year." Her free hand rubbed up and down his arm. "I'll be here until the baby comes. Let's not spend our time together discussing my desire to learn more."

He had to look at the bright side of things and work to make her not want to leave. "At least he gave us permission to court." He kissed her cheek.

Mrs. Fellowes waddled into the kitchen, the

children following behind her. "What did the judge have to say about the two of you?"

His heart pounded in his chest, knowing he could touch Lilah and show her how much he cared when he wanted. "He said I may court Lilah, but I have to move back to the bunkhouse."

The housekeeper nodded. "That will leave a room for Darrin and Dooley. As soon as he gets his things out, Darrin, you can move you and your brother's things in. I'll move Dooley to that room the next time I check on him."

Darrin sat in a chair at the table. "Brody, we don't have to take your room." The boy didn't look at him, as if he were the one causing a problem.

He put a hand on the boy's head. "You can have the room. I don't want it. The bunkhouse will be fine for now." He winked at Lilah and her face darkened a lovely pink.

Judge Radley entered the kitchen. "Where's breakfast?" he asked, taking his seat at the head of the table.

Mrs. Fellowes and Lilah jumped into action, putting food on the table.

As soon as he'd finished eating, Brody retrieved his belongings from the room upstairs and headed to the bunkhouse.

The hands were still eating as he reclaimed his old bunk and placed his belongs in the trunk under the bed.

He wandered into the kitchen and took his usual seat, pouring a cup of coffee.

Buster was the first to say anything. "Lilah taking those kids into the house get you throwed out?"

Grinning, he shook his head. "They are taking up all the beds. Mrs. Fellowes told Darrin to come get his and Dooley's stuff and to move into the room I've been in. Guess she feels I'm well enough to live out here."

Smithy stared at him and pointed a fork full of hotcake at him. "There's somethin' else. You wouldn't be grinning like you won a poker pot from bein' tossed out of the house."

He wanted to make it clear to everyone, and especially Sy, that Lilah was off limits. "You're right. The judge sent me back out here when I told him I wanted to court Lilah."

There were hoots and slaps on the back from everyone but Sy. He sat sipping coffee, his eyes downcast.

"What are the jobs today?" he asked Buster.

The foreman rattled off each man's job for the day.

He barely heard what Buster had to say. It wasn't lack of sleep that had him daydreaming. The knowledge his grandfather wasn't against him courting Lilah, had given him added energy and sent his thoughts to their next chance meeting. Tonight after dinner, he was going to take her for a walk to a secluded place where they could talk about this university and do some more kissing.

"Come on." Stubbs slapped him on the back.

The cowboy was to the door before Brody roused himself and headed after him. Outside, he stopped Stubbs. "What are we doing?"

The hand grinned. "You got it bad, but then we knew that." He nodded to the corrals. "Buster wants you to get the other two horses out of there that you want. Then we are to go check the fences on the southern border."

A full day. He'd be too tired by nightfall to even think of kissing Lilah.

***

Lilah sat on the porch reading to the children and keeping an eye out for Brody. He'd been sent with Stubbs to check the southern fences. Now that everyone knew how they felt about one another, she didn't have to hide her anticipation of seeing him again.

"Why'd you stop?" Amelia asked, as she once again stared down the road.

"Sorry. I'm distracted." She smiled at the child and continued reading where she'd left off. The sound of many horses' hooves had her shutting the book and standing. Sheriff Davies, Sandy and Roy, along with four men rode into the barnyard.

"Darrin, go get the judge," she said, turning the boy to the door and then walking off the porch to meet the sheriff. The Double R hands peeled off from the group at the barn.

"Sheriff, what brings you and these men out here?"

He tipped his hat and stared past her at the children. "You starting up a school?"

"No. These are the Lund children. Their father left them alone and Mattie was seriously injured. We're taking care of them." She glanced at the men with him. "Why are you here?"

"I asked them here." Judge Radley stepped off the porch. "I see you found some men to help. I'd offered my hands but I need them all right now."

"I understand. Where was the last place you saw

268

Talbot?"

Her heart picked up speed. The sheriff was after the escaped prisoner. She was glad Brody and the others wouldn't have to deal with the killer.

"Let's go ask Buster." The judge turned to her. "Lilah, go get some water for these men."

She ushered the children into the house and headed to the kitchen. Returning to the front of the house, she found the men dismounted and standing in the shade of a tree. She carried the tray with glasses and a pitcher of water over to them.

"Nice place," one of the men said as he took a glass of water.

"We like it," she responded and held the tray out to the last man.

"You the judge's daughter?" the man who spoke before asked.

"No. I'm his ward."

"Same thing." His eyes held the same gleam she'd witnessed in Angel's eyes. An expression she now knew had nothing to do with her and everything to do with greed.

A shiver slithered up her spine. She set the tray down and turned to head back to the house.

"You could be a little more hospitable." The man grabbed hold of her arm.

She glanced at the others. They all were intent on staring at their water. Anger shot through her. He had no right to touch her let alone call her inhospitable when she'd brought them all water.

"Release my arm."

"What's going on?"

Lilah's heart raced at the sound of Brody's voice. She felt his presence beside her. Her gaze was locked with the man still holding her.

"I believe the lady asked you to let go." The threat in his tone grabbed her attention. He stood next to her, his pale eyes narrowed and glaring. His fisted hands raised to about his waist.

The other man released her arm and smiled. "Just being friendly."

Brody stepped forward and slugged the man in the face.

"No! Brody!"

Chapter Thirty-three

Brody ducked the punch the man returned and slammed his head into the man's gut, shoving him back against the tree.

"Stop!" shouted a male voice.

He pulled his head from the man and received a blow to the jaw. Before he could throw a punch his arms were wrenched behind his back, and he was pulled away. He glared at the man being restrained by the sheriff.

When he'd walked up and saw the man holding Lilah, he'd wanted to rush forward and yank his hand from her arm. Then she'd forcefully asked the man to release her and he'd refused. That had unleashed his small amount of control.

"What do you think you're doing, son?" Grandfather stepped between him and the man the sheriff was backing up.

"He grabbed Lilah and wouldn't let go when she asked." He twisted his head and found her standing back, her eyes wide.

"You can't go fighting every man who talks to her."

He swung his attention back to his grandfather. "He wasn't talking, he had a hold of her arm and wasn't letting go even when she asked him."

His arms were released.

Buster stepped around in front of him to stand beside his grandfather. "The judge is right. You can't cause trouble every time a man comes near your girl."

Glaring at the two older men standing in front of him, Brody bent and picked up his hat. "He was hurting her. I won't apologize for stepping in." He shoved his hat on his head and walked by Lilah. She started to reach out to him, but he continued on to the barn.

Why didn't she speak up and tell them the man had been hurting her? He stomped over to the barn and sent the dogs, kittens, and children all fleeing as he entered, slamming the door open.

Gus sat in the light of a window scratching Mattie's crutches with his knife. The man was doing a wonderful job making the sticks smooth.

"You the one making all the ruckus out there?" Gus asked, motioning to a wooden box beside him like the one he sat on.

"I guess so. I didn't start it. One of the men with the sheriff grabbed Lilah." He rubbed a hand over his jaw where the man had connected with a punch.

"And bein's how you're sweet on her, you came to her rescue." Gus stopped smoothing the wood and studied him.

"Yes. None of the others with the sheriff were going to do anything."

The older man chuckled. "That girl has been warding off randy men since she turned sixteen and became an eyeful. She could have handled the situation and had left the man scared to ever treat a woman like that again. Now, he can just boast he got into a fight over a pretty girl." He pointed his whittling knife at Brody. "And you'll have to prove to your grandfather you aren't hot-headed and won't fly off the handle every time a man looks at Lilah."

He wanted to argue with the man but everything he said made sense. He'd have to apologize to both his grandfather and Lilah. He'd apologized for few things in his life. This would be the one time he was genuinely sorry.

"How are the crutches coming?"

Gus smiled. "She can try them tomorrow. I have some more smoothing that needs done." His smile dimmed. "That girl has become so sorrowful, I hope this will brighten her life."

Brody stood and put a hand on the man's shoulder. "I'm sure it will. I better get to my chores and not upset anyone else today."

His talk with Gus left him with lots to think about. Outside, he was happy to see the sheriff and his men had left. The unsettling part was knowing they roamed the ranch and he'd no doubt run into them at some point. But that was one apology he wouldn't be making.

After the chores, he entered the kitchen hungry for supper. Mrs. Fellowes stood at the stove, stirring a pot.

Mattie sat at the kitchen table putting rolls into a bowl.

Lilah entered, followed by the two youngest girls. "Amelia, you take the bowl of rolls into the dining room." She picked up the small bowl of butter. "Rosie, you can put this on the table."

Both girls beamed with happiness and left the kitchen carrying their bowls.

The moment Lilah spotted him her lips started to tip into a smile then stopped. He took a step toward her, then motioned to the door.

"I need to talk to you." He didn't want to apologize in front of the girl and the housekeeper.

She stood to the spot as if she'd planted roots. "We can talk here. There's work to be done." Then she moved, picking up a large pot off the side of the cookstove.

He moved closer to her. Steam moistened her face as she lifted the lid off and started to pour ranch beans into a bowl.

He took the large pot from her and dumped the contents into the bowl.

She motioned for him to put the pot in the sink. When he turned from the sink, he caught sight of the backside of her skirt leaving the kitchen. She wasn't making this easy.

Quick strides took him out of the kitchen and into the dining room. He made eye contact with the two girls and sent them back to the kitchen. Lilah straightened from putting the bowl on the table and he was there. Close enough the spattering of freckles across her cheeks blended with the deepening color of her skin.

"I want to apologize for this afternoon, but you're making it difficult." He placed his hands on the backs of the two chairs she stood between, corralling her in one place.

"There's a meal to be put on the table." She tried to push through his arm, but he wasn't letting her get away. Not until she'd heard him out.

"It can wait a couple of minutes." He stared into her eyes. "Lilah, I'm sorry I threw a punch this afternoon. I should have realized you could handle yourself."

"Yes, you should have. Do you think he's the first man to put his hands on me like that?" Her eyes flashed with anger. "Buster and the judge have taught me ways to get away from unwanted advances."

He raised a hand and skimmed his fingers over her cheek. "I shouldn't have riled so quick. I promise to let you handle things, but if it looks like you can't, I'll step in." He leaned down, hovering his lips above hers. "Because I will never let anyone hurt you." Waiting to see if he'd been forgiven didn't take long.

Her lips pressed to his, and he wound an arm around her, pulling her close. This wasn't the time or place to lose himself to her kisses. He drew back and eased his arm out from around her.

"I'll see you at supper." He backed out of the room and headed for his grandfather's office. Time for another apology.

***

Lilah hurried through helping Mrs. Fellowes with the dishes. She stood in her room, patting her hair. She'd combed lavender through her locks and was ready to meet Brody out on the front porch. After the meal, he'd asked her to meet him and they'd go for a walk.

She left her room and peeked in at the children. They were all snuggled in their beds, giggling. "Sleep tight, I'll see you in the morning."

Downstairs she started to say something to the judge, but noticed he was sleeping in the chair. Mrs. Fellowes glanced her way. She didn't smile but there wasn't any reprimand about staying out too long.

On the porch, she found Brody leaning against a post. He turned at the sound of the screen door opening.

He had caught her attention when she first met him, but now that he wore the cowboy hat, boots, and work pants, he took her breath away. She stopped an arm's length from him and enjoyed the view. She sighed.

Brody held his arm out to her, and she slipped her hand through the crook of his elbow. It was still light. Though the heat of the sun lingered on the ground, the air was cooling.

"Where are you taking me?" she asked, noting he walked up behind the house.

"Somewhere quiet where we won't be disturbed." He squeezed her hand against his body, causing heat to spread up her arm and swirl in her chest.

They strolled through the trees and skirted large boulders that had rolled down from the crown of rock on the top of the hill to their north. The sun cast a soft, end-of-the-day glow onto the hillside when he stopped.

He'd brought them to a small flat spot on the side of the hill where they could look down on the buildings and two of the hay meadows beyond.

"This is beautiful!" She wrapped her arms around his neck. "I think I'm going to like being courted."

He lowered his head and their lips met. She'd thought of little else but kissing him again after his apology before supper. Now, on the hill all alone, they could kiss until they were both exhausted.

The angle of the kiss changed, his breath came in puffs against her cheek as his tongue slid across her lips as if tasting them. What did his mouth feel like? She followed his lead, parting her lips. Their tongues touched, and she opened her mouth in surprised. He didn't retreat as she had done. The intimacy of part of him inside her, sent heat coursing to her area between her legs.

She clutched his shoulders as she squeezed her legs together trying to make sense of the throbbing. Her knees gave way. Brody pulled out of the kiss and helped ease her down to the ground. The warm soft bed of grass smelled earthy.

"Are you not feeling well?" he asked, lying beside her, his head propped on an arm.

She felt as if she had a fever. And all from his kisses. "I…my…" How did she tell him of the sensations she didn't even understand?

He leaned close, kissing the tip of her nose, her cheek, her neck. Her eyes closed as he nuzzle her neck.

"You smell good. Like a flower." His lips returned to her lips.

His body shifted closer. His arm wrapped around her middle, drawing her close. "Why are you so still?" he whispered in her ear.

Instead of wondering about the sensations, she decided to explore them. Rolling to her side, she faced him. Her breasts squashed against his chest, her lower body molded to his. There was a hardness that pressed against her throbbing mound. The sensation caused her already stimulated body to push closer.

A whimper escaped her as she wiggled closer and wished she could satisfy the ache.

"Oh, Lilah, don't tempt me." He captured her mouth with his. His tongue tangled with hers.

The arm under her, circled his neck, drawing them closer, holding him tight as he seduced her mouth. She grasped his hip with her other hand, pulling his lower body tighter against her. Her body rocked, rubbing the throbbing area against his hardness.

He shifted and she moaned, missing the contact. His lips drew away, and he leaned his forehead to hers.

"We can't…" He drew in a long breath. "This will lead to…"

"You can't leave me throbbing in my woman parts." As soon as the words came out she wondered at the boldness of her tongue.

Brody chuckled and pulled her head to his chest. "I have the same problem."

She shoved back. "You have woman parts?"

He laughed and kissed her, a quick peck on the lips. "No, my manhood is throbbing and about to burst."

"Really?" She'd been on the ranch and knew the male put his part inside the female to make babies, but she'd never thought there were sensations before it happened that could be so frustrating and wonderful. "I never knew mating could be such a varied mix of sensations."

Chapter Thirty-four

Brody wiggled to alleviate the ache and need that had engorged his dick. He'd bedded a few girls while in New York. All willing and looking for a husband. He'd been lucky that none had become with child. Holding and kissing Lilah was different. He wasn't going to bed her on the grassy hillside. He wanted to make love to her on a soft, fluffy bed. Fulfill all her needs and love her until she was so limp all she could do was smile.

Her bold comment told him she was going to be all he'd ever need to satisfy his male cravings. And she'd already shown him she could fill his heart with love. He had to prove to her, he could make her happier than going to a university.

As much as he hated leaving her unsatisfied, he wasn't going to risk losing her by making love to her here. He stood and pulled her up into his arms. "It's time to take you back."

"I don't want to go back. Not yet." She wrapped her arms around his neck. Standing on her tiptoes, her breasts pressed against his chest, reminding him of what she had to offer.

He wrapped his arms around her, picked her up off the ground and kissed her until they were both fighting for air. With her feet in the air, she didn't have a way to press her mound against his still throbbing dick.

Settling Lilah on her feet, he unwound her arms from his neck. "That's the last kiss tonight. I'm going to have to go sit in the stream to cool off and not walk into the bunkhouse with a bulge in my pants."

She stepped back, and in the dim light of the half moon, she stared at his bulge. When she reached out as if to touch, he backed up.

"Oh no. I'm having enough trouble not exploding. You touch me and I'll be a goner."

"Is that…" She bit her lip and her wide eyes peered into his. "Your man part?"

He gulped. She was so innocent of the ways of a man and woman. The things they did this night and the things they talked about were to be shared between a married couple.

"Yes." He grasped her hand and led her down the side of the hill. "How much do you know about a man and woman coming together?"

"Only what I've seen of the animals on the ranch." Her tone reflected she didn't quite understand it all.

"It might be a good idea to ask Agnes questions. She's a married woman and could help you understand." He kept a steady pace down the hill.

"What about you? How much do you know?"

His feet stalled.

She tugged on his hand, turning him to face her. "Have you been in a woman?"

He'd never been able to lie to someone he cared about. His mother, Maria, and now Lilah. He cradled her head in his hands. "Men have a need that has to be sated. If they aren't married, they find a willing woman or pay for one."

Her eyes widened. "Like whores?" she whispered.

"Some men do pay those women."

Her eyes narrowed. "And you?"

"Not me. Where I grew up there are always willing women." The second the words came out he regretted them.

"Willing? What do you mean?"

"There are widows, eager to be held. Young women who aren't ready to marry but want to have an enjoyable evening." He tugged on her hand, making her start walking again.

"How many have you... You know?"

"Where I come from it's how a man learns to fulfill his wife. By bedding willing women who have experience, I learned how to make who I marry happy." That was the truth. Every woman he'd bedded had told him what they liked and being an eager young man, he'd learned to please. Of those there was only one he'd slept with more than once. They weren't in love, they had just both needed a warm body to hold to vanish their loneliness for a few hours.

She was quiet until they were just about to the house. Lilah stopped, again turning him to face her. "How do you know the difference between sating a need and loving someone?"

His heart kicked into his ribs and a lump came to his throat. He grasped her shoulders and leaned down, nearly nose to nose with her. "My heart didn't pound in my chest when I held others and I didn't kiss them until I was breathless." He settled his lips on hers.

When she opened her mouth, he dove in, delighting in her acceptance and charging his senses with her taste. The kiss lasted until he couldn't think or breathe. Her lavender scent was as intoxicating as any whiskey and her sweet taste rivaled any confection he'd ever stolen.

Still holding her shoulders, his forehead once again resting against hers, he whispered, "That kiss tells me you are the only woman for me."

She sighed. "And you are the only man for me."

He pulled her into his arms and hugged her.

A light beamed across the porch from the front door. "It's time for Lilah to come in," Grandfather's voice boomed.

"Good night." He kissed Lilah and released her, giving her a nudge toward the house.

He waited in the shadow of the tree until she'd entered and the door shut before walking to the stream behind the bunkhouse and splashing cold water on his face, head, and back of his neck. Once his body had settled back to normal, he headed into the bunkhouse.

***

Lilah rose the next morning tired and grumpy. Her body hadn't settled down until the wee hours. While it raged, she'd thought about what Brody had said. As soon as breakfast was cleared from the table she would visit Agnes.

He entered the kitchen, laughing with Darrin and Dooley. The sight of him interacting with the children always softened her heart. This morning was no exception, but her heart raced and her body started a low throb like the night before, just by looking at him.

"Morning." He hung his hat on a peg by the door and crossed the room, dropping a kiss on her cheek.

Her face heated as the children all watched and giggled.

"What's so funny?" Judge Radley asked, as he entered the kitchen for his morning meal.

"Brody kissed Miss Lilah on the cheek," Amelia said, hiding her mouth behind her hand.

The judge peered at her and then Brody. "I want you both in my office after the meal."

"Because I kissed Lilah's cheek?" Brody didn't take his chair, he stood like a bear protecting his cubs. Only she was pretty sure it was her, he was protecting.

"We'll not discuss this in front of the children." Judge Radley sat.

"It's best we talk about this in his office," she conceded. Also not wanting the children to hear whatever the judge had to say or what Brody might spout.

He didn't sit, he just stared at his grandfather.

She walked around the table and put a hand on his shoulder. "Sit. We'll discuss it after the meal."

He sat but grabbed her hand and pulled her down into the chair next to him, all the time his gaze remained on his grandfather.

The children chatted during the meal but the adults and Mattie were quiet.

After the breakfast, Lilah rose and started to help Mrs. Fellowes.

"I and the children can take care of this. Go on and get this conversation over." The housekeeper took the dishes from her hands and nudged her toward the doorway.

Judge Radley stood in the hallway waiting. Brody followed her out of the room and into the office. He closed the door behind them. She took the chair in front of the desk as she had the morning before and Brody took his place behind her, a hand on her shoulder.

The judge sat behind his desk and studied them a moment. "When I accepted you wanted to court Lilah, I didn't expect you to make spectacles in public."

"How is kissing her on the cheek a spectacle?" His hand on her shoulder tensed.

"The children—"

"Will know how I care for Lilah and see that they are in a caring household. My kissing her cheek isn't any different than if I kissed Amelia or Rosie on the cheek." His face drained of color and he knelt beside the chair. "I'm not saying what I feel for you is the same as the two children. It isn't, you know that."

For the first time that morning, she laughed. "Yes, I know what you meant." Her gaze drifted over his sincere face and then narrowed on Judge Radley. "I agree with Brody. By our showing our affection for one another in front of the children, they will know they are in a loving environment. One that I hope they wish to stay in should their father ever return."

Judge Radley shook his head. "If you feel free to kiss in front of the children how will you restrain yourselves when out in public?" He thumped a hand on the desk. "You are taking this much too fast. Had I known your idea of courting was kissing her at all times, I wouldn't have agreed."

"There is nothing that can slow down our feelings for one another." Brody stood, his hand remaining around hers.

His solidarity with her added one more reason she loved him.

"We shall see. I'm headed to Venator this morning. I have something to pick up from the stage." The judge stood.

She took this as a dismissal and headed for the door.

"Lilah, stay," the judge said.

She glanced at Brody. He stopped at the door, looking as if to say something.

"Go on, son. This is household business I need to talk to her about." The judge leaned back in his chair.

Lilah smiled at Brody and returned to the chair. The door clicked and the older man leaned forward.

"Can you put all the children in one room for a couple of nights?" He studied her.

"Yes. Why?" She couldn't think of any reason to leave a room open.

"I'm picking up a guest at the stage. She'll be staying with us for a few days. You'll need to clean the room you vacate the children from and make it inviting." His smile made his eyes twinkle.

"Is it an old friend who is coming?" she asked, thinking it was about time the man found a woman that interested him.

"Yes. It's an old friend." He turned his attention to papers on his desk.

She left the office smiling. Now where had he picked up a woman friend over the years?

Chapter Thirty-five

Brody spent the morning helping Buster sort the horses in the corral. The ones they would keep and the ones his grandfather had contracted to the army. He spotted Gus carrying the crutches toward the house before noon.

"Mind if I see how Mattie's crutches work?" he asked Buster.

"Go ahead. It's almost meal time."

He jogged from the barn up to Gus. "Ready for her to try them?"

The man grinned. "Yep. I think the little lady is going to be pleased."

At the house, he went in search of Mattie. He found her in the kitchen helping Lilah and Mrs. Fellowes prepare lunch for the children.

"Mattie, Gus has your crutches ready. Want to come outside and try them?"

She stopped spreading preserves on the bread. She

didn't answer him, only glanced at Lilah.

"If these crutches work, you can walk around and play with your brothers and sisters," Lilah said, moving toward the girl. "You won't have to depend on anyone to help you get around while that leg heals."

That seemed to be the words the girl needed to hear.

She pushed up onto her well foot. Standing, she spoke. "I don't want to try them outside with everyone watching."

Lilah smiled. "You can try walking in the sitting room." She glanced at him. "Have Gus bring the crutches into the sitting room and keep the children outside."

He nodded and headed back to the front porch. All the children were gathered around Gus asking questions.

"Hold up, all of you. You sound like a flock of chickens." He waded through the children to the man holding the crutches. "You go on in. She wants to do this inside."

Darrin started to dart by him. Brody reached out, capturing the boy by the shirt collar. "And she doesn't want gawkers. Everyone is to stay out here with me." He waved at Gus. "Go on in. They're waiting for you in the sitting room."

Gus crossed the porch and disappeared into the house.

"Why can't we go in?" Buddy whined.

"Yeah, she's our sister," Darrin added.

"Because she wants to try her crutches without all of you watching and asking questions and making her uncomfortable. She'll come out when she's ready."

Sourdough rang the meal bell.

"Come on, let's go eat," he said, heading toward the bunkhouse.

"Children, your lunch is ready," Mrs. Fellowes called from the side porch.

All the children ran back toward the house, even Buddy and Betsy. He shrugged and entered the bunkhouse. Mrs. Fellowes would have to keep them away from Mattie.

He'd stepped onto the board walkway in front of the bunkhouse when he heard the jingle of harnesses. Glancing toward the road he spied his grandfather driving the buggy back to the ranch. He had passengers. When he said he had something to pick up from the stage, Brody thought the old man had meant packages.

By the time the buggy stopped in front of the house, he was running across the barnyard to meet it. He couldn't believe his eyes. Maria and Emma sat in the back seat of the buggy.

He reached up grabbing the child and hugging her tight. Then he held his arms up to the woman who had helped him through hard times and he'd helped her. She dropped into his arms and hugged him tight.

"We thought we'd never see you." She leaned back. "You are even more handsome."

He laughed and set her on the ground. "How did you get here?"

"When I saw how attached you were to these two I sent some letters off." His grandfather stepped up beside Maria. "Mr. Peck found them and arranged for their trip out here."

He was glad to see the mother and daughter. Happy they were no longer living in the tenements, but… "Why did you bring them here?"

The front door opened. Lilah and Mattie, using her crutches, stepped out onto the porch.

He strode to the porch and smiled at the girl. "Look at you!" His gaze drifted to Lilah.

She stared at Maria and Emma.

Lilah wondered why the judge would bring a beautiful woman, and equally as pretty little girl, to the ranch. She'd thought he was picking up a woman his age. As she stepped off the porch, the girl ran up to Brody, throwing her arms around his legs.

He reached out to her, but she didn't respond. Why did the child hug him like she knew him? The woman moved up behind him, touching his arm as if she did it all the time.

Her gaze bounced from the child, to the woman, to Brody. Who were these people? Why were they so intimate?

As if he heard her silent question, he drew the child from his legs.

"Lilah, this is Emma and her mother, Maria. They were my neighbors in New York City."

She stared into his eyes. What wasn't he saying? The two appeared to be very familiar with him.

"Lilah, please take Maria and her daughter up to the guest room so they can freshen up before the noon meal." Judge Radley ushered the woman and child past Brody. His gaze still held hers.

"We need to talk," he said, again, reaching out to her.

She nodded but followed the mother and daughter into the house. She closed the door and turned to the woman. "I have a room made up for you upstairs. With the children in the house, we are running out of beds."

She started up the dark stairway and stopped at the end of the hall. At the room Brody had resided in not that long ago.

"It is a pretty room. Gracias." Maria entered, followed by her daughter.

"How well do you know Brody?" she asked, unable to keep the thought locked up.

The woman smiled and her eyes sparkled. "He has been a very good friend to us. We are the reason he was arrested. I have never felt so bad as when I heard the police caught him."

"Did you go to his aid?" She didn't understand how they could have been the reason for his arrest.

"No. No one would have believed me. If Brody had not stolen food and medicine for us after my husband died, I would not have my Emma. She was very sick." Maria removed her hat and placed her coat on a peg. Then she knelt and relieved the child of her bonnet and coat.

The room had a nice breeze blowing through, but her anger didn't heed the cool breeze.

"Why would he risk jail to help you?" She knew he had a caring heart. Look at how easily it was to persuade him to bring the Lund children back to the ranch.

"We have been close for a long time. When my husband and I came to New York City we lived next to Brody. He was the one who brought the old lady with medicine to me when I could not bring Emma to the world. He was with me when the police told me my Jorge was dead." Maria sighed. "It hurt bad when he told me he was coming here. I-we had come to rely on him to survive."

Lilah tried to understand the relationship between this woman, her child, and Brody. But her heart squeezed with fear. Fear he loved Maria and the child and had only been dallying with her, much like Angel. It was a good thing she would be going to the university. Put some distance between them.

Another part of her wondered if he had asked his grandfather to bring these two here. That he felt as incomplete without them as Maria did without him.

She couldn't stay in the room any longer. She needed air and space to think.

Without a word, she bolted from the room, ran down the stairs, and out the back. She couldn't face anyone, especially Brody, at this moment. She needed time to think.

Walking briskly, she headed up the canyon behind the house. Her mind whipped through all the special times she and Brody had shared. Last night, when he'd brought her to life. Making her want something she didn't understand but knew she needed. Replaying the kisses and his touch, her body hummed. What they had and experienced together had to be love. A bond that no one else had with him.

Maria's face when she spoke of him came to mind. The woman loved him. But did he love her?

She trudged on, thinking, cursing her body that heated each time she thought of Brody's kisses, and then thinking some more.

Catching her breath, she stopped at the top of the south ridge. Pride filled her chest as she gazed down at the harvested meadows and the stacks of hay in each one. She was a part of this ranch. A part of all its accomplishments. If Brody was torn between Maria and her, she'd just have to make him see she would be the best wife for him. He was the first man to come along that she wanted and could see in her future. She was going to do whatever it took to make him love her.

"Well, what have we here?"

She swung around and took a step backwards.

Talbot stood not ten feet from her.

Chapter Thirty-six

Brody paced back and forth in his grandfather's office. He couldn't believe the gall of the man to bring Maria and Emma all the way here. "Why didn't you tell me what you'd done?"

"I thought you'd be pleased to see your friend and her daughter and to know they could start a new life in the west." The older man sat behind his desk, a smug expression on his face.

"There's more to this. Are you trying to keep me and Lilah apart? Did you think bringing Maria and her daughter here would cause trouble?" He hadn't seen Lilah since she'd taken the two into the house. The mother and daughter were in the kitchen helping Mrs. Fellowes.

"No. At first, I just wanted to investigate the reason you were arrested. Follow up on your story. Then Mr. Peck said there was indeed a widow and her daughter who lived next to you. He took her statement about what happened.

That riled. The man had taken him in but still didn't trust him. "So you thought I was making up why I was arrested? Have you believed anything I've said since coming here?" He'd thought this man, his grandfather, had realized he wasn't like his father. This conversation was telling him otherwise.

"You have to see this from my shoes. My only daughter was taken from me by a smooth-talking, good-looking man. You come here, a handsome young man who is smooth-talking my hands, my housekeeper, and my ward. Hell, I've even fallen for your smooth-talking. I had to make sure you weren't like your father for Lilah's sake."

"Lilah's sake or your own?" He'd had enough. Finding out the judge had been secretly investigating him again, scorched his gut. He had to find her and see if she believed him a honey-tongued liar as well.

He stormed into the kitchen. "Where's Lilah?"

Mrs. Fellowes shrugged. "She went through here an hour ago. Looked upset so I figured she was going to go sit a spell under her favorite tree."

"Where is it?" he asked, heading for the door.

"The tall one, up the creek a ways."

He shoved the screen door open and strode up behind the house, his gaze on the tree. She wasn't there, nor were there any signs she had been there. He spun in a circle, searching for her. Nothing.

He headed back to the bunkhouse and barns. He searched each building and asked everyone he saw if they'd talked to or seen her. No one had seen her since taking the woman and girl into the house.

His chest squeezed with panic. Where could she be? He went back to the house and found Maria still in the kitchen.

"Did you say something to Lilah?" He leaned against the doorframe, watching the woman. She'd always been a beauty. But he'd only thought of her as a friend or an older sister. Yes, he could say he loved her but like a brother would a sister.

"I told her how you helped us and were a good friend." Maria's lashes hovered low, hiding her eyes.

"What else did you tell her?" His heart raced at the thought she'd said something that made Lilah doubt his love for her.

"Nothing. The more I talked the more agitated she became." This time the woman raised her lashes, and he saw she had said something that sent the younger woman away.

He slammed out of the kitchen and stood on the porch. Where would she have gone? I haven't checked to see if her horse is missing. He strode to the barn and checked the corral. Dusty was standing in the corral with the other horses. Someone would have seen her if she'd taken off down the road. That left the hill behind.

And the man who sought revenge on the judge.

With a rope in his hand, he caught his horse and saddled it before he'd even made a plan.

"Where're you going?" Gus asked, walking into the barn.

"Lilah's missing. I'm going up the draw behind the house and see if I can find her." He led the horse out of the barn and mounted up. "If I don't come back in an hour, best send some men looking for both of us."

He spun the horse and loped by the house and up the draw, searching the trees and boulders along the creek for any sign of the woman he loved.

The farther up the draw he went without seeing her, his fear for her grew. She knew better than to head out on her own. There may be a posse after Talbot but he'd managed to avoid the ranch hands for several months.

If the man had Lilah, there was no telling what he would do. He stopped his horse at the same spot he had a month ago when he'd witnessed activity on this ridge. After tying the horse to a bush, he crept up the side and peered at the trees on top.

There wasn't any movement in the shadows of the trees. But a small flicker at the edge of the trees caught his attention. Something caught on a branch, fluttered in the breeze.

He retrieved his horse and walked to the grove of trees. A piece of cloth the length of his finger and twice as wide had been shoved on a broken twig on the tree. He plucked the scrap of material from the tree and held it in his hand. The faint scent of lavender evoked memories of kissing Lilah. This had to be from her. But why?

Staring out across the ridge and down to the meadows at the end of the ridge, he wondered what to do. Go for more men or sit here and wait?

His gaze dropped to the ground. A set of hoof prints and shuffle marks disturbed the dirt. He dismounted and dropped to his knee to better examine the tracks. A horse dragging something. He followed the marks. No. There were footprints. Small footprints.

Then drag marks.

For the first time since realizing Lilah was missing, he smiled. Talbot had her, but she was leaving an easy to follow trail. One even a greenhorn like himself could see. He tied his bandana to the tree where he'd found her scrap of fabric, hoping the ranch hands found it and followed their tracks.

***

Lilah couldn't believe she'd been so stupid as to walk right up to Talbot. She'd tried to get away, but the man was quick as a cat. He'd caught her, breathed his foul breath in her face, and just as quickly tied her hands in front of her. Now he continued down the south canyon. It was rugged and rocky. She could no longer drag her feet and leave marks, but her skirt caught on the rough rocks, leaving bits and pieces. When they arrived to wherever this man was taking her, she had a feeling her skirt would be several inches shorter.

While the man scared her, an even bigger fear at the moment was his horse riling up a rattler and it lashing out at her as she wandered by. The hot sun beat down into the rocky canyon making it twice as hot. No breeze cooled her skin. And she'd left the house in such a huff, she didn't have a hat to keep the sun from baking her head.

"Can I have some water?" she asked, for the third time.

"Not until we get to my hiding spot." He hadn't looked back once to see if she was still walking behind his horse. Of course, he'd probably know if she fell since he had a hold of the rope that tethered her to him and his horse.

Even though she had many questions, she wasn't going to waste her energy on talking. She had to concentrate on putting one foot in front of the other and watching for snakes.

***

Brody groaned when the dirt trail vanished into the rocky canyon. He didn't have any idea where he was, but he could tell the only way to make it down this canyon was to stay low in the chasm where the falling rocks hadn't quite filled the bottom. Several steps in, he noticed bits of fabric attached to the rough rocks. Lilah had come through here.

Anger boiled. She was still walking from how low on the rocks the tufts of cloth were snagged. As his horse gently placed his feet, he cursed the man who made Lilah walk through here. He had no doubt the canyon was home to snakes. He kept his eyes and ears tuned to the rocks and anywhere he thought a snake could be hiding, following the canyon downward.

Ten minutes after entering the rocks, he spotted two dots moving out into the sage brush flat land at the bottom of the canyon. He wasn't far behind. He prayed the man didn't look back and see him making his way down the rocky ravine.

Chapter Thirty-seven

Lilah could barely put one foot in front of the other, this time dragging her feet was due to weariness and not trying to leave a trail. Talbot led her over a small rise and down the other side. She glanced up and stopped. The rope jerked her arms, propelling her forward.

Talbot rode his horse into a cave. The entrance smelled of rodents, but he continued into the darkness. She stumbled and stubbed her toe on what felt like a rock.

"I can't see." Fear clenched her chest and she couldn't breathe.

"Follow the rope."

Her feet had stopped again. The rope jerked her forward. She put out her tied hands to stop the fall. Her weight on her hands and the weariness of her body made her wish to stay right there on the cold, musty ground.

A light glowed ahead of her.

"Get to the light." Talbot's rough voice came from the direction of the light.

They'd traveled far enough in she couldn't see the outside light. She shivered and shoved up off the damp floor.

Making her way to the light, she discovered a small camp. This was where the man had been hiding out. His horse didn't seem the least bit disturbed by the darkness. The one lantern spread a ten foot radius of light.

He yanked on the rope, pulling her to him. "We're goin' to be nice and cozy in this here cave."

She turned her face from the sour breath.

He untied the long rope but kept her hands tied together.

Her gaze took in the crates of food, the pile of blankets, a hunk of fresh meat, and a pile of hay. The only thing she didn't see was water.

"I'd like a drink." She sunk onto a crate, giving her tired legs a rest.

He produced a canteen, handing it to her.

She unscrewed the top and drank sweet, cool water. From the burning sensation on her face, she knew the sun had blistered her skin. The curse of having freckles and light skin. She splashed water into one hand and patted it on her scalding skin.

"What do you think the honorable Judge Radley will do when he discovers you're missing?" Talbot reached out and took the canteen from her.

"Send out a search party." If the man didn't know about the posse looking for him, she sure wasn't going to tell him.

"They'll never find us here." His confidence didn't help lessen her fear.

"There must be others who know about this cave." She'd never heard of a cave in the years she'd lived with the judge. Was it on the ranch land or had they traveled off the ranch? That would be why no one ever found him. He came and went from this cave and the rocky canyon leaving no tracks. If this wasn't Double R property, no one would have any reason to look here.

He dug around in the ashes of a fire pit and tossed dried sage brush onto the red coals underneath. "I'm hungry. How about a nice steak from one of the judge's prime cattle?" The man laughed and sliced two steaks from the hunk of meat sitting on the top of a crate. He plopped the meat in a skillet and set it over the tiny flames licking at the sage brush.

"I need to. You know." She had needed to relieve herself for some time but wasn't going to have him watching while she did. Here, she could step into the dark and perhaps get away from him.

He grinned. "Step out into the dark if you want, but don't even think about getting away."

She knew the direction they'd walked into the camp. Not wanting him to suspect she was going to try and get away, she stepped out of the light several steps the opposite direction. Once she took care of business she tried to walk around the outside of the circle of light without being seen.

"You best get back in here before you get lost in this cave." Talbot turned the steaks and stood. He squinted in the direction she'd stepped out of the light.

She stood to the side of him, headed the opposite direction he stared. Careful to not make a sound, she barely picked her feet up and started forward into the dark. Her toe hooked on another rock and she went down. This time crying out as a rock gouged her ribs and scraped her temple.

"I told you not to try and get away." He picked up the lantern and headed her direction. Reaching down, he jerked her to her feet. "You might as well get comfortable, you'll never find your way out of here." He sat her on the crate and went back to cooking.

Tears trickled down her cheeks, partially from the sting of her injuries, but mainly because no one would find her and she had no idea what this man had planned for her.

***

Brody followed the tracks through the sage and rabbit brush. Lilah dragged her feet again, only this time it didn't look intentional. The drag marks weren't as deep and they were constant. He stopped at an opening in the ground. It was twenty feet across and eight feet high. The prints he followed continued on into the cave.

He realized the chance he'd take walking in. For all he knew Talbot was waiting for him. But he couldn't stop now. Lilah was tired and in danger. He tied his horse to sage brush on the top of the knoll hiding the cave. If the ranch hands were following, they'd see his horse and look around. Then they'd see the cave. He hoped to have her out before they arrived.

Back at the opening, he slipped in, staying close to the edge of the cave wall. The scent of rodents followed him downhill until the light from the opening barely showed him the way. A few more steps and he was in such damp darkness his breath was stolen and he lost sense of direction.

Slowly, one step at a time, he backed up until the light chased away the eeriness of the dark. He didn't have a lantern. They'd see him coming if he did have one. But he had to find a way to get back out of the dark.

He walked outside and up to his horse. The lariat on his saddle wasn't as long as he would probably need, but it was all the lifeline he had. At the edge of the darkness, he rolled a large rock onto the end of the rope. Holding the rope in his left hand, and running his right hand along the cave wall, he headed into the darkness. The going was slow as he bumped his shins on rocks and scrambled around piles. What felt like several miles, ended up to be only the length of the fifty-foot rope. When the end sat in his hand, he sighed. He'd yet to see any light from inside the cave. All he had to guide him now was the wall.

Placing the end of the lariat over a large rock, he continued on, keeping one hand on the hard-packed earth and rock on the side of the cave. He'd traveled what felt like the same distance as the rope when he saw a faint glow of light ahead. His right hand continued to feel the wall as he softly placed each foot until he flanked the ring of light.

He stood still a moment, noting Talbot was by the fire and Lilah sat on a crate across the circle of light from the killer. The man had cached supplies enough for several months. After moving one foot and stubbing his toe on a rock, he dropped to his hands and knees. It was the quietest way he could think of to get to her.

Talbot rose, carrying the sizzling frying pan toward Lilah. Brody crouched, ready to rush into the circle if the man tried to harm her.

The killer stabbed something in the pan and handed her the fork. A large piece of sizzling meat hung from the utensil. She accepted the food and scooted to the back of the crate.

Brody continued, with his gaze on the backside of the crate where she sat. His knee landed on several sharp points and his head bumped a large hard object as he crawled over a small pile of rocks. He cursed, thinking he'd have to get himself and Lilah over the rock pile when they escaped.

She set the fork and half-eaten piece of meat on the crate beside her. Her head dropped forward, chin to her chest. He had trouble believing she fell asleep even knowing the miles she'd walked.

To touch her might frighten her into making a sound. He'd have to whisper to her that he was there. But to make sure Talbot didn't hear him in the quiet of the cave, he'd have to get so close he was almost touching the back of her head.

He glanced at Talbot. The man had spread out the pile of blankets and looked ready to turn in. Good. He'd wait for Talbot to be settled in for the night and he'd catch Lilah's attention and get her out of here.

Within minutes, snoring echoed through the cave.

Lilah couldn't believe the man could fall into such a dead, loud sleep so soon. But she was glad. She flicked the meat from the fork and started to work on the rope knotted around her wrists.

"Lilah."

She sat upright, staring at the sleeping man.

"Behind you," the voice whispered again.

She spun on the crate and made out the shape of a man behind her. "Brody?" she whispered back, hardly believing the greenhorn had followed them into the dark cave. Her heart squeezed with happiness that he'd found her.

"Stick your hands out here."

She did as she was told. Her hands pulled apart and the rope lay in her lap. A hand captured hers.

"Come on."

She followed him into the dark, then stopped.

He pulled her into his arms. "We have to keep going," he whispered in her ear.

"Do you know which direction to go?" she asked, remembering how she'd been turned around in the darkness earlier.

"I followed the wall in and strung a rope as far as it would reach. We just have to get to the wall and keep it to our left side." He released all but her hand and started slowly through the darkness.

It seemed like they'd walked for hours when Brody stopped. She heard a slap.

"I found the wall. We'll go slow. There were lots of rocks along here." He held firm to her hand, leading her through the darkness.

"Shouldn't we see some light by now?" she asked, feeling like they were going the wrong direction.

"This has to be the way. The wall is to my left and I feel like we're gradually going up. I walked downhill coming into the cave." He squeezed her hand. "It just seems like we've gone a long way because you can't see anything."

She hoped he was right. Her legs had become heavy weights. "I can't go any farther. I'm too tired." Her hand fell from his. They'd never find one another in the dark. "Brody!" she said in a panic.

"I'm here. His hands bumped into her. Moments later his arm closed around her.

Tears burned her sun-blistered face as she cried into his shoulder. "Don't leave me," she whispered.

"I'll never leave you." He kissed the top of her head.

She wanted to believe that, but her mind went to the scene this morning when Maria and the little girl arrived. "But you left Maria and Emma." Her heart twisted, wondering how he could leave someone he loved.

"Maria and Emma were neighbors. I didn't love them like I love you." His fingers gripped her chin and tipped it up.

She couldn't see his face or if he smiled, but the gentle way he held her chin gave her hope.

"I love you and would never leave you." His lips brushed against hers. "Why do you think I'm here? When I realized Maria's arrival, which by the way, I knew nothing about, had upset you, I went looking for you." He kissed her again. Longer. When he stopped, he said, "That was smart of you to leave such a good trail." He kissed her, again.

She had forgotten how tired she was as his kisses gave her hope and strength. He'd followed her because he cared. Because he loved her!

He drew out of the kiss. "Can you keep moving? I told Gus to send someone after me, or us, if I didn't come back in an hour. I left your piece of clothing, as well as my bandanna, in the tree on the ridge and hope they follow our tracks. I even left a clue at the top of the rocky canyon and my horse is tied on top of the cave entrance."

She nodded. He'd been thorough in making sure they had people looking for them. She believed in him and his love. *I should have never doubted him.*

"I can make it as long as you don't let go."

"I'll never let you go." He kissed her again before drawing away and grasping her hand.

She sighed. Her heart was healing. Filling in the cracks that had started while Maria talked. Another question came to her. "Did you bed Maria?"

He stopped, pulling her into his arms. "I'll never lie to you. No. She was there for me when my mother passed, and I was there for her when her husband passed. She is like an older sister to me. And Emma like a niece. I spent a lot of time with the two. Maria would cook dinner for me and I would watch Emma when Maria needed."

She should have listened to her heart. If she had, they wouldn't be in this dark cave. "I'm sorry. I let my head tell me you loved Maria and Emma."

He stopped, pulling her close. "I do love them, but not the way I love you." Brody held her tight and kissed her with a sweet caress of lips. "I love you as a man loves a woman. I want you in my bed every night and standing beside me during the day." He kissed her again. "When you lost your parents and came to live with the judge, did you ever climb into his lap and hug him but think of your father while doing so? Or while helping Mrs. Fellowes, pretend it was your mother?"

She nodded. There had been times she'd missed her parents so much she had pretended the two adults in her life were the ones she missed.

"Maria and Emma were the family I yearned to have. They were my comfort." He snuggled his face against her neck. "Had I already met you, I would not have been over at Maria's house so much. I would have been courting and marrying you."

She giggled as he tickled her behind the ear with his nose. The conviction behind his words struck her. She'd hoped and dreamed that someday a man would come along and show her undying love. She understood now, that while Angel had been dashing and exotic, he hadn't loved her with the depth of love that Brody showed her every time he looked at her.

"Yes. If I could talk grandfather into it, I would marry you next week."

"But what about my going to school." Even as she said the words it wasn't as important to her as it had once been. The thought of being away from him for the length of time it would take for her studies—her heart thudded to a halt. How would she endure being away that long?

The sound of a horse and the glow of a light shot her heart into her throat and froze her limbs.

Brody pressed her against the side of the cave, shielding her with his body.

Chapter Thirty-eight

Brody covered Lilah with his body. He glanced back at the growing glow. It had to be Talbot looking for her. Lucky for them the light didn't reach the side of the cave where they stood.

He wrapped his arms around her, drawing her down onto the ground behind a small pile of rocks he could make out from the shadows of the lantern light. Holding her close, keeping her from harm, his mind flashed to her words. She still wanted to go to the university. Her desire for learning was stronger than her love for him.

The light moved by and the idea to follow the glow to the outside struck him. "Come on." As he grasped Lilah to help her stand, water splashed. How could there be water in a cave? Perhaps there was a way out that way? But they couldn't walk through water in the dark.

"Where are you girl?" Talbot called out. "This here's the end of the line. The lake in here ends any way out from this side. If'n you're lost in here, you'll die of starvation, never getting out."

Damn! They'd gone the wrong direction. He must have crossed the cave and all this time they'd been walking deeper into the darkness.

They would have to follow the light now and hope the man wouldn't notice them since he knew Lilah was lost in the cave.

The splashing continued for a few minutes before the man came back their way. He held Lilah down behind the rock again. Once the light had passed, they stood and followed the glow, remaining in the darkness beyond the light. There were fewer rocks to dodge walking in the middle of the cave, however, if he lost the light, they would be confused as to which direction to go if he didn't keep the wall close. By staying where he could reach out and touch the wall at any moment, he was guaranteed of continuing the right direction.

Talbot walked his horse by his camp and moved on through the cave toward the opening. Before long dim moonlight was visible at the cave opening. Talbot stopped just inside the entrance and blew out the lantern.

Brody stopped and pulled Lilah into his arms. He placed his lips next to her ear and said, "He's waiting for you to try and make a break for the opening."

She nodded.

"We'll wait here. He'll have to eventually give up." He sat on the ground and pulled her down on his lap, wrapping his arms around her to keep her warm. "Go to

312

sleep," he whispered against her ear.

Her body relaxed and soon even breathing told him she was sleeping. He didn't dare nod off. Being this close to the opening, he wasn't going to miss a chance to slip out.

Holding her in his arms, he thought about her desire to learn about cattle breeding and bookkeeping. Both things he knew nothing about. As much as it hurt, he'd have to let her go. Have to let her learn what she could and hope she came back to him.

His heart started thudding in his chest when Talbot dismounted and led his horse out of the cave. If he noticed the horse on top of the knoll, he'd know someone was in here with Lilah. That would make the man more anxious to find them.

A horse nickered. Damn! Another nickered back. He had to catch Talbot off-guard. It was their only chance. He gently shook the woman sleeping in his arms. "Wake up. Lilah, wake up."

She sat up straight. "Is he gone?"

"He went outside. You stay here. I heard my horse nicker. He knows there's someone else in here. Our only chance is to surprise him." He stood and scrambled over the rocks up to the side of the cave entrance the man disappeared.

Rocks of all sizes were strewn about the entrance. He picked up one, not too heavy to hold over his head, but large enough to knock a man out.

Listening, he waited.

Rifle shots rang out.

Brody moved to drop the rock but heard someone scrambling down the side of the knoll. He raised his arms, and Talbot burst into the cave.

He brought the rock down on the man's head and shoulder, propelling him to the ground. The killer landed with his body humped in the middle over a boulder. Brody ripped the pistol from the killer's holster and picked up the rifle Talbot dropped.

"Here." He handed the rifle to Lilah as she ran up to the spot. "Hold that on him while I tie his hands."

The sound of horses rumbled down over the side of the knoll. He didn't take his attention from the man folded over the rock. He pulled Talbot's arms behind his back and tied them with his suspenders.

"Talbot come out with your hands in the air!" shouted someone outside the cave entrance.

"He can't." Brody shouted back.

"Brody?"

He recognized Sandy's voice. "Yeah. Lilah and I just caught him."

Sandy, followed by two others were silhouetted in the breaking light of dawn beyond the cave.

He yanked Talbot up, but the man was unconscious and nothing but dead weight.

"Roy, Sy, grab him and haul him out to his horse." Sandy took the rifle from Lilah. "You two ready to get out of here?"

Brody put his arm around her shoulders. "Yes, we are." They left the dark cave and walked out into the golden glow of a beautiful summer morning.

Roy and Sy had tied Talbot over the saddle on his horse. Brody walked over to his horse and mounted, lowering a hand down to Lilah.

"I don't have a riding skirt on," she said, glancing

at the area behind his saddle.

"I don't plan on you riding back there." He leaned over, grasping her around the chest and under her arms. He pulled her up sideways onto the front of his saddle. His backside as far back as he could. She sat in his lap, dangling her legs off one side of the horse. He wrapped his arms around her and followed Sandy. Sy rode behind them and Roy led Talbot's horse.

He studied Lilah's face. She had blisters, scrapes, dirt, and blood on every inch of her face, but he'd never seen a prettier woman. She had a genuine heart and courage. He plopped his hat on her head. "I don't think you want any more sun on your face."

She put her hands up, hiding behind them.

"Don't hide. Let everyone see how strong you are." He kissed her ear. Her hair hung in tangled hanks. She'd been through so much.

"I'm not strong. If I had been strong, he wouldn't have tied me up in the first place." Her tone revealed her disgust with herself.

He turned her face to his. "Strength isn't how much you can lift, it's how much you can endure without giving up." He kissed the tip of her nose. "You didn't give up. Even as I moved toward you in the dark you were working to get free."

Lilah stared into his eyes. She'd been strong because she wanted to get back and fight for him. She looped her arms around his neck. "You're what made me strong."

"Me?" Skepticism shimmered in his eyes.

"You. I'd decided I had to get back to the ranch and fight for you. I wasn't going to let Maria take you away from me." She dropped her gaze. Now, knowing how he felt about her, she was a fool to have walked away.

"Look at me." His tone was tender.

She peered into his eyes.

"Maria won't take me from you. I'm yours. And I'm going to fight for you. I understand you want to continue learning to help here at the ranch." He had to swallow a couple times to get the words to come out. "And I'm willing to wait for you."

"Really? You don't mind if I go to the university and you'd be here ready to marry me when I get back?" True happiness bubbled inside her for the first time in a very long time. Not since her parents' deaths.

His gaze lost a bit of its glow. "I won't like having you gone." He touched her cheek. "But knowing you're coming back to me, I'll have something to look forward to."

She thought about months without seeing him. Without his kisses and caresses. Would a university teach her anything more than she could learn from Judge Radley's books? A thought was forming. The idea made her giddy. He wanted to stay at the ranch and work alongside his grandfather. Perhaps she could make them both see her solution would work.

She was relieved when Sandy skirted the rocky canyon Talbot had dragged her through. They soon were walking down the road from Mule to Venator. Relaxing, she leaned against Brody's chest and closed her eyes. The brief nap she'd had at the entrance of the cave had done little to snuff out her tiredness.

***

Brody straightened in the saddle and held Lilah

close as Sheriff Davies and the posse rode down off a hill toward them. They were almost to the road leading to the ranch buildings. He wanted to get her back to the house and have Mrs. Fellowes doctor the blisters and scrapes on her face.

The sheriff stopped in front of Sandy. "That Talbot?" he asked, pointing to the body draped over the horse.

Brody nudged his horse up beside the hired hand. "Yes. He'd kidnapped Lilah."

The sheriff glanced at the woman in his arms and cringed. "How did he get her? We've been all over these hills for days."

"She climbed the south ridge and found him. Or he found her. He tied her hands and made her walk miles through a canyon and down a rocky ravine to a cave. He has supplies stashed in that cave to last him a month." He glanced down at the sleeping woman in his arms. "I followed the trail she left and was about to get her out of the cave when these men arrived. Their chasing him back into the cave gave me the chance to surprise him."

"He alive?" Sheriff Davies asked.

He shrugged. "Don't know and don't care. He's killed Double R cattle, wounded a Double R hand, and kidnapped Lilah. Don't care what happens to him as long as he never shows up around here again."

Glancing over his shoulder he said to Sy, "Hand Talbot over to the posse. I want to get Lilah to Mrs. Fellowes." He urged his horse forward. Before long he heard the cadence of the other horses behind him. He grinned. Slowly, he was gaining the respect of the hired hands.

At the barnyard, children came running from all directions.

"Is she alright?"

"What happened to Miss Lilah?"

"How come her face is bloody?"

Lilah stirred.

"We're home," he whispered in her ear.

Buster held his arms up to help her from the horse. He lowered her into the foreman's arms.

"What are you doing? I can walk." She swung her legs, and Buster set her on the ground.

Brody dismounted, handed the reins of his horse to Buster and put an arm around Lilah, leading her to the house.

"I'm fine," she said, but she didn't pull away.

"I want Mrs. Fellowes to tend to the blisters on your face and make sure you get plenty to drink and eat." He wasn't taking any chances on her collapsing.

They walked to the back door. He stopped inside the kitchen. Maria had on an apron and was mixing dough. Mrs. Fellowes was standing over a steaming pot.

"Oh my!" the housekeeper exclaimed upon seeing Lilah. She hustled over and took her by the arm. "Come sit on my bed while I clean up your face and put petroleum jelly over those scrapes."

Maria stared at Lilah.

Brody walked over to Maria. "What are you doing?"

Her hands stalled in the dough and her eyes held his. "Your grandfather offered me a job helping Mrs.

Fellowes and Mrs. Malone."

"Grandfather!" he bellowed and headed for the office.

Chapter Thirty-nine

Brody stepped into his grandfather's office and slammed the door shut.

The old man jumped and opened his eyes. He'd been sleeping in his office chair.

"You didn't ask me before you brought Maria and Emma here, and now you have hired her to be the new housekeeper?" He stalked over to the desk, placed his hands on the top, and leaned across the wood expanse at his grandfather.

"I figured if you were willing to go to jail for the woman and child you must have feelings for them." He waved his hands over his desk. "I wanted you to have a wife and family. I wanted you to stay at the ranch."

He straightened and paced. "I don't love Maria that way. She was a good friend. She gave me family when I thought I didn't have any. But I don't want her here. She's the reason Lilah was compelled to wander off on her own." He stopped and stared at his grandfather.

"Talbot kidnapped her."

The old man stood up behind his desk. "We have to go get her!"

Brody shook his head and waved him back in his seat. "She's here. Mrs. Fellowes is doctoring her."

"Doctoring? How bad is she hurt?" His grandfather started around the side of the desk.

He put out an arm stopping him. "She'll be fine. She's a strong, intelligent woman. I followed the trail she'd left and found her and Talbot in a cave."

"Where's Talbot?" The old man narrowed his eyes, studying him.

"Sheriff Davies has him. I don't know if he's alive or not. Frankly, I don't care." He put his hands on the older man's shoulders. "I love Lilah. She loves me. I don't want to wait for her to come back from the university. Give us your blessing to marry and I'll attend the university with her." Peering into pale eyes like his own, he said, "And we'll come back here and help you run the ranch, Grandfather."

The old man's eyes glistened with tears. "You called me grandfather."

Brody wrapped his arms around the older man and hugged him tight. His grandfather hugged him back. They stood that way for several minutes before the judge stepped back.

"I think Lilah's parents would approve of marriage to a fine young man as you. And I approve of sending you to the university with her."

His heart thrummed in his chest. "Thank you, Grandfather." He hugged the older man again, then strode out of the room and down the hall to the kitchen.

Mrs. Fellowes stepped out of her room.

"How is she?" he asked, quietly.

"She'll be fine once I get some food in her."

He smiled. "Good. I think I have something else that will help."

The housekeeper grinned, patted his arm, and hustled over to the stove. He noticed Maria wasn't in the kitchen. He wasn't going to let that distract him. He entered the bedroom.

The woman he loved sat on the edge of the bed, using a mirror to dab petroleum jelly on her scrapes.

She looked up and her already red cheeks deepened in color. "I'd prefer you not stare at me so. I'm a mess."

"You're beautiful." He crossed the room and knelt beside her.

"No I'm not. My face…" She dropped the mirror face down in her lap. "I'm horrific looking."

"All I see is a beautiful woman." He leaned forward and kissed her lips, careful not to press on any of the scrapes. He drew back and stared into her eyes. "I just had a talk with my grandfather."

Her eyes widened. "What about?"

"Marrying you." He couldn't believe the woman he wanted to spend the rest of his life with was sitting in front of him, holding her breath.

"I have an idea about that." She held up a finger.

"I told him if he'll let me marry you before you go to the university, I'll go with you and join you in the classes."

She sat back, blinking her eyes. "You'd do that? Attend school with me?"

"To stay with you, yes."

He expected her to show more happiness. She just sat there studying him.

"I have an idea, too. What if we get married and I don't go to the university, but we read your grandfather's books about cattle breeding and he can show me how to take care of the books?"

He studied her glistening eyes and raised eyebrows. "You'd stay here and marry me? And we could learn about cattle breeding together?"

"Yes."

"You're sure you don't want to learn from real teachers?"

"All I want is to stay with you." She flung her arms around his neck. This time she kissed him, but without regard to her injuries.

He joined in, pushing her back on the bed and indulging his need to know she was well, by running his hands down her sides and over her hips.

"Ahem!" Mrs. Fellowes throat clearing, brought them both up for air and sitting on the side of the bed.

"I'll not have this kind of going's on in my room, on my bed." She shoved her fists on her ample hips.

"Yes, Ma'am," Brody said, not even trying to hide his smile. He grasped Lilah's hand and drew her to her feet. "Is that food ready? I'm starving," he said, leading Lilah out to the kitchen and a table set with two steaming bowls of stew.

***

Lilah sat on the porch waiting for Brody to join her for a walk. She'd spent all of yesterday and most of the night before bringing Buster and Agnes' new son into the world. He'd been a fighter. Both were resting

323

comfortably with Maria caring for them and the family.

She smiled.

Brody had been adamant about Maria leaving the ranch to not cause her anymore unrest. But with Mrs. Fellowes aging, the Lund children living with them permanently since their father was discovered dead in Pendleton, and Agnes needing help until her health bounced back and she could take care of her family, Maria was a big help. And Sandy had taken a shine to the woman and her daughter. The two had married the week before, after Sandy, Roy, and Clem built a small cabin for Sandy's new family to live in.

She studied the addition Brody and Gus were building onto the main house. It had two bedrooms and an inside bath. One room would be Judge Radley's, the other was for her and Brody. When the addition of family bedrooms was complete, they were to be wed. Her heart raced and her body hummed thinking about sleeping next to him every night. The addition wasn't going fast enough for her.

Whistling drew her attention to the handsome man walking toward her. The grin on his face was infectious. Her lips turned up and her heart soared. The heat from looking at him chased away the evening autumn chill.

"Miss Wells, would you care to walk with me this fine evening?"

She shoved her arms into the sleeves of the coat she wore around her shoulders and stood. "Mr. Yates, I'd be pleased to join you on a walk."

He held out his arm, and she hooked her hand through the crook of his elbow. They'd been taking a walk every evening since he'd rescued her from Talbot and they'd told his grandfather they were getting married before the end of the year and not attending the university. She hugged his arm and sighed.

The weather had become stormy and unpredictable. They no longer wandered up to their grassy love nest. Now they walked up into the trees and circled back around to enter the animal barn and spend a couple of hours driving each other to a heated frenzy with their touching and kissing. She couldn't wait much longer to become Mrs. Brody Yates and feel the completion of their love.

Tonight was no exception. Her heart pounded in her ears and her body throbbed. She needed him to make the sensations go away. "We'll marry soon. Brody, please." She thrust her hips against the bulge in his pants.

She'd talked with Agnes as Brody had suggested and learned exactly what it was he held back from and what would relieve her agitated state. Agnes said she was surprised he'd been able to refrain from making love to her. Most men in love didn't have that much control.

"Lilah, we have to wait." He kissed her forehead, temple, and chin.

"Why? There is no reason we need to wait, unless you really don't want me." She had her fingers wrapped in his, now, two inch-long hair, holding his face in front of her. Moving her hips, she brushed against his hardness again and watched the heat flash in his eyes.

His mouth came down on hers. The kiss wasn't soft and tender. He devoured her mouth as if he were a starving man. His hips moved against her, and his hands, which had already unbuttoned the front of her dress for him to suckle her nipples, slid down her sides and gathered her skirt.

"I'd prefer making love to you with us both naked but since it's November, we're in a barn, and someone could walk in on us, this will have to do." His fingers found the split in her drawers and teased her woman parts, making her moan.

He covered her mouth with his and withdrew his hand.

She shook her head, trying to tell him not to stop. His mouth released hers.

"Don't stop," she whispered in a husky voice.

"I'm not." He slipped his arms through his suspenders and slid his pants and drawers down.

Her first glimpse of his maleness started her heart thudding. She knew what came next but her body stiffened at the thought.

Brody felt Lilah's hesitation. She'd pushed him harder tonight to bring them together completely. Once she'd realized what she was asking, her desire had waned. He grabbed his pants to pull them back up.

Her hand caught his, stopping the motion. "Kiss me, bring the fire back," she whispered, raising up to his lips.

That was the courage in her that he loved. Even though she was scared, she wanted to fulfill them both. He captured her lips, seducing them with his lips, teeth, and tongue until she wriggled under him and pressed her mound to his pulsing dick. He grasped her skirt and spread her legs with his.

Her opening was wet and slick. Slowly, he nudged

inside of her as he lapped and sucked first one nipple and then the other. Her lovely breasts had been first bared to him the night after he'd saved her from Talbot. Each night she'd been bolder and bolder with her explorations of his body and allowing him to explore hers.

Tonight. It was the ecstasy they'd both been wanting. He pressed deeper. She froze, then moved against him, and he started the rhythm that pounded in his heart. Their mouths merged and their bodies melded together. He thrust and ground against her until he was about to burst. Her head fell back and she moaned long and lusty.

He released, reveling in the love and sanctuary she gave him.

Her arms wrapped around his neck, and she pressed kisses all over his face. "Agnes said when a man and woman in love come together it is magical." She dropped her head back. "I saw stars while in a barn!"

He cradled her head in his hands and kissed her soft and long. "My heart beats with yours. Soon we'll marry and start a family." He'd wanted a family of his own for so long he couldn't believe it would happen soon.

Lilah smiled. "You already have a family. Me, your grandfather, Mrs. Fellowes, the ranch hands, and the children." She kissed his lips and leaned back. "You don't have to be born in a family to become family. It's the people you surround yourself with and that you love and respect that make up your family."

"I told Grandfather you were strong, beautiful, and

intelligent." He nipped her neck and moved inside her, starting his desire for her all over again.

Chapter Forty

Judge Radley held a bible and smiled at her as Lilah stood beside him in the barn. He held a bible and smiled at her. Knowing he was pleased with her marrying Brody and had asked if he could read the marriage vows, her heart overflowed with love for the man who had become her second father.

Everyone from the ranch and some of the local ranchers, along with her friends from Burns and Venator were standing in the barn waiting for the ceremony to begin.

Her smile started slipping with each minute that passed and no sign of Brody. Had he changed his mind? He wouldn't run off and not tell her. Would he? She glanced at Maria, standing next to Sandy. She nodded and smiled.

Hurried footsteps had everyone turning to the barn doors.

Gus burst through the doors. "Don't worry. He's

coming." He closed the doors and joined the other ranch hands.

A murmur rose from the crowd. She picked up her skirt and headed to the doors.

"Lilah, come back here. Gus said he was coming," Judge Radley called to her.

Roy and Clem stepped in front of the door. "He'll be here." Roy said, smiling.

She scanned the row of hired hands and realized now that Gus had arrived, Buster and Brody were the only ones missing. The foreman would get her groom here. But what if he was injured. She spun around and hurried up the aisle to Mrs. Fellowes.

"Maybe Brody needs your assistance," she said, grasping the woman's hands.

"I'm sure he's fine. Go on back up by the judge and wait." The housekeeper patted her hands.

Tears burned her eyes. What was wrong? Why wasn't he here, and why wouldn't anyone check on him?

The doors burst open.

Brody strode down the aisle and up to her. He grasped her hands tightly with his.

"You're cold," she whispered.

"Tell you about it later," he whispered back and faced his grandfather. "We're ready."

The judge read the vows and said the line she'd been waiting for since Brody burst through the barn doors. "You may kiss your bride."

Brody took her into his arms and stared into her eyes. "You are all the family I need." His lips descended on hers. The kiss, sweet and tender.

The crowd whooped and Mrs. Fellowes, Agnes, and Maria, pulled sheets off the makeshift tables laden with food.

Brody couldn't wait any longer. When everyone was busy eating, he grasped Lilah's hand and led her out of the barn. He'd been dreaming of this moment for weeks.

"Where are we going," she asked.

"I was late because the road was a mess between here and Burns." He still had a slight chill from the trip he'd made.

"When did you leave? We saw each other last night." She blushed.

Darrin and Dooley had walked in on them in the barn last night. Luckily, they'd only been kissing and no one was undressed. "When I left you at the porch, I harnessed up the horses and headed for Burns. My present to you had to be picked up or there wouldn't have been a wedding night."

"I don't understand."

He led her into the house and down the small hallway in the new addition. He opened the door and waited. He'd promised her a large goose down mattress and that was what he'd brought home from Burns less than an hour ago. Gus and Buster helped him haul it into the room. He'd put the new sheets and blankets on it himself.

"The bed. It's beautiful!" She looped her arms around his neck and kissed him.

"Glad you like it." He picked her up and laid her gently on the bed. "It's time to start adding to our family."

331

Note from the Author

Thank you for joining Brody and Lilah on their journey to discover love. This book is set in an area not too far from where I live. The cave in the story is an actual cave where we take family and friends who visit. There is a lake in the cave. It was first used by the Paiute Indians. They barricaded themselves in after discovering the Bannocks were on a raid to kill them. Later the cave was discovered by the whites and in the early 1900's was used as a picnic destination by a local resort. They had small docks and rowed boats out in to the lake. Now it is owned by the Masons and used once a year for a gathering. The rest of the year it is open to the public. There aren't any signs, only locals know how to find it.

If you enjoyed Brody's story, please leave a review. It is the best way to let an author know you enjoyed their book.

All my work has Western or Native American elements in them along with hints of humor and engaging characters. My husband and I raise alfalfa hay in rural eastern Oregon. Riding horses and battling rattlesnakes, I not only write the western lifestyle, I live it.

I love to hear from fans. You can contact me through my website: http://www.patyjager.net
Blog: http://www.patyjager.blogspot.com
Newsletter: http://eepurl.com/1CFgX
By joining my newsletter you get access to my books for free. Join and find out how.

You can find all my books listed at:
Goodreads:
http://www.goodreads.com/author/show/1005334.Paty_Jager
or my website: http://www.patyjager.net

Letters of Fate
Davis
Isaac
Brody

Halsey Brother Series
Marshal in Petticoats – Gil's story
Outlaw in Petticoats – Zeke's story
Miner in Petticoats – Ethan's story
Doctor in Petticoats – Clay's story
Logger in Petticoats – Hank's story
Halsey Brothers Series – Box Set
Halsey Homecoming trilogy
Laying Claim– Jeremy's story
Staking Claim – Colin's story
Claiming a Heart – Donny's story
A Husband for Christmas - Shayla's story

Other Historical Western Romance
Gambling on an Angel
Improper Pinkerton
For a Sister's Love
Western Duets: Volume One
Western Duets: Volume Two
Western Duets: Volume Three
Western Holiday Duets

Western Anthologies
Sweetwater Springs Christmas: A Montana Sky Short
Story Anthology
Rawhide "N Romance: A Western Romance Anthology
Silver Belles and Stetsons: A Western Christmas
Anthology

Contemporary Western Romance
Perfectly Good Nanny

Historical Paranormal Romance
(Native American)
Spirit of the Mountain
Spirit of the Lake
Spirit of the Sky

Windtree
Press

Thank you for purchasing this Windtree Press
publication. For other books of the heart, please visit
our website at www.windtreepress.com.
For questions or more information contact us at
windtreepress@gmail.com.

Windtree Press
www.windtreepress.com

Hillsboro, OR 97124